Signed Confessions

Guilt and a desperate need to repent drive the antiheroes in Tom Walker's dark (and often darkly funny) stories:

- A gullible journalist falls for the 40-year-old stripper he profiles in a magazine.
- A faithless husband abandons his family and joins a support group for lost souls.
- A merciless prosecuting attorney grapples with the suicide of his gay son.
- An aging misanthrope must make amends to five former victims.
- An egoistic naval hero is haunted by apparitions of his dead wife and a mysterious little girl.

The seven tales in *Signed Confessions* measure how far guilty men will go to obtain a forgiveness no one can grant but themselves.

Signed Confessions

Stories

Tom Walker

Fomite
Burlington, Vermont

ISBN-978-1-937677-36-7

Library of Congress Control Number: 2012950689

Fomite
58 Peru Street
Burlington, VT 05401
www.fomitepress.com
Author photograph by Parish Photography
Cover art from Drawception.com - copyright 2012 Nihildom Inc.

For Lila, Alex, and Maggie

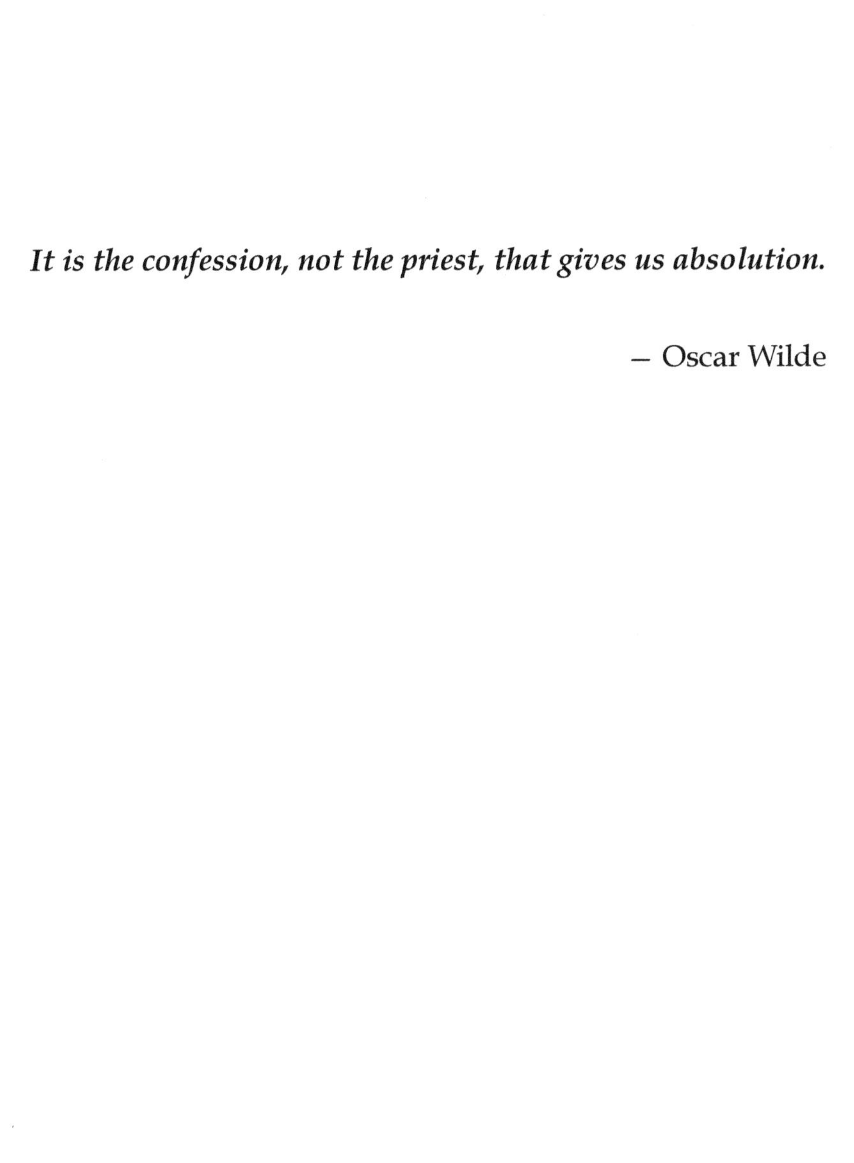

It is the confession, not the priest, that gives us absolution.

— Oscar Wilde

Table of Contents

Acknowledgements

"Blessed Are They That Mourn" originally appeared in the fall/winter 2004 issue (Volume XXV, Numbers 3 and 4) of *The Texas Review*.

"Making Amends" originally appeared in the spring 2012 issue (Number 13) of *Kerem*.

The author is grateful to these periodicals for permission to reprint.

Blessed Are They That Mourn

Consider all that follows a signed confession.

Before my thirty-three-year-old son Matthew died last winter, I hadn't thought of Billy Vandemeer in ages. Living in a new century, three times married and divorced, I'd managed to forget Billy's name. Matthew's death put me in mind of Billy because Billy's father, like my son, took his own life.

Matthew was my only begotten, my sole seed. What father survives the death, by any cause, of his progeny without guilt? Nature's course has been subverted, the natural law requiring that our children outlive us contravened. As a longtime Assistant District Attorney, I am big on the law, an upholder. Law civilizes. Law is to Americans what philosophy was to the Greeks. There should be a law against suicide. Law begets law as fathers beget sons. If the child ends his own life, the father's guilt is unbearable, and mine was compounded by the fact that our Dallas police pried from Matthew's hand the silver Beretta 950 Jetfire single-action I had given him on request. His death was no accident: Matthew was killed by a .25 ACP round fired by his right hand from that loaded pistol into his right temple.

When I gave him the Jetfire—a slightly upgraded version of the Beretta I myself carried under Texas conceal-and-carry law

—he'd seemed neither depressed nor suicidal. He'd seemed grateful. He'd claimed he needed some protection from a male rival in a hurry. I assumed it was some husband or boyfriend. I was quick to give him what he needed. How in the name of God was I supposed to know that three months later, he would use the gun on himself?

As if the action were perfectly self-explanatory, there was no letter of explanation or note of apology or good-bye. Nothing. "Killing yourself is a Fuck You sign waved in the faces of those you love," a best seller on the subject of suicide told us in the seventies, and I think it was Daniel Webster who said,"There is no refuge from confession but suicide, and suicide is a confession." Matthew had something to confess, I knew in my heart, and the face in which he waved his Fuck You sign was my face.

Have you ever tossed and turned through a dream so ridiculously dire and catastrophic that at some point you realize you're dreaming? There is relief in the realization even as the nightmare continues and you can't awaken from it. Matthew's suicide was like that. I kept waiting for something or someone to grab me and shake me to wake me up. Since it couldn't really be happening, I clung to my denial. A skeptic by nature, a Doubting Thomas by profession, I'd seldom believed the suicides in plays or novels or movies; I dismissed them as plot contrivances. Oh sure, suicides happened in real life, but not in my family. Not to my son. Better, almost, that he'd been murdered. To me suicide was murder, the murder of oneself. The ultimate act of cowardice. Even attempted suicide should be against the law.

Trance-like in my denial, I sleepwalked through the funeral

arrangements, the casket selection and obituaries, the Rosary and Requiem High Mass and cemetery internment and all the other gloomy business I had to negotiate. But I never woke up. Finally, I had to face the fact that my only son, my sole seed, my little Matty, was dead. Dead by his own hand.

—⁓—

But my confession is not about Matthew's suicide. Or the mistakes I made as a father that in any way enabled it. *Nolo contendere*, I will not contest. It's about what I did to Billy Vandemeer one cool sunny day in the fall of 1953 when he and I were thirteen but so close to being young men that the hours of our boyhood were numbered.

On a dreary grey September afternoon two weeks earlier, while I was taking my piano lesson at school from our music teacher, Sister Maria Goretti, Billy's father had come home early from the Big D Auto Garage where he worked as a mechanic. He sent Billy to the corner grocery for a pouch of Bull Durham tobacco and some rolling papers. He then took from a locked closet the 12-gauge double-barreled Model 24 Winchester shotgun he and Billy used to hunt dove, went into the kitchen, and fired it point-blank into the faces of Billy's sisters, Carolyn (ten) and Gretchen (eight), while they sat snacking on milk and Oreos at the table.

Next, police concluded, he went to the connubial bedroom, sat on the edge of the bed, positioned the shotgun between his knees, his mouth over the barrels, and depressed the trigger with his thumbs. The top of his head was blasted off; gouts of blood, pieces of brain and skull fragments were plastered to the ceiling. Billy got back from the store before his mother, Alma Vandemeer, got home from her job at the neighborhood day nursery. It was his fate to discover the three virtually headless corpses. He didn't bolt and run away screaming — he held himself together and dealt with the situation like a grown man, picking up the phone and dialing 0 for Emergency. Whereas Alma went into shock and had to be sedated.

This most bizarre crime in many a Dallas moon sent my church parish (St. Joseph's) and our stupefyingly dull fifties suburb into a tizzy of shock, disbelief, morbid curiosity, gossip, and speculation. Our local media — bored with barrio knifings, the Korean armistice, McCarthy red-baiting, and big-league baseball's lopsided pennant races — shamelessly milked the tragedy. On their front pages every day for a week, both Dallas dailies treated it like chapters in a grisly pulp serial, complete with photos of the five smiling Vandemeers at some happy event, a birthday party perhaps. It was all ghastly, yet nobody could get enough of it. How we ghouls enjoy horror from a safe distance. And I may have been the worst ghoul of all, because I kept a scrapbook of the case. No one knew I was doing this; at school I was known as a square, a wonk, a "brain," and my scrapbook would've been evidence *prima facie* of my dorkiness and dweebiness, though such words were yet to be coined in 1953.

Accidental shootings were nothing new to a violent city like Dallas, but Mr. Vandemeer was the first man I'd personally known to shoot himself on purpose. Remarkably, in a state where guns outnumbered people, forty-seven years would pass before I knew another. The second man would be my son.

⸻

At the Rosary and the funeral, nobody came up to me and said Matthew was "in a better place now." You can guess why. Nevertheless, he received a ritual internment with all the trimmings, so to speak, in a Catholic cemetery; since Vatican II in the early sixties, suicides had been granted full Church burials on grounds that anyone *non compos mentis* (mentally ill) enough to take his own life could not be held morally responsible for taking it. As a man of law, I found that logic circular, a papal Catch-22; as a lapsed-Catholic agnostic, I could not have cared less one way or the other. To me, all ritualistic burials, with their morbid hoopla, were primitive wastes of time and money; I'd already arranged to have myself cremated without ceremony. But my devout Catholic parents—my mother, especially—were relieved that the Church gave Matthew the deluxe treatment, as though it provided a highway to heaven, his final mortal sin notwithstanding.

My parents! Cruel to say, what a pain in the ass doddering old parents are. Two days after the funeral, exhausted from fatigue, having gone full-speed with little rest for a solid week, I nevertheless made myself drop by to check on them at our old two-story family house where, against my counsel, they insisted on living alone. Rummaging up in the attic for mementoes of Matty's youth, I came across that scrapbook of clippings about the Vandemeer killings I'd compiled back in 1953. Grief for my son—who'd never married, whose crazy mother was

5

dead, and who (not affectionately) liked to address me as "Honorable Prosecutor" — had sent me up the rickety ladder to that attic in search of baseball cards, Little League uniforms, science projects, and other memorabilia amid the cobwebs and darting cockroaches and layers of dust. What I found instead was a moldy scrapbook from my own boyhood. A chronicle of murder and suicide.

I squatted like a baseball catcher and removed the scrapbook from its sodden carton. The attic was dark but for the weak light from a triangular plate-glass window. As I shone my flashlight on the yellowed faded pages, I had a vertiginous moment of nausea. But I made myself read on.

Soon it was evident that if I'd assembled those clippings to solve the mystery, I had failed. Pieces of the puzzle were missing. And what insight I'd gained from my eighteen years as an Assistant Dallas County D. A. would shed no more light on the Vandemeer case than my flashlight could. I knew that deranged killers seldom kill for reasons they can logically explain. Yet questions cry out for answers. "Why?" Dallasites demanded to know in 1953. Why would Mr. Vandemeeer kill his innocent little daughters? Had he been abusing them? There was no indication of that. Why use the shotgun rather than the loaded Army .45 the police found in the night table beside the bed? Why, if his crazed impulse or intent was to slaughter his progeny, did he spare Billy? Because Billy was male and he was a misogynist? Then why spare Alma? A police psychologist suggested that wife and son had been spared to care for one another because soon there wouldn't be a man around the house.

Not even Lenny Bruce or Mort Sahl could have topped that, but the psychologist was serious.

If Mr. Vandemeer had been losing his marbles, as we said in the fifties, wouldn't Billy and his mother have had some inkling of it? Both claimed they hadn't. But I had a hunch they knew more than they let on. The man was a Korean War hero, a platoon sergeant decorated for valor in the 1950 Battle of Pyongyang City. Had he, I wondered up in the attic, been a victim of Post-traumatic Stress Disorder? "Shell-shocked," we called it back in the day. Returning war heroes could be trigger-happy; I had seen enough war movies to know that.

But what did I really know? I had barely known the Vandemeers. At my all-boys' school, I'd steered clear of Billy; Gretchen and Carolyn attended a girls' school; I had spoken to Mrs. Vandemeer—a tall, gawky woman with a nervous air—exactly once, at a church Bingo. Mr. Vandemeer I knew only as the lantern-jawed, crew-cut, muscular fellow who dropped the others off at Sunday Mass in a green '51 Studebaker and picked them up forty-five minutes later. He wasn't Catholic. So far as we knew, he wasn't anything. He didn't go to church.

Nobody in our parish knew the Vandemeers well. They were Yankees—Pennsylvania Dutch transplants to Dallas's blackland prairie. Not standoffish but not Texas-friendly either, they'd seemed a normal enough blue-collar family, nouveau middle-class in the boom years of Eisenhower's first term but unable, it was said, to afford a TV. On a Sunday drive weeks before the tragedy, my parents and I had driven by their house, a tacky cottage financed, my father supposed, by the G. I. Bill. "Why, the

Vandemeers are *poor*," my mother lamented. "Isn't that *sad?*"

For reasons that should be obvious, the Rosary at the funeral home and Solemn Requiem High Mass the next morning at St. Joseph's were closed-casket affairs. The Mass must've broken St. Joseph's attendance record, because it was Standing Room Only. Newspapermen, TV crews, and the sort of parishioners seldom seen at church clogged the aisles. Monsignor Steinkruger, our pastor, officiated in his silk-brocaded black chasuble. As the Mass ended, the St. Joseph's children's choir sang the haunting Gregorian chant for the dead "In Paradisum" and six pallbearers with long faces rolled the coffins down the center aisle, out through the front door.

Billy and his mother followed — he manfully solemn in an ill-fitting coat and tie, she weepy in a floppy hat with a black veil, his hand protectively at her elbow. After a few steps, she began to wail. I had never heard a more awful sound. Her legs sagged beneath her — I didn't think she'd make it to the vestibule. I pitied her, but something coldblooded in me was grateful not to be the only "only child" in our class anymore. Only children were rarities in the seventh grade at St. Joseph's; if you were one, your parents might be practicing "artificial birth control," a crime against nature, a mortal sin. And you were probably an accident. A mistake.

Billy went on to finish the fall semester at St. Joseph's, and a few days after the funeral, I had him over to my house. Had he changed? I'll get to that. The following January, Alma sold the haunted bungalow and enrolled him in a public school out in Oak Cliff, a blue-collar suburb where she'd found them a cheap apartment. And in June, the month I stopped taking piano, she and Billy moved back to Philadelphia to live with her parents. That was the last we heard of them.

—∿—

My mother was calling me, her old-lady vibrato soaring up to the attic like a laryngitic mezzo-soprano's. "The Young and the Restless" had ended, so she and my father were free to badger me anew with questions about Matty. They were in worse denial than I, and the soap opera provided a respite from their grief. But what could I tell them that they didn't already know? They'd been closer to him than I had. Like his crazy dead mother, they had spoiled him, indulged him, pampered him, waited on him hand and foot. And refused to reproach or discipline him with tough love when warranted: that thankless task fell to me. I didn't spare the rod, either, and Matty resented me for it. I won't deny that sometimes my tough love was a little too tough. *Nolo contendere.*

I yelled to my mother that I'd be down in a minute. My legs had begun to ache from squatting; I rose to stretch them and continued to read standing up, breathing the poisonous mold of the scrapbook's pages but caught up in a grim fascination. Unable to stop reading, I would come back another day, maybe tomorrow, for whatever of Matthew's I could find up there.

But my mother kept calling me. She was deaf and hadn't heard me. When had she ever heard me? The woman drove me insane. The prosecutor in me longed to indict her for what I did that October afternoon in '53. Having Billy over had been her idea — during supper a few days after the funeral, she had suggested it.

And that particular supper had begun so nicely, with baseball palaver between my father and me, the men of the house. Man talk. "World Series starts tomorrow," he'd reminded me. "Dodgers and Yanks. Think your Brooklyn bums have a chance?"

"It's their year, Dad. Duke hit three-thirty-six. Furillo hit three-forty-four. Jackie Robinson hit —"

"It never would have happened," my mother interrupted with one of her classic non-sequiturs, "if there had been no guns in the Vandemeer house."

The subject of guns was a bone of contention between them; if my father kept a gun in our house, she didn't know about it. "Objection," he droned in his courtroom voice. "Hon, the man could have bludgeoned those kids with a hammer."

"And used it on himself? Honestly, Reece." She addressed me gravely: "I think you should have Billy over one day after school next week."

The bite of hot mashed potatoes I'd taken stuck in my throat. "Why?" I asked.

"To show sympathy, dummy," my father said, chewing. "Why do you think?"

"You won't regret it," she added. "When we show compassion to others, God rewards us a hundredfold."

My father nodded in agreement. I rolled my eyes. It was a familiar routine. I had reached the age when all of a sudden, and distressingly, one's parents have turned into predictable dolts like the parents in TV sitcoms.

"We've shown sympathy, Mom," I protested. "We sent a card. We sent flowers. We even sent a *ham*."

"Sustained," my father ruled. "We did send a ham. A honey-baked."

"Stop with the bench talk, Reece. I don't mean token gestures. I'm talking about reaching out to that little boy with love and hospitality."

"But he's never been here before," I whined. "It's gonna seem like I'm invitin' him 'cause I feel sorry for him."

"Well, don't you?" Now she was going to preach—I saw it in the prim set of her lips. "Blessed are they that mourn," she quoted, "for they shall be comforted. That's from the Sermon on the Mount. Our Lord meant you, young man."

"Right," my father said. "Pass the gravy, guy."

I passed it with a puzzled frown. I hadn't understood the Jesus quote. Who was supposed to be mourning, me or Billy? Wasn't I the comforter? Religion often made no sense to me.

"Billy won't come," I said. "He's gonna think it's weird I'm even *askin'* him. We're not friends."

"He needs a friend," she countered. "The day will come when you'll lose a loved one and need a friend."

"A friend in need," my father murmured, buttering a hot Pillsbury dinner roll, "is a friend indeed." He actually said that.

I took my last shot: "I've got piano recitals next week."

"Piano recitals," he scoffed. "You should be playing football, not Mozart."

"I agree," I said. "But baseball, not football."

"He doesn't play Mozart, Reece. He plays Chopin. I played Chopin. And he doesn't have a recital on Wednesday."

"In that case," said my father, "enter it on the docket. Wednesday it is."

"I'll make you and Billy your favorite pie," she cajoled me. "An Eagle Brand lemon icebox pie. With Graham Cracker crust."

"I don't want some stupid *pie,* Mom! I don't want Billy here!"

I had gone too far. My father set down his knife and fork and stared at me the way he had the one time he'd taken me fishing and I'd girlishly recoiled from the wriggling earthworm he'd handed me to bait my hook.

"Tell me, guy," he said. "Are you scared of this poor kid because his dad was looney tunes?"

"No, sir."

"Are you sure?"

"I'm sure."

"Then it's settled. Objection overruled, case closed, *res judicata.*"

Have I mentioned that my father was an attorney? I hated him. He added, "You have that boy over Wednesday after school. Play some catch with him. Watch the World Series. And save me a piece of that pie."

I was silently furious. My mother had won again. She always won. I was losing respect for my father. She wanted me to be like her—a bleeding heart, a do-gooder who quoted Scripture and played Chopin. And he was fine with that. He thought he was strong, but he wasn't. He yearned to be a judge. Thank God he never became one. I hated him.

I had lied to him. I was scared to death of Billy Vandemeer. Partly for the reason my father suggested but also for a bigger reason. I had seen Billy in action.

Some case history. Despite being a Yankee and sounding it, he was the most popular boy in school; I was probably the least. To the extent that he knew I existed, his attitude toward me was derisive. I was the only seventh-grader who wore glasses, so Billy nicknamed me "Specs." Once everyone was calling me Specs, Billy re-nicknamed me "Liberace," for I was also the only seventh-grader who took piano. I hated being Liberace even more than I did Specs after an eighth-grader told me Liberace was a "homo." I wasn't sure what a homo was, but I knew it wasn't good. I was a nearsighted pianist, an only child, a mediocre athlete, and a straight-A student. Being known as a homo on top of all that could be a death warrant.

Now, with the hindsight of decades, I could see that Billy hadn't meant to single me out for contempt. He'd saddled other classmates with offensive nicknames too, permanent ones, and even "Jap," "Super-Spic," "Chocolate Drop," and "Penis Breath" had accepted them good-naturedly. Why? Because Billy was Billy. Or, as he called himself, Billy the Kid.

Billy the Kid was everything I wasn't. He was cool, I was square; he was tough, I was soft. He was strapping and good-looking, with sleepy grey eyes and long lashes (picture Robert Mitchum at thirteen) and a grin that could charm a cobra. I was that pimply-faced nerd with glasses who's always blowing his nose or asking to go to the bathroom. Sure, I made straight A's, but so what? The nuns gave Billy B's for never cracking a book and A's in conduct even though he cussed when they weren't around and told dirty jokes at recess.

And got in fights. We were forbidden to fight, but Billy got by with it. He never got caught. He seldom started a fight, but he'd get into one without much provocation. Most of our schoolyard scuffles amounted to just wrestling and rolling around on the ground, but Billy was a headhunter who went for the face. The sickening thing about watching him fight was the workmanlike way he went about it, as though he'd been trained by a boxer. And he had. His dad (he bragged) had fought in the Golden Gloves. Twenty years later, taking little Matthew to prizefights at the Dallas Coliseum, I would realize how well-trained Billy was.

The first boy I saw Billy the Kid beat up was Walter Joe Mc-Clain, the school bully. The *casus belli* was an idle threat Billy had taken as a challenge. Walter Joe was an overgrown fourteen-year-old, dumb as a post, with a promising future as a petty criminal: He extorted lunch money from smaller boys. Billy had been at St. Joseph's hardly a week when he happened on Walter Joe tormenting Arnold Windmeyer, a sixth grade sissy, in the lavatory.

On Arnold's stubborn days, when he wouldn't relinquish his lunch money, Walter Joe would drag him into a stall and threaten to stick his head into an unflushed toilet. Arnold would then surrender the change and go without lunch. I never understood why he'd resisted to begin with. He knew what was going to happen.

One morning during recess, as I was washing my hands at

the sink, Walter Joe dragged Arnold into the bathroom once more. I longed to defend Arnold but would've been no match for Walter Joe and didn't want to become his newest victim.

"Cough it up," Walter Joe demanded. "You little shit." Arnold denied having any money and they headed for the nearest stall. Both knew the drill, the ritual.

Then Billy the Kid walked in. "Both of you scram," he ordered. "The Kid needs to take a crap and you're in his stall."

"Use another stall," grunted Walter Joe, not turning around. "Or I'll kick your butt too."

"Let him go," Billy said. "You goddam son of a bitch."

Walter Joe turned around in amazement. Not even he cussed like *that*. With witnesses present, his reputation was at stake. But something warned him to cut his losses and back away.

"For a new kid," he grumbled, "you've got a big mouth, Vandemeer." But he let Arnold go.

Arnold scuttled out of the bathroom like a cockroach. From a distance, safely invisible, I stayed to watch what would happen next. Walter Joe tried to leave too, but Billy blocked his path. "I thought you were gonna kick my butt," he said.

"Next time," Walter Joe muttered.

"Naw. Do it now."

Walter Joe tried to shoulder Billy aside. The Kid punched him in the nose with a left jab. The bigger boy screamed. Billy followed with a short right hook to the jaw. He grabbed Walter Joe by the collar, dragged him back to the stall, and forced him to his knees. He pushed his head into the toilet and flushed it. Edging closer, like a gawker at a traffic accident, I saw blood dripping from Walter Joe's nose into the pink swirl of water as Billy jerked his head up and down. I can still hear Walter Joe sobbing, gulping, begging for mercy.

Walter Joe McClain didn't ever bother Arnold Windmeyer again. He began missing school and soon dropped out of St. Joseph's. Billy became known as a hero, a white knight who could protect the weakest among us from not just the Walter Joes of our world but the non-Catholic bullies from Beacon Hill, the public school two blocks away. Even our Holy Father, Pope Pius XII, would have blessed Billy for that, even though he frowned on fighting. It was a sin.

I was the only person on the planet who didn't think Billy hung the moon. I saw him as a mean kid who liked to hurt people. But to whom could I say that? The nuns and priests were the officers of his fan club. (The nuns didn't even mind Billy's being left-handed, though they'd been known to call left-handed kids "children of the devil" and force them to be right-handed.) My classmates would've said I was just jealous of Billy. Arnold Windmeyer happily would have given Billy his lunch money every day had Billy asked for it.

Life was not just. That was the fact of life I had yet to learn. There are people to whom the rules apply and people to whom they don't. Some people get away with murder, others with nothing. There is no justice, especially not in courtrooms. I had to go through law school at the University of Texas at Austin and become the Number Two man in the Dallas County District Attorney's office to learn that fact.

No, life was not fair. Consider. Was it fair that I should raise my son to be a man's man, a hunter, a fisherman, a lover of the clean life, a subscriber to the Hemingway code of valor, only to see him violate the code and (like Hemingway and Billy's father) commit the ultimate act of cowardice and unmanliness? No, I don't think that was fair. Do you?

Unlike my father, though, I didn't just stand around like some referee, enforcing the rules while my son fought his demons alone. Whatever they were, and I didn't know what they were, I tried to help him fight them. After his crazy mother died, I redoubled my efforts. But the harder I tried, the harder he pushed back. Sweet gentle Matthew grew to hate me for telling him he was not fighting the good fight, not fighting like a man. Later he accused me of being judgmental and preaching the macho gospel of Hemingway and Mailer. He stopped coming round or returning my calls. Yet the night I gave him the Jetfire, we drank beer, talked sports, planned to go dove hunting, buried the hatchet, even hugged each other. Remembering that night keeps me sane. I would see him alive just once more.

⁓

Now, sweating up in that airless purgatory of an attic, breathing dust and mold, I wondered how differently my life and Matthew's might have turned out had Billy declined my invitation. Since the funeral, the Kid hadn't struck me as all that needful of compassion, and I saw this as further evidence of his callous insensitivity. Dead father and dead sisters or not,

17

he seemed as much his old self as ever. On his first day back, he almost got into a fight with a towering eighth-grader who'd blocked him too vigorously at touch football. They had to be separated, and Billy was once more hailed as a hero.

Obediently, before that day ended, I'd invited him to my house. I managed to corner him in the cafeteria without a single sycophant at his side: no mean feat. I phrased the invitation in a way that he might decline it: "Hey, Vandemeer. You couldn't come over after school Wednesday, could you?"

The heavy-lidded eyes unveiled with curiosity. "Wednesday? What for, Liberace? You givin' a piano recital?"

"Hey, you don't *hafta* come —"

"No, really," he said, putting on a straight face. "I'd like to see your mansion. But what would we do?"

I shrugged. "Have a snack? Play catch? Watch the Series?"

The World Series! Billy loved baseball and the Vandemeers didn't own a TV.

"Yeah, sure," he said. "I'll come."

⌇⌇⌇

Billy's dig about my "mansion" had not passed unnoted. My family's rumored affluence embarrassed me. Affluence is relative, and ours was modest by any measure. Our parish encompassed an economically mixed neighborhood bisected by an actual pair of railroad tracks that almost never saw a train. On the wrong side of them lived poorer, blue-collar families like the Vandemeers in bungalows built after World War II; on the right side lived comfortably upper-middle-class families, like mine, in older two-storied houses of Georgian brick with attics and up-stairs porches and chimneys and sweeping front lawns. Ours wasn't a mansion—my father, a liberal defense attorney, accept-ed too many *pro bono* cases to afford a mansion. But it was im-posing, with white columns in the Colonial style framing the porch and a hilly front yard graced by Texas live oaks.

At three-twenty that day, Billy and I rode our bikes to my house from school. Needless to say, I would not mention the tragedy that had befallen him. Or that I'd kept a scrapbook of it. He couldn't wait to watch the Series game. He almost ran me over as he followed me through the maze of anteroom and liv-ing room, with its Steinway grand, and chandeliered dining room, through the kitchen and into the den housing our 17-inch black-and-white Emerson TV console.

Turning on the set, I felt a pulse of hope. Our love for base-ball was the only thing Billy and I had in common. This was Game Six, the Yankees leading three games to two. I rooted for my Dodgers—Texas had no major league teams then—while Billy pulled against them. A native Philadelphian, he hated the Dodgers because they'd virtually owned the Phillies since 1950.

In the eighth inning, my mother served up slices of lemon icebox pie and tall glasses of cold milk on TV trays. To my cha-grin, she hung around for a response; Billy's compliments seemed to satisfy her, and they must've been sincere, because he wolfed down two pieces. I noticed that his table manners were crude. No surprise.

In the top of the ninth, the Yankees led by three runs, and I was in despair. But the Dodgers' Carl Furillo tied the game by lining a three-run opposite-field homer into the right-field seats. I stood up and cheered.

"Won't matter," Billy muttered. "Your Brooklyn Bums are gonna lose."

And they did. In the bottom of the ninth, the Yankees' feisty second baseman Billy Martin knocked in the winning run with a single to center. The '53 Series was history. I sat glumly silent as we watched the Yankees players celebrate in their clubhouse, spraying one another with champagne.

"Tough titty, Liberace," Billy crowed. "But what can you expect from a team with niggers?"

I bristled. "Jackie Robinson is a great player. And the word is Negro."

"Niggers choke under pressure. That's why the Dodgers never win the World Series." He bounced up, put on his red Phillies cap, and pounded his raggedy baseball glove. "C'mon, Liberace, let's play some catch…"

—∿—

We walked out to the driveway—the same red cobblestone driveway I could see now, decades later, through the triangular window from my perch in the attic. My legs were weak with dread. Billy was the star pitcher on his Pony League team. Rumor had it the Phillies were scouting him. He'd probably started that rumor, but I'd heard Billy could throw a ball through a carwash without getting the ball wet, he threw so fast. Also, he was left-handed—a southpaw; in baseball lore southpaw pitchers could not throw a straight ball; their pitches always had some

20

late movement. How was I going to catch him?

Fortunately, the one thing I could do well was catch. My reflexes were sound, and my first baseman's mitt — a Rawlings "Claw" my father had given me for Christmas — was large and sturdy. (Once or twice, he'd even found time to play catch with me.) It was a glorious afternoon, crisp but sunny, with a scent of burning leaves in the air. Billy and I tossed the ball back and forth until our arms were loose. Then he began to wind up and throw harder. His pitches were no faster than my father's, though, and I had no trouble with them.

"Hey, Liberace," he called. "Got a catcher's mask?"

No, I said, and asked why. "'Cause I feel like cuttin' loose and don't wanna hurt you," he said.

That was insulting and condescending. "Throw your smoke," I challenged. "I don't need a mask. But no curves, okay?" I squatted and held up the Claw as a target. "Bring it."

"It's your funeral," he warned.

With his straight-overhand motion, he threw only fastballs, but they accelerated with a late rise. I had to get my leather up fast. He threw what coaches called a "heavy" ball — it exploded into the Claw like a cannon-fired shot put. I feared it might knock the mitt off my hand. I caught his pitches high, in the webbing, rather than low, against the palm; if I missed one, it could break my nose or shatter my glasses.

As he threw harder, I began to perspire, fogging my lenses. Every pitch was a white blur before it rocketed into my glove. I felt trapped and panicky. How I hated Billy. I'd always hated Billy a little, but now I hated him a lot. Okay, he had warned me that I might get hurt. But still.

Now, up in the attic, lost in my memories of that day, I realized he'd been venting some pent-up rage. But how was I to know that? Miraculously, somehow I hung in there, snagging every pitch, gaining confidence, until he tired and began to slow down.

"Whew," he finally said, grinning, out of breath. "I'm pooped."

Limp with relief, I could only nod.

"You're not a bad catcher, Liberace."

"Gee, thanks."

"I mean it. Hell, you're better'n my Pony League catcher."

It was the best compliment I'd ever received. At that moment, I could've forgiven Billy everything. I remember the grudging smile on his face, the sun-refracted nimbus round his red cap, the chirping of a bird in a tree. But something ruins the tableau. It's the blurred image, behind Billy, of fat Hartley Newman cruising up the driveway on his new red Schwinn three-speed.

Hartley, who was fourteen or fifteen, didn't know Billy. He attended Beacon Hill and lived far up the street, atop the hill, in a genuine mansion. The Newmans were rich, oil-rich. But Hartley's loutish manners and swinish obesity were proof that money didn't buy breeding or class. I called Hartley Newman "Hardly Human," but it never seemed to bother him. You couldn't insult Hartley Newman, because he didn't listen.

"Scram, Hardly," I told him.

But Hartley eased further up the driveway, straddling his bike. He braced it with his left foot. Brows furrowed, craning his neck, he squinted at Billy.

"What're you starin' at, Fat Ass?" Billy asked him.

"Ain't you that Billy Van-somethin'-or-other?"

Billy tossed his glove onto the lawn and approached Hartley with a menacing swagger. "Billy Vandemeer," he said. "What of it?"

"Beat it, Hardly," I warned. "Leave."

It had the feel of the day Billy beat up Walter Joe McClain, and I did not want to see Billy beat up Hartley on my front yard. I was feeling too good to watch that.

Hartley wouldn't leave. He said, "I seen your pitcher in the paper. Weren't you the guy that had his father kill his sisters?"

O God, I thought. *Had his father kill his sisters.* I rushed between them before Billy could hit him. But Billy wasn't going to. He'd stopped moving. He looked dazed and stricken.

Hartley farted. A muffled fart, but I heard it. "You're him," he persisted. "You're the guy. Ain't you."

Billy looked down and nodded.

"Get outa here, Hardly," I warned again.

"Didn't your daddy kill himself too? Why'd he do somethin' like that?"

Knock him off that bike, Billy! I wanted to scream.

But Billy just stood there, staring at some invisible object six inches from his face. Hartley edged closer and added, "He musta been crazy."

That was too much—I lost it. I gave Hartley the back of my hand. I purposely missed his face, but the swipe glanced off his shoulder and caught him upside the ear.

"*Ow!*" he squealed.

"Scram!" I ordered. "Beat it!"

Hartley spun his bike around and took off down the drive-way, fat legs and buttocks churning furiously. From a safe distance, he turned his head and yelled back something we couldn't hear.

Billy stayed in his daze, as though waiting for me to snap my fingers and bring him out of it. I will never know what was going on inside his head during those moments. I'm no head-shrink, but I suppose some door of denial had been kicked in, the carnage revisited, the traumatic tape replayed in his mind's eye. My impulse was to comfort him, throw my arm over his shoulder, give him a hug. But something stopped me.

"Jeez, Billy!" I scolded him. "Hartley's nothing! Why didn't you *say* something? Why didn't you hit him?"

"I'm thirsty," Billy said in a small voice.

At that moment I knew I'd never be afraid of Billy Vande-meer again. "Goddam it, wake up," I demanded. It was the first time I'd ever said "goddam" and it felt good.

His eyes unglazed. "Can I have a glass of water," he said.

I motioned toward the house. "Go get one."

The fact that he took his time—he may have gotten lost—annoyed me more. When he reappeared, I said, "Go home, Bil-ly." For once in my life, I was in the driver's seat, calling the shots, and it felt wonderful.

"I don't want to go home," he said.

The plaintive admission spoke volumes. *I don't want to go home.* It got to me—how could it not?—but I resisted. "Go away!" I yelled. "I don't want you here! I didn't want you here in the first place! You make me sick!"

Billy's shoulders looked to sag. He seemed disoriented. He found his bike, mounted it, and slowly pedaled off. I watched his red-capped figure recede until it disappeared in the direction of the tracks.

Heading back to the house, I picked up the glove he'd tossed on the lawn and forgotten. I hadn't noticed how small it was. Soft and worn, dark and ragged, it didn't have a lace connecting the fingers or a webbing between the index finger and thumb. It was a "dead-ball-era" glove. A relic. A hand-me-down. His dad's.

—∿—

"What's gotten into you?" my mother asked that night over supper. "Four pieces of fried chicken and now seconds on pie?"

My father chuckled. "He's a growing boy. Let him eat. I'll have some more pie myself." He gave me a wink. "Our son probably worked up an appetite playing baseball with the Vandemeer boy."

"How did that go?" my mother asked me. "Your game of catch?"

"Okay," I said.

"He seemed well mannered for a Northerner," she commented.

"Yeah," I muttered. "I guess."

"Having him over was the right thing to do, wasn't it," she crowed as she sliced the pie. "Father Steinkruger says charity is its own reward."

"Monsignor Steinkruger," I corrected.

"It wasn't so bad having him over," she said. "Now was it."

"I hear tell," said my father, "that Billy throws a baseball ninety miles an hour. Judge Calhoun's son plays on Billy's Pony League team. Word is, Billy has big-league stuff."

"He's not that good," I said.

"He's not? Hearsay, is it?"

"He's certainly well-mannered for a Yankee," my mother reiterated. "I think he's handling his terrible tragedy like a little soldier. Don't you, darling?"

"I guess," I replied with my mouth full of pie.

"And you'll have him over again?" she asked.

"No, ma'am."

She looked disappointed. "Why not?"

"He's had the boy over," my father told her. "No need to force them to be pals if they don't want to. By the way, fella, what happened to your Dodgers?" He grinned as he rubbed it in. "They sure got beat."

"They did," I mumbled, chewing.

I could not resist adding, "Billy said it's 'cause they have Negro players." The dismay on their faces was priceless. I had won the round.

—⁓—

My mother was calling me again. In a rage I slammed the scrapbook shut and sent it spinning like a rectangular frisbee, pages flying, toward a corner of the attic. And in that corner I spotted it. Billy's old glove.

Coated with dust, it was small enough to have lain unnoticed all these years. I crept over to it, picked it up, and held it in my hands. For no reason, I started to cry. My mouth trembled, my eyes blurred, I tasted the salt of the hot tears that streamed down my cheeks. My shoulders began to heave. Grief crippled my hands, and then they could only twist the glove, without ceasing, as if it were a rumpled leather handkerchief. Unable to stand the sound of my whimpering, I wept into the crook of my arm to muffle it, and then I stuffed my mouth with half my fist to stifle it.

Even at Matthew's funeral I hadn't cried. Why was I crying now? But then I asked myself why the hell I shouldn't be crying. Wasn't I in mourning too? Was mourning for women only? I'd goddamn well mourn if I wanted to. I had been on the verge of tears for days anyway.

Maybe, it occurs to me now, other things were bottled up inside me as well. Maybe I was also mourning for those nine convicts I had prosecuted and sent to death row when I could've asked for life. Or mourning for those two old fools downstairs, not dead yet but soon to be, who'd never had a clue as to who I was and never would. Or mourning for my first wife, Matthew's crazy mother, who'd called me the hardest man she'd ever known thinking it would hurt me. But I wasn't really crying for them. I was crying for my son, who the week before he died had told me about the man who was threatening his life. His rival for the affections of another man.

It was like an uppercut to the solar plexus, but the prosecutor in me had suspected what was going on. There had been circumstantial evidence, but I'd refused to consider it. More denial. Matty's eleventh-hour confession had only infuriated me. "Don't say another word," I warned him. "I won't even listen to you. Shut up. Jesus Christ, Matty! You make me sick!"

My tears kept coming, I couldn't stop them. It was ridiculous. I felt like such a fool. Should I go downstairs and face my parents with my eyes red and wet and my face twisted up with grief? With so many tears stored up, I wondered who else I might be grieving for. There had to be someone. Myself? No, it was too early and too late for that. But there was one other person. Dead or alive, wherever he might be, I was mourning for Billy Vandemeer.

—⁓—

I wish I could end my confession on that cathartic note. Absolution and forgiveness are often granted the penitent with wet eyes. Tears can sway a judge and jury. I should know — they had cost me enough convictions in the courtroom.

But I have one more sin, one more crime, to confess. On that October night in 1953, after I'd cleared the table, finished my homework, taken my shower, and slipped between the sheets, my mother knocked on my door and padded into my room in her robe and bedroom slippers. With a shy smile, eyes luminous in the semi-dark, she sat on the edge of my bed. I dreaded what might come. A bedtime homily. A parable extolling the poor meek losers of the world. Another lesson from Jesus's Sermon on the Mount.

"I want you to know," she said, touching my shoulder, "how proud we are of you for having Billy over. We won't make you do anything like that again."

I nodded. "Thanks, Mom. But you know what? I'm glad you made me." It was true, but not for the reason she thought.

"I love you." She bent down and kissed my forehead.

Afterwards, too pumped up to sleep, I reached under my bed for Billy's tattered baseball glove. How soft and pliant the leather was, as if cleaned and oiled a hundred times with loving care. If it had been his dad's, might it possess some occult power? I would keep it. Not to use, since I wasn't a southpaw and it was a rag, but just to have. I'd tell Billy someone had stolen it off the lawn.

Queerly excited, I put the glove on my right hand and began smacking its worn pocket, awkwardly and unnaturally, with my left fist. Gently at first but then harder. And soon, in the darkest part of night, I lay there pounding Billy Vandemeer's old baseball glove in a kind of frenzy.

CONFESSORS

Walter had just turned forty when it happened. How would he remember it at fifty? As an old-fashioned "nervous break-down?" A mild psychotic episode? A midlife crisis? It had been the strangest interlude of his life—that lost weekend which lasted three months, that going AWOL from the conscription his sexless marriage had become, that taking on a new identity with a made-up name.

Laid off from another job, nagged by a fat unhappy wife, needled by an acne-scarred Goth teenager (their son) addicted to violent video games, Walter had decided to run away from home. He didn't run, but he did walk. He told them he was leaving (neither took much notice) without saying where he was going or for how long. He packed a suitcase and a clothes bag and hurried out of his suburban house to the taxicab that waited, throbbing, at the curb.

Walter lived in a very large city ringed by suburban cities. He hid out, under an alias, in the bowels of "old" downtown—a dark stifling one-bedroom dump in a slum. Its Salvation Army furniture, lime-green shag carpeting, and free cable were its redeeming features. With a twinge of regret, but as a symbolic gesture, he slipped off his wedding ring and hid it under the mattress. He had his unemployment checks re-routed to his new digs. He watched old black-and-white movies in the morning and drank orange-flavored gin while he watched them at night. He never slept unless he'd passed out. Meals on Wheels, whom he'd lied to that he was disabled, brought him lunch and supper and the food was actually edible. Lacking a telephone or cell phone or iPhone or any other fucking kind of phone ensured that no one he knew could reach him. For the time being, at least, Walter had disappeared. Holed up in this impregnable refuge, this dark forbidding fortress, he felt absolutely safe and secure. Invisible, even. No enemy could find him.

The first week was wonderful: a vacation, a respite, a recuperation. Better than playing hooky from school. "Hell is other people," some French existentialist he'd read in college had written, but Walter had escaped from the hell that philosopher was talking about. By locking himself in, he had locked other people out, and there was exhilaration in escape from them.

After a week, of course, he began to long for human contact and his fortress began to feel like solitary confinement. But he'd expected that. It was time for Phase Two. Before running away from home, he'd gone on the Internet, listed the city's support groups, and made a call to each. Years earlier, in his late twenties, Walter had attended an open A. A. meeting with a recovering alcoholic friend and found it surprisingly moving and edifying. Even entertaining. He'd never forgotten that experience. Now was the time to revisit it and see where it might lead.

So he ventured out of his dark seclusion into the light of day like a bear coming out of hibernation, and soon had a different support group for each day of the week. Alcoholics Anonymous, Gamblers Anonymous, Overeaters Anonymous, Sex Addicts Anonymous, Suicide Attempters Anonymous, Kleptomaniacs Anonymous—he'd joined them all even though he'd never stolen or gambled or been addicted to sex or attempted suicide, and barely qualified as an alcoholic.

"My name is Roy and I'm a glutton," he'd lied to the disgustingly obese members at his first Overeaters Anonymous meeting. He'd used the alias "Roy" at his Alcoholics Anonymous meeting too; Roy Rogers had been his boyhood Western hero. Roy was a manly name, dashing and romantic. He wondered if it derived from the French word *roi,* which meant king. Roy Rogers was the king of the cowboys.

"Hi, Roy," the members droned in unison.

"I may not look it," he told them, "since I'm barely overweight, but I'm a foodie. A glutton. A pig with a tapeworm. A gourmandizer. A chow hound. I don't eat to live, I fucking live to eat. That's why I hate my life and why I'm here. And I feel better already, because I'm saving my life. By the way—anyone know where the snack bar is?" It was unpardonably corny, but it earned laughter and applause that made him feel accepted. Like one of the gang. For the rest of that day, he really did feel better about himself.

Phase Two worked out well. Support groups provided the modicum of human contact Walter needed to keep from going stir crazy without the hassles or headaches of social intercourse. They kept his mind off his problems and put them in perspective. It was consoling to learn that people obviously better educated, better looking, and better off than himself had managed to wreck their lives worse than he had his. Paradoxically, empathizing and identifying with their failures made him feel less like a failure himself. Listening to their woeful histories—darkly sad but often funny too, like the shticks of Jewish comedians just out of rehab—was balm for Walter's battered psyche. Every bio was a reality show, a tearful psychodrama leavened with comic relief. The members sometimes laughed until they cried.

"How do you fail at being a failure?" one waggish little man asked the Suicide Attempters Anonymous group. "I managed to. I tried to shoot myself in the head, but I survived with minimal damage. They rushed me to a hospital where miracle-working surgeons, God damn them, were there to save my life. They expected me to be grateful. I called them every foul name I could think of. They figured I was crazy—they just laughed it off. They'd put a metal plate in my head and told me I could get HBO now without paying." The group seemed unsure how to respond until the Suicide Attempter started to laugh, and then they too were laughing, and Walter, faking it, was laughing harder than anyone else but wondering how much of the story was true.

Compassion poured from his soul at the group meetings like cream from a carton. Each confraternity of damaged men and women became for him a family more deserving of love than his own. He was like those faceless anonymous spectators in the back rows at courtroom proceedings. He told himself he was there to audit, watch, laugh, cry, empathize, understand, commiserate. And most of all, to *learn*. One day, of course, when he was healed and felt strong enough, he would return to his family. But there was no hurry.

For support groups that made him participate actively, he had to fabricate a personal history. Forced to "share" or "testify" or "witness," he made up a sob story for each. Having minored in creative writing, Walter didn't lack for imagination or verisimilitude. But why make things up? Why not just tell his true story, expose himself as the others did, acknowledge his failures as a husband and father and breadwinner? He had his reasons not to. Making stuff up kept things under control; telling the truth might mean surrendering that control, and in his fragile, helpless state he couldn't risk it. He dared not divulge his weaknesses and bare his innermost soul to a bunch of losers who wouldn't understand. He was willing to sit in judgment on their lives but unwilling for them to sit in judgment on his. (With his luck, they'd judge him unfairly and leave him feeling suicidal). He had lain on the couches of psychiatrists who hadn't helped him. How could addicts and sickos and weirdos and total strangers?

What he took from the meetings instead was like the joy evangelicals receive when one of them steps forth to accept Jesus as savior, confess some sin, and beg to be forgiven. Vicariously, Walter was being forgiven every day, and forgiving others just as often. He was still sane enough to suspect he'd gone a little crazy, but so what? He'd suffered an emotional breakdown; neurotic and infantile behavior was allowed. He was a man half-blind groping his way through a thunderstorm. Any port in the storm was welcome. What felt right was right.

And what he was doing felt right. Support groups were working for Walter.

Confessors Anonymous, his Wednesday group, was his favorite. Based on a discipline called Catharsis Therapy he'd read about in *Psychology Today,* it granted forgiveness to guilt-ridden penitents who could not forgive themselves. Members confessed to the Group their deepest secrets and blackest sins. In Walter's chapter, after probing (and often merciless) cross-examination by the other members and a thirty-something moderator, in a white robe, who looked like Jesus and called himself Christophe, penitents received forgiveness and absolution. The healing closure—the catharsis—would follow. Walter would then join the other confessors in applause and congratulations. Some members wept, but there Walter drew the line. He refused to become maudlin or hysterical. He still had his pride.

"We are saved by the catharsis called love," Christophe explained at Walter's first Confessors Anonymous meeting. (With his long hair and beard, his sandals and robe, he reminded Walter of Jeffrey Hunter's Jesus in the sixties movie *King of Kings*.) "And the ultimate expression of love is forgiveness. We must forgive and be forgiven. But the only person who can forgive us is us. The theologian Reinhold Niebuhr is emphatic on this."

The members nodded gravely. Walter doubted they knew Reinhold Niebuhr from Reingold Beer, but he did, having majored in philosophy. He'd heard that Christophe held a chair in the philosophy department of some university, but he didn't believe it. Maybe it was the Jesus look, or the insanely blazing blue eyes, or the Group name Christophe had chosen, or the limp moist handshake, but he mistrusted Christophe. And it bothered Walter that while the other support groups were either free or inexpensive, Confessors Anonymous exacted a steep membership fee and monthly dues. Still, it was his favorite group, the one with the most interesting members, and he looked forward to its meetings.

Confessors Anonymous, Christophe emphasized, were not just those who heard confessions but also those who made them. Once you had confessed and been forgiven at a meeting, you could forgive yourself and doff your hair shirt of guilt. No confessor remained unforgiven if he or she sincerely repented. Forgiveness was a slam-dunk. The Group had just three rules: anonymity (each member used an assumed first name); no socializing or fraternizing (except during smoke breaks); and strict confidentiality (what happened in Group stayed in Group). Breaking any rule meant expulsion and the withholding of forgiveness.

"And I'll know if you've broken a rule," Christophe warned. "And which one." Not only was this guru Christlike, Walter thought with a snigger, but Godlike. Omniscient.

—∿—

Confessors Anonymous met for two hours each week in the ground-floor conference room of an old hotel that had seen better days. The Group, a dozen strong, sat on folding metal chairs around a long wooden table that was battered and scarred, with Christophe at the head. The fluorescent ceiling light was bright enough for a police grilling. Smoking was not allowed, but after the first hour came a ten-minute break during which smokers fled the building to light up. Confessors, Walter noted, were even heavier smokers than Alcoholics Anonymous. He had started smoking again just to fit in.

In his first four meetings, Walter heard confessions that jolted him. The quartet of penitents included an attorney who'd paid her shyster sister-in-law $500 to take the bar exam for her; a gay schoolteacher who as a teenager was regularly molested by his father and "by golly enjoyed it" because it was the only time the man showed him any affection; a loan officer who'd embezzled $100,000 from his bank and secretly made restitution but never rid himself of the compulsion to turn himself in to the police; and a retired Army Captain who, in 1968, had assigned a Second Lieutenant he disliked to a patrol under fire in the Mekong Delta, where the junior officer was wounded in a Viet Cong ambush. Each confessor was forgiven, though several members had trouble forgiving the gay schoolteacher.

Walter (Group name Roy) spent days rehearsing the confession he would make at his fifth meeting. While Christophe and the members listened intently as a judge and jury, "Roy" described how, one Saturday night when he was seventeen, driving drunk in his parents' Ford Fairlane after a party, he'd fled the scene of an accident. Speeding along the dark road that led to their subdivision, he'd sighted a hitchhiker on the shoulder.

Ragged and disheveled, some Hispanic wearing a headband and a T-shirt, probably an illegal who camped in the woods, the wretch held his thumb aloft. Why he'd be hitchhiking at this hour Walter had no idea.

Walter, or Roy, decided to give the hitchhiker a scare. He sped up along the shoulder. He meant to just miss him but failed to swerve in time and clipped him with a *thwack*. Comically, the hiker somersaulted through the air, head over heels, into the brush.

"I never slowed down," Roy confessed. "I floored the accelerator. All of a sudden I was cold sober. I'd never been so scared. I almost crapped my pants. I couldn't turn around and go back—I already had one DWI and couldn't afford another. If the poor guy was dead, I could've gone to jail for years. I drove home, crawled into bed, and lay awake till dawn trying to decide what to do. In the end I did nothing."

It wasn't total fiction—it had actually happened to his black-sheep cousin Jack, a malicious prankster. No one but Walter and Jack knew about it. Walter related it with such anguish in his cracking voice that the other members (save one) bought every word. During the cross-examination, the embezzler asked, "What happened to the wetback?" "I don't know," Walter said. "I never heard or read anything about him." "Maybe he was hitchhiking because he'd had an accident or run out of gas," the gay teacher surmised. "Did they find a car nearby?" "Not that I know of," Walter replied. "God damn it, did you try to find out!" the Army Captain barked. "I tried everything I could to find out!" shouted Walter. "I drove around the area the next morning and took a look. I even got out of the car. I found nothing. No one. As if I'd dreamed it up."

"Maybe you did," a fourth member offered. "Maybe your whole story is dreamed up."

There was a hush. As if in shock, everyone stared at the speaker. Her Group name was Andrea and she sat directly across the table from Walter. Perky and red-haired, with bangs and a pony tail, Andrea fell just short of pretty. Startled green eyes shone like headlights in her freckled face. She always wore (he'd noticed) expensive-looking pumps, silk cowgirl shirts, and designer jeans. Everything about her hinted of advantage or privilege.

"Is your story made up, Roy?" she pressed him.

Walter felt himself blanch. He had not expected to get caught.

"Of course not," he responded with an ersatz indignation. "Why would I make up such a thing? I can still see the face of that man in my headlights."

Andrea smiled knowingly. "Does it look like a deer?"

"Ease up, Andrea," the gay teacher warned.

"You ease up," snapped the female attorney. "Andrea has the right to interrogate."

"Confessors, please," urged Christophe. "Let's proceed with our judgment. Roy has carried this cross since he was seventeen. That's well over half his life. Shouldn't he be forgiven?"

"He should be," said the embezzler. "There's nothing he can do about the poor devil now."

The gay teacher said, "If you had killed him, Roy, you'd have heard or read about it."

"Maybe you injured him but didn't kill him," the Captain suggested. "He probably got up and staggered off and got a ride on the highway. You're a coward and a deserter but not a killer, Roy. I mean, you *could've* killed the beaner, but you didn't. I don't condone what you did, but I forgive you for it now."

Walter breathed relief. The vote didn't have to be unanimous, and he had a majority. The attorney summed up, "Here's my judgment. You've tormented yourself all these years about an evidently inconsequential incident, Roy. Cease and desist. Grant yourself peace. Technically, you committed a felony by fleeing the scene of an accident. You could have gone to jail. Maybe you should have. But it's time you closed the case on this matter. It's a *fait accompli*. A *res judicata*. I vote to absolve and exonerate and forgive."

One by one, except for Andrea, who voted "present," the other members voted the same way. So did the moderator. "Roy, the Group's verdict lets you off the hook," Christophe announced. "What you did was despicable, but you've confessed and repented. Guilt can be useful, but yours serves no purpose. Don't drink and drive again. At least not on nights when *I'm* out hitchhiking."

There was polite laughter. Christophe flashed his beatific smile. Walter felt as if he'd been acquitted of an actual crime. Tears welled in his throat. He wondered if this was how stage actors felt after a great performance. He had lost himself in his role and actually become Roy, a guilt-ridden coward. Maybe he was Roy.

But Andrea, he saw, had not been taken in. She was smiling

at him with mild contempt, her lips pursed in amusement.

—◦◦◦—

Against his better judgment, unable to resist, Walter sidled up to her during the break. She was standing outside the hotel entrance, furiously puffing on a cigarette. The small leather purse in which she kept her Virginia Slims probably bore a Gucci or Louis Vuitton label. Her sterling silver lighter shone and sparkled. Walter lit up too.

Exhaling smoke, Andrea sought to apologize. "I'm sorry I was a bitch in there. It was nothing personal."

"That's all right. Did you really doubt my confession?"

"I did. I'm not sure why."

"Well, at least you were honest. Are you skeptical about Christophe, too?"

"Very skeptical."

Walter chuckled. "Don't you trust anybody?"

"I know Christophe. His real name is Irving Finkel and he used to be an est trainer. I'll bet you heard he gave up a lucrative career as a psychotherapist to found Confessors Anonymous."

"No. I heard he held a chair in some philosophy department."

She laughed delightedly. "That's even better! These saintly gurus come equipped with the greatest bogus resumés!"

"If you think he's a phony, why do you come to his meetings?"

She blew a jet of smoke and smiled cagily. "That's a good question, Roy. Why do you?"

Walter wondered if she might be telepathic. A psychic or a modern-day witch. What if she could read minds? She would know the truth about him. She was perhaps fifteen years his junior, and he'd been taken with her since Day One. Her tight silk cowgirl shirt showed thimble-like nipples; her body looked hard and taut; he felt a stirring in his loins. No, he told himself. Don't even think about it.

"You're not like the others in there," she said. "There's something different about you."

"There's something different about you, too. What makes us special?"

She gave a shrug. "We could be kindred spirits. Soul mates. Want to meet for a drink afterwards?"

She watched his reaction. "Oh, don't look so scared," she said.

Walter felt the tingle in his groin again. "It's against the rules, remember?"

"Who would know? Christophe?"

"He said he would."

"That's more of his chest pounding. Let's go for a drink afterwards."

Walter shook his head. "Better not."

She wrinkled her freckled nose in disappointment. "Your story painted you as chicken. I guess it was true."

Walter felt the back of his neck prickle. He looked around.

"All right," he said. "One drink."

〜

They'd arranged to meet in an anonymous little bar, cool and dark and intimate, that Walter knew of because it was within walking distance of his apartment. They chose a booth toward the rear. Andrea was well spoken, with just the barest hint of a twang, and Walter had a hunch she'd tried to rid herself of it. Soon they were breaking another Group rule by discussing the other members and Christophe and mimicking them. But they did not reveal their real names or divulge other personal information. Or mention Walter's phony confession.

They didn't have one drink, either. They had three, and she matched him martini for martini. Soon they were touching each other across the table and giddily playing footsie underneath it. Walter felt he'd known Andrea for a long time. There was something familiar about her.

The next thing he knew, he was leading her up the wooden staircase that ran alongside his apartment building to the kitchen entrance. Entering, he was afraid she'd comment on the stuffiness and squalor, but she didn't. She only began removing her expensive silk blouse.

Taking this pert little redhead into his bed, breaking the Group rules, not to mention his marriage vows, was the boldest thing Walter had ever done. But the gin had emboldened him, and he'd never wanted a woman more, and by God he was going to have this one. His prick was tumescent before they reached the bedroom.

She was a true redhead—a first for him, which was exciting. He had read in *Psychology Today* that there are sex types, discrete as blood types, that determine a couple's sexual chemistry. He had not believed it until now. Andrea was clearly his sex type. With his wife, sex had always been a chore, a challenge, and failure a possibility. This felt more like child's play, lighthearted, unhurried, without goals. Like the wet dreams of his adolescence, sex with Andrea was almost too effortless, and he feared he might be dreaming. He could not make a false move. It was as if her body were an appendage of his, like the hand he used to masturbate.

They came together, and without pausing she positioned herself on top. And then spoon-fashion, draping her right leg over his right hip. And then in another embrace. It was proving to be a fuck fest. She was a sexual gymnast, nimble and supple as a contortionist, and that, he supposed later, was why making love with her was so easy. In the missionary position she could press the soles of her feet against her ears. She was partner-proof; any man could've had good sex with her; even he could. Apparently multi-orgasmic, she came again and again, each time with a girlish whimper and then a hiccuping sound.

Finally limp with exhaustion, they shared a cigarette, passing it back and forth like lovers in some black-and-white forties movie. Walter thanked her and told her he wanted to see her again. *"Vell, vy not,"* she murmured in a husky Marlene Dietrich voice, and they both laughed. They skipped the post-coital conversation that would have led to further violations of Group rules, and after a time of cuddling there, gloriously nude and feeling very close, she made an excuse to leave. She rose, dressed, and let herself out the kitchen entrance as he watched from his bed like a sultan—sated, supremely satisfied, and unable to believe his good fortune. Could this really have happened to him?

"See you next week, *Roy*," she called from the door with a

canny smile and a wave of her hand. "Let's do this again."

When she was gone, Walter felt like whooping in self-congratulation. A sexy, intelligent, not bad-looking young woman had wanted to go to bed with him. That was flattering in itself, and then she'd said she wanted to come back. So what if she hadn't believed his confession? Why should that matter? The others had believed it. It only meant that she was smarter than they were. He liked intelligent women. And this one was a wizard in bed, too.

He could not stop congratulating himself. Apparently, he not only had survived his nervous breakdown but triumphed over it. He was going to be just fine. Now the world was his oyster.

⸙

Walter had been raised in a faith he no longer believed in that was big on pomp and ceremony and ritual. Religiously, he and Andrea acted out their illicit ritual after each Confessors Anonymous meeting for the next three Wednesdays. She wore the same chic, expensive cowgirl outfit and red pumps. They were careful to ignore each other during the meeting. They met at the same bar afterward, enjoyed three martinis at a leisurely pace, hurried to Walter's apartment (which he'd aired, cleaned up, and even redecorated), jumped into bed, and fucked for hours.

Walter had never thought to enjoy casual or impersonal sex —he saw himself as too deep and substantial a person for that. But with Andrea he reveled in it. The anonymity—the fact that he didn't know her name or anything else about her—was an aphrodisiac. He was as phallic and potent as a satyr. It was the most exciting time of his life, and he refused to jeopardize it by

45

wondering how long it would last. Andrea was his ministering angel—week by week, he felt himself growing stronger and more confident.

He had become a new man. Walter may have been a wimp, but Roy was a stud. He quit going to his other support group meetings and counted the days until Wednesdays rolled around. He cut down on his drinking and slept soundly every night. Occasionally, with a stab of remorse, he'd remember his wife and son, but never for very long. They were the past and he was living in the present. Someday he'd go back to them, but not right now. He read, he went to movies and restaurants, he took long walks. It felt so good to be alive.

Inevitably, as lovers will, he found himself wanting to open up to Andrea. Reveal who he was, learn who she was, tell her about his sad fat frustrated wife and acne-scarred teenage son, his failed careers and suffocating suburban existence. But he stopped himself from doing it. Why bring up the things he had run away from to save his soul? Why piss on his own parade? Why ruin a perfect love affair by wanting it to be something more?

—ᜑᜑᜑ—

But everything changes, even if we don't change it. For Walter things changed drastically after the Group meeting at which Andrea shared her shameful secret. She'd put it off for as long as Christophe would permit, but finally it was time to fess up or leave the Group.

In the halting voice of a nervous child, she described how, in her late teens, she'd been raped by a mentally challenged uncle who'd come to live with the family because he was homeless. When she told her parents—whom she described as "Dallas rich, Dallas religious, Dallas dumb"—what he'd done to her, they made it seem like *her* fault ("the way you parade around in those short shorts and halter tops!") and forbade her to tell anyone. With a one-way plane ticket the uncle was dispatched to Darlington, Wisconsin to live with cousins on her father's side. Andrea was instructed to pretend the ugliness had never occurred; it could only embarrass the family and soil her reputation. Time healed all wounds, her father reassured her, and what had happened actually happened to many young women.

Christ! Walter thought angrily, listening to her. No wonder she hadn't wanted to share. He could not believe what he was hearing.

But the unbelievable parts were yet to come. Andrea resumed her tale of woe. A month later, she turned up pregnant from the rape. Her parents told her they'd had enough; love had its limits; they suggested she leave home and move to another town. She could visit at Christmas and other holidays. Her father gave her a thousand dollars to spend as she wanted and make a new start. "The well's dry now," he added.

She was talked out of an abortion by her twin sister, the wife of a wealthy televangelist. The twin sister was even more "pro-life" than the televangelist, but Andrea worshipped her. Andrea consented to have the child and, with the televangelist's help, have it adopted by a couple in his ministry. He had a waiting list of affluent childless couples wanting Caucasian babies, preferably blue-eyed males.

Late into Andrea's second trimester, her obstetrician detected a problem. State-of-the art sonography was employed, the fetal heartbeat monitored, the amniotic fluids drawn. The fetal anatomy was studied and analyzed with real-time sonography. Money being no object (the televangelist and his ministry were footing the bills), a second opinion was gotten from a nationally famous Houston obstetrician.

Both doctors agreed that the fetus was anencephalic: missing a major part of its brain. "You are carrying a child that will not survive outside your womb," the Houston obstetrician told Andrea.

"And may not survive inside it," the first obstetrician added.

Again Andrea considered abortion; again her sister talked her out of it, citing a problem pregnancy, worse than Andrea's, in which an allegedly anencephalic baby had not only survived but grown up to become a Pentecostal deacon. Walter kept himself from laughing, but none of the other confessors as much as smiled. Christophe appeared to be weeping.

Andrea gave breech birth to a baby boy with a frog-like face and deformed cranium who'd been dead two weeks. "I'd been a walking coffin for the poor little freak," she sobbed. "I felt guilty for getting raped. Guilty for not reporting it. Guilty for not having an abortion when I should've. I knew I was being punished but didn't know which of those things I was being punished for. I thought I'd done what was right. I didn't *want* him to die."

She was fighting back tears. "Please forgive me," she whimpered. "I didn't want him to die."

"I forgive you, Andrea," Christophe declaimed with his arms

outspread as if to embrace her. "You are a beautiful human being."

Walter winced and rolled his eyes but voted with the other Confessors to forgive. Bypassing the interrogation, the Group absolved Andrea of everything she'd done wrong, even though she'd done nothing wrong, and the catharsis was complete. Andrea tried to smile like a plucky cowgirl, but her chin was trembling. She refused to cry. Walter yearned to get up, walk around the table, kneel beside her, put his arms around her, and bury his face in her lap. He was in love with her, he realized.

—∞—

In bed that afternoon she was as cold and unresponsive as his wife and unable to reach an orgasm. Walter, having gotten off twice, chalked it up to her having confessed. Maybe they should've skipped sex today, he thought. As they shared their ritual postcoital cigarette, he sensed a profound change in her. In confessing, had she revealed more than she'd intended? Maybe she wasn't as tough as she tried to appear. Maybe she wasn't tough at all.

Whatever the answers, he needed some right now. He would proceed gingerly. "Sweetheart," he began, "something bothered me about your confession. You seem so independent—so much your own person. So smart, so strong. How could you let your dumb sister and brother-in-law make the biggest decision of your life for you? I mean, it was your body, not theirs, and —"

"My sister's not dumb," she said in a dull voice. "Wanda May's a smart woman."

"I'm sorry I called her dumb. But how could you let them?"

"I don't know. Maybe that's the sin I was confessing."

She took a drag off their cigarette, exhaled, and her eyes widened with fear as she turned fully toward him. "Are you disappointed in me? Are you judging me?"

"Or course not." I love you, he wanted to tell her, but he was afraid to.

"The Group forgave me. Christophe forgave me. Do I need your forgiveness, Roy?"

"Don't do that. Please."

"What are you saying then? You think my story was made up?"

"Of course not, sweetheart. Just not in character. No big deal." He faked a smile. "Who are you, Andrea? What's your real name? My name is Walter and I'm an alcoholic. Say hi to me. I was a member of half a dozen other support groups when I met you."

As a bid for levity, or perhaps intimacy, it failed. She turned her face away. At length she sighed. "All right, Roy or Walter or whoever you are. It's confession time again. My story was a fake. A lie."

Silence.

Then: "Don't play with me, Andrea. That's not funny."

"I'm not playing. My story was made up."

The ceiling began to spin and then the room to tilt as if on an axis. She was serious, he realized with alarm. His impulse was to reach out and pull her body against his and tell her it didn't matter whether her story was real or not. But it did matter.

"What are you saying?" he asked in a cracking voice.

"That I lied. And I hate liars." She stubbed out their cigarette in the ashtray. "So look, mister, if you and I are going any further, and I want to, because I think we have something, we need to be totally honest with each other. No more lies, okay? I'm a stringer for *Rolling Stone*. I'm researching a feature about the comeback of seventies-style support groups and self-help programs."

Walter felt sick. He struggled to find his voice. He couldn't.

"It may be a cover story," she added.

"Please tell me no," he croaked.

"Oh, come off it. I'm not confessing to a *homicide*. Like you did."

He stared at her. "You're a reporter? A fake? This ruins everything."

"What? No, it doesn't. Why should it?"

"I was moved by your story."

"So? I was moved by yours until I realized it was bullshit."

"Now you're not real. I can't trust you."

She sat bolt upright and yanked the sheet up to her chin. "Look who's talking!" she hissed, green eyes ablaze. "Why the hell are *you* at Confessors Anonymous? You're an impostor too. I told you I suspected it that day when we were smoking on the break. Now that I know you shall we say intimately? I'm sure of it."

"It's not the same thing, Andrea. Your story and mine."

"Why not? What makes you special? Your confession was so obviously counterfeit. You're not the wild and crazy type of guy who'd run over somebody in a car. You're a sweet timid little boy and a stickler for rules. I had to push you into bed. You were scared to break *Christophe's* rules. I'll bet you've never gotten a traffic ticket. Even drunk, you wouldn't have done what you said."

"A drunk teenager will do anything."

"I've seen you drunk. You don't change much."

"It happened twenty-five years ago."

"Stop lying, God damn you!" Her voice was like a knife slicing a glass. "Your story was a lie and so was mine. So what? You should be *glad* I'm not some rape victim or human coffin or basket case. I'm a serious journalist."

Walter had no response. He'd been lied to, tricked, cheated, betrayed. Nothing she could say would change that. His lips quivered. The ceiling was tilting again; would it never stop? He tried to swallow, but his throat was dry.

"I'm a serious journalist," she repeated in a small voice, as if he hadn't heard the first time.

"You're also an actress," he muttered. "You deserve an Oscar. You fooled everybody."

"Well, *you* didn't. Even Christophe is on to you. I happen to know he's on to both of us."

Now he could only sit there, naked and silent, on the edge of the bed, his elbows on his knees, his head in his hands. He felt like throwing up.

"Get out," he told her.

"What? Hey, wait a minute —"

"Get out. It's over. I joined the Group to study people in pain. Not magazine hacks."

She gave her tough little chuckle. "You joined the Group to study people? It's not supposed to be a science project, asshole. Don't worry, Professor — I won't mention you in my story." She bounded up, pulled on her designer jeans and silk shirt, and stepped into her red high heels. She stumbled, almost falling, and then grabbed her leather purse.

She smiled at him fixedly, with contempt. "You're a coward and a cipher," she sneered. "You're hiding out from your*self* in this dump. Aren't you."

"Maybe I am."

She turned and stormed out. He heard her heels clunking down the wooden staircase. Minutes later, Walter remembered that he still didn't know her name or address or phone number.

—*ww*—

Walter skipped the next two Confessors Anonymous meetings, but returned to his other support groups. Now he needed support worse than before. They offered scant comfort, however, since he was there in body only. When he wasn't brooding about Andrea—fantasizing about her hard little breasts, the copper-penny taste of her mouth, the whimper and then the hiccuping sound she made when she came—he was glancing at his watch, needing a drink, a smoke, a place to whack off. He missed her with a dull ache in his loins, a gnawing at his heart. He had known it would end at some point, but hadn't expected it to hurt like this.

Day after day, he paced the green shag carpet in his apartment like a prisoner in a jail cell or a leopard in a cage, agonizing over what to do. Now he felt well enough, strong enough, to go home. But did he want to? He missed his wife and son, certainly; how could he not? For all their faults, he missed them. He had never meant to stay gone forever. If he returned to Confessors Anonymous and Andrea took him back, he might never see them again. But then he and Andrea could resume on an honest basis, make a fresh start with real names, real identities, and bid the Group good-bye. Perhaps move to another city in another state. Surely she had enough material for her damned *Rolling Stone* article by now.

But did he want Andrea back? That was the question. Should he gamble his future on a woman he knew nothing about except that she was his sexual type, fucked liked the Whore of Babylon, taught him a new position each time they got into bed, and made his cock so stiff that it ached? Should he take such a risk? Some days he thought yes; others, absolutely not. He changed his mind more often than Hamlet. First he'd despise her again for lying, fabricating a confession that moved him so deeply, conning him into believing it. Then he'd remember that he'd done the same thing to her. Or tried to. And she was right when she said being an undercover writer for *Rolling Stone* was a lot better than being a damaged victim of rape and incest. A basket case.

She'd called him a little boy because he'd acted like one who's just learned there's no Santa. Now it was time he acted like a man. He should forgive her and ask her forgiveness. Forgiveness was the highest form of love—Reinhold Niebuhr said so. And he loved Andrea. Of that he could be certain. He was also sure that she loved him. No woman, not even his wife, had fallen in love with him the way she had. No other woman might ever.

What to do? Waking up on Wednesday morning with a throbbing erection, he decided. He would try to get her back, if only for a while. He had to buy himself time. He needed a clearer picture of who she was and what she offered him besides porn-star sex and some acting ability. He needed to be certain about their connection.

It was time for Phase Three. He would go back to Confessors Anonymous.

⸎

But she wasn't at the Wednesday Group. She too had missed the last couple of meetings. No member had seen her since the day she'd made her confession. He asked them all. During the break, he even cornered Christophe in the hallway.

"I need to find Andrea. Do you know what's happened to her?"

The moderator knitted his brows. "Has something happened to her? Members often skip meetings for weeks at a time. Members come and go. It's not unusual."

"She said she knew you personally."

"She knew me professionally." Christophe eyed him with suspicion. "What do you want with her?"

"I'm in love with her."

Christophe glowered. "You're out of the Group, Roy. You broke my rule about socializing."

"Fine, I'm out. And we did more than socialize. Screw your rule."

"No, screw *you*. See, I can talk dirty too."

"Please tell me how I can find her."

"I wouldn't even if I knew. We protect the privacy of our

55

members. You've probably damaged her recovery. I shouldn't tell you this, but Andrea is a sick girl. Didn't you hear her confession? She can't forgive. She can't forgive *herself.* She goes into fugal states. She doesn't know who she is. She's in denial about what happened to her."

"She says she made that up."

"Every word was true. She was my patient when I was a therapist in Dallas. I brought her into my Group when I founded it. She'd been winning at her therapy. Her confession was a breakthrough. And now you've sabotaged everything, damn you."

"She said you were just an est trainer."

Christophe smiled ruefully and shook his head.

"I have to find her, Christophe. What's her real name?"

"I don't know. Who was she this time? The CIA spook? The Broadway method actress? A *New Yorker* stringer on assignment to write about support groups?"

Walter looked down. "It was *Rolling Stone.*"

"And you believed her? Andrea's denial takes the form of pathological lying. She becomes delusional. The rape trauma made her promiscuous. The last thing she needed was sordid sex with a dishonest person."

"Why am I dishonest?"

"Because your confession was a fake, Roy. I knew it at the time. I assumed you had a good reason to lie. Apparently, you didn't. Did you join the Group to get laid?"

"Of course not. Please, Christophe. If you hear from her —"

"Stay away from my Group. Stay away from me. Leave and don't come back."

Walter spent days looking for Andrea but had no way to find her. He went to the bar where they'd drunk and asked if anyone had seen her again. He sought her face in other bars, in restaurants, theaters, even in specialty shops that sold designer Country-Western couture. He called *Rolling Stone* in New York City and made a fool of himself by describing her in detail and asking if they'd assigned a stringer matching her description to research a story on support groups. He learned nothing. For three consecutive Wednesdays, he cased the Confessors Anonymous meetings from his parked car, watching Group members enter the hotel and emerge two hours later.

He never saw Andrea. On the third Wednesday, he approached one of the members as the man was climbing into his SUV. It was the embezzling loan officer who wanted to turn himself in. Somehow Walter felt he could trust him.

"She likely won't be back," the embezzler said. "I've been support grouping for years, Roy. Many of us need long-term help. But Andrea struck me as the sort who just wanted to make her confession and get on with her life. If we see her, we'll tell her you're looking for her. Christophe won't. He's never forgiven anyone he's kicked out of Group…"

⁓

Walter finally went home to his wife and son. There was no reason to hide out from them any longer. With Andrea gone, he desperately needed human contact. He was shriveling up without it. And he missed his family. He rationalized that he was not returning by default but because it was the right thing to do. He was stronger now, his loved ones needed him. Fate had made his decision. What wants to happen will. The thing with Andrea had wanted to happen but then had wanted to end. To suffer a natural death. He had to let it go.

When he returned home, his wife and son were overjoyed with relief. They had been to the police, the morgue, even a missing persons agency. There were no recriminations or questions. No explanations were demanded. His son embraced him —something he hadn't done since he was five—and his wife, who had lost weight and was no longer obese, hugged him and kissed him and wept into his shoulder. Walter cried too. His absence had been good for everyone.

He would be granted a second chance. Not many deserting husbands and fathers were so lucky. He found a new job, a better one. He stopped smoking again, stopped drinking. He joined an exercise club. *Mens sana in corpore sano.* He had no further need for support groups. He didn't fully stop thinking about Andrea, or their Wednesday afternoons together, but he did stop tormenting himself with remorse and regret. "The only person who can forgive us is us," Christophe had said, mangling Niebuhr's syntax. Walter had forgiven himself.

And then, as fate would have it, Walter thought he saw her one afternoon three years later, on a busy avenue downtown. His heart lurched in his chest. She was walking briskly, a block ahead, on the other side of the street, wearing a chic leopard-skin outfit with red pumps and carrying a large brown handbag. A rich redhead in a hurry. But she was taking choppy little steps that were not how he remembered Andrea walking. He chased after her, faster and faster, weaving through swarms of well-dressed men and women, bumping into some, until he was close enough to yell, *"Andrea! Andrea!"*

She didn't stop or turn around. Couldn't she hear him? When he caught up to her, she spun round and faced him as if to ward off an attack. He recognized the startled green eyes, the red-haired bangs, the freckled nose. But something was different. Something was wrong. The woman was not Andrea.

Then it came to him. The sister. The twin sister. The meddling born-again twin sister.

Andrea had mentioned her name, but he'd forgotten it. Out of breath, lungs burning, he apologized for startling her. He explained that he'd met her sister in a group and known her as Andrea. The woman looked around in distress, but he saw that she was no longer afraid. She seemed to be weighing a decision.

He asked, "Can we go somewhere and talk? Just for a minute?"

She nodded. He guided them to a Starbucks around the corner. They sat down at a small round table. He said, "Please tell me how I can find your sister. She knew me as Roy. It's vital that I talk to her. I need to—apologize."

The woman regarded him sympathetically; to his surprise, she reached out and touched his hand. Her fingers were icy.

"I'm sorry to have to tell you this, Roy," she said. "My sister passed away a few months ago. Her name was Agnes May Suggs. I'm Wanda May. She had one of those intra-cranial brain aneurisms? We were real shocked, 'cause she'd always been so healthy. Physically healthy, I mean. You know, real sassy and full of life and vim and vinegar?"

Walter felt a chill. No, he thought. Not dead. No.

"It happened one morning she was out jogging. She had a brain rupture and some bleeding and all of a sudden she was *gone*. Women get aneurisms more than men. Did you know that? I'm sorta scared, 'cause I'm at risk. I'm her twin and it runs in families. I can only trust in Gawd. May His will be done."

Walter put his face in his hands.

"She mentioned you once. She told me she'd met this wonderful man named Roy in a club she'd joined and she was in love."

Walter fought back tears. In a breaking voice he said, "We parted on—not the best of terms."

"How you parted didn't have nothing to do with her death, Roy. She's happy now. Agnes May was a good person but unhappy. She had something real bad happen to her when she was young. She lost a baby and blamed my husband and I for it. We never knew why. And she would not yield herself up to the Lord Gawd to be forgiven."

"She didn't need to be forgiven."

"She's in a better place now, Roy."

Walter was silent. Wanda May picked up her leather handbag. "I'm late for a network luncheon," she said, rising. "My husband is pastor of First City Pentecostal. You've probably saw him on TV." She mentioned a name.

"I have," Walter lied, rising. "I'm glad we met, Wanda May," he lied again. He didn't like this woman. He extended his hand, but she ignored it.

"I'm sorry for your loss," he said.

"And I'm sorry for yours." Her mouth was smiling, her eyes were not. "You have a blessed day, you hear?" With mincing steps, Wanda May headed for the door.

The following Wednesday, Walter drove to the dilapidated hotel where his Confessors Anonymous meetings had been held. He arrived fifteen minutes early. It was unlikely that the meetings would still take place there, at the same hour, after three years. But he took a chance. There was one more thing he needed to do. It was silly, it was childish, but he needed to do it.

Entering, he was dismayed to see a man in a shiny grey suit and a tie standing, with a clipboard under his arm, at the open door to the conference room. But as Walter approached, he recognized him. Christophe's hair was still long, his blue eyes still blazed, but his beard was gone, his face smooth and fuller, his expensive-looking suit impeccably tailored.

They shook hands. Christophe's handshake had gotten firmer. "Hello, Christophe. You have a new look."

"So do you, Roy. Your aura is healthier."

"I was afraid you wouldn't talk to me."

"Forgive is what I do. I'm sorry I was tough on you last time. Forgive me."

"Andrea's dead, Christophe."

The moderator nodded sympathetically. "I heard. Her name was Agnes May Suggs. She was a beautiful human being. She died of a brain aneurism. She went quickly. Be thankful she didn't suffer. Heaven has another angel now."

Walter decided he still didn't like Christophe.

"Roy, you don't blame yourself, do you?"

"For her death? No."

"Good. You shouldn't."

"I want to rejoin the Group. Just for one meeting."

"Why?"

"To make a confession. A real confession. Not a phony one."

"Do you want to make it today?"

"Please."

"Go on in. Wait—do you want a new name?"

"Yeah. I'll be Walter this time."

"Welcome, Walter. We all need forgiveness. And the only person who can forgive us is us."

Making Amends

For forty years — most of his adult life — Milton Caleb Kooze brooded over every insult he received. He nursed grudges, picked at scabs, flayed his psyche like a medieval flagellant. He tormented himself by lusting for verbal vengeance the way other men lusted for women or power or gold. He lay awake nights sharpening rapier-like ripostes that had failed to materialize at the critical moment.

But lately, for reasons mysterious, Milton found himself brooding just as obsessively about insults he'd meted out. They had cost him friends, acquaintances, lovers, colleagues, students — even enemies he'd cherished who'd written him off and refused to have anything further to do with him. They'd cost him his first wife, too, though about that he could not complain. Even on her best days, Brenda had been a harpy, a harridan, a virago and a shrew. A castrating bitch wife fit for a Hemingway hero like Francis Macomber.

This nursing of guilt was worse than nursing grudges. Milton wondered what was happening to him. Was he mellowing out in his limp-schlonged golden years? Hearing some long-stifled voice of conscience? He had no use for cowards, the *pakhdnim* who get religion in the top of the ninth because they fear what awaits them once the game is over. He liked to think of himself as a "mean old Jew," tough as an old boot, whom you messed with at your peril. So maybe he deserved his new torment. His putdowns had broken bones, drawn blood, left scars, and now he was being punished for them. Milton Caleb Kooze didn't believe in God, but he did believe in the Law of the Deed, which made sure you reaped what you sowed. That was in the Old Testament. Milton didn't believe in the Old Testament either, but the King James Version was English literature of a pretty high order and Milton taught English at City College.

One night, unable to sleep at all, he reviewed the insults he'd been proudest of: the barbed zingers, knees to the groin, knockout punches, the zowies. As a montage of ugly scenes unspooled in his memory, his cruelty sickened him and he hardly recognized himself. Once more, to her face, with other family members present, he was calling his obese unmarried three-hundred-pound Aunt Louise "a battleship with nipples" and "The Countess of Monte Crisco" and reducing her to tears. At a wedding party, he was calling an overdressed matron he barely knew a "walking garage sale of a certain age." In a letter to the *Times,* he was calling a late Orthodox rabbi loved and mourned by the Jewish community of Queens "a Henny Youngman wannabe that finally got the hook."

That was the kind of insult Milton felt especially bad about because the insulted party was dead and it would be hard to apologize to him and take it back. Another late victim had been his first mother-in-law. At a party celebrating her ninetieth birthday and not meant to be a roast, he was toasting her again: "Dear Nitchka, you will never get old. You are already there. Older than dirt. Older than Methuselah. Older than Melchizedek and George Burns and that ancient Sara in the Bible. Older than God. It's amazing that at your age you don't need glasses but still drink your Manischewitz straight out of the bottle. You don't have an enemy in the world because you've outlived your enemies and their children and their children's children. Even your Whole Life insurance policy has expired. Happy ninetieth, Nitch. You don't look a day over eighty-eight."

No one but Milton had laughed, and the crone was mortified, her big night ruined. Not even on her deathbed, when he confessed he'd lifted every word from the coffee table best seller *Playful Putdowns for People You Love,* had she spoken to him again.

—⁓—

How could he have said such things to anyone? And why was he only now feeling remorse about them? The guilt had begun several weeks ago with a dream. In it he was insulting a student unrecognizable to him in one of his English classes. She was a gum-chewing "Goth," in shiny black leather, whose network of metal body piercings probably extended to her clitoris. Embodying everything he deplored about the Millennial Generation, she had just asked why "Shakespeare wrote his plays in prose but his sonnets in, like, poetry."

In the dream he'd ordered her to stand up. Then he commenced to dress her down. He heard himself call her a "black-head," a "pustule," a "slattern," and a "receptacle." In his inner ear, his barking was deafening, but he knew he was in good form, his metaphors apt, turns of phrase deft, epithets worth anthologizing. He had never felt as good humiliating a student in his teaching career. It was better than a sex dream.

But then, as he menacingly approached the girl, who slouched beside her desk smacking her gum with a smirk, the dream went awry. She seemed to shrink, to grow smaller, younger, until she was a baby-faced child, six or seven, in a schoolgirl uniform. His harangue grew thunderous—he could see that the other students, small children also, were terrified. The little girl's mouth formed a horizontal figure eight. She stumbled backward. She squinched her eyes tight as a tear squirted out of each. There was a dripping sound. Milton saw that she was standing in a puddle of urine.

He came awake. Bathed in a cold sweat, he felt a shame he'd never known before. The ugly scene hadn't happened, but it could have—that's how plausible and real it seemed. He longed to resume the dream and reassure the child, all the children, that he wasn't really a monster, an ogre, or a brute. But he couldn't get back to sleep.

—ᨆ—

Milton told his best friend about his late-life crisis. She was his only friend—his second wife, Ruth, whom he called Baby Ruth. He didn't tell her about the dream—he was afraid to tell anyone about that. Even Baby Ruth would be frightened.

"Baby, it's costing me sleep," he whined. "I keep seeing their faces when I berate them. They look like Christ's face when the Roman soldier gave him the vinegar-soaked sponge as he thirsted on the cross. Do you think I'm going bonkers? *Meshuga*?"

Baby Ruth shook her head. "Milton, it's normal to feel remorse at our age. We've gained wisdom and maturity and objectivity. We realize we've sinned as much as we've been sinned against."

That sounded reasonable, but then she had to ruin it by saying, "You can't do that when you're young. They say youth is wasted on the young."

Milton groaned. Her fondness for the hackneyed phrase was the only thing he disliked about Baby Ruth except maybe her always saying "at this point in time" (redundant) and pronouncing the word "interesting" with four syllables (trendy). He was an English teacher, forever editing.

"I've been sinned against *more* than I've sinned," he kvetched like King Lear. "I've insulted no more than a hundred people. Thousands have insulted me."

"Well, you know what they say. What goes around comes around."

"Who says that? They should die slowly, in excruciating pain."

"Life is a mirror, Milton. It shows us a mean face when we scowl at it in a mean way."

Milton flinched. He hated mangled clichés even worse than those precisely worded. But he was willing to let Baby Ruth mangle hers. He could not hurt her feelings for the simple reason that he could not afford to lose another wife. He would need Baby Ruth to care for him in his dotage, which had begun earlier than expected. He could not afford to lose another friend, either. He was down to his last one.

"Think of this as an opportunity," Baby Ruth suggested. "A moral awakening after a long sleep."

"Now I'm Rip Van Winkle? Tell me what to do."

"Make amends to the people you've insulted worst. Tell them you're sorry. Ask them to forgive you."

He thought about it. "This I won't do," he said. "It sounds like Alcoholics Anonymous. I'm not some goddam alcoholic." Actually, he was a borderline alcoholic and they both knew it.

In a softer tone he added, "I never wanted to be an insulter. It didn't come naturally to me. I only became one out of self-defense."

"Well," Baby Ruth sighed. "You know what they say."

"I do, so don't say it —"

"It's the Golden Rule. Do unto others the things you want them to do unto you."

"But what if they're not kinky like I am?"

She didn't get the joke. "Cruelty is a double-edged dagger," she added rather gravely.

"Stop, already. Tell me what to do."

"Will you do it?"

"No. But tell me."

"Okay, Milton." Baby Ruth took his face in her hands and gazed, lovingly, into his eyes. "We'll hold a lottery of insults. We'll write the initials of thirty people you've insulted on little white balls and jumble them in a bingo blower. For a start, you'll draw five balls and make amends to each person."

Milton was amazed that Baby Ruth would suggest such a thing. Had she forgotten that the women he'd insulted worst, skewered and barbecued, chewed up and spit out, were his old lovers and first wife? She was still jealous of those witches. ("True love never dies," she liked to say. "Nor does false love, if truth be told." Another mangled cliché, but he liked the Shakespearean ring.) Didn't she realize that making amends would reconnect him with women he'd loved? Women who, God forbid, might still love him? Milton was vain enough to think they all did.

"What if the people I apologize to won't forgive me?"

"Doesn't matter. Forgiveness would be a bonus, but don't expect it."

"I can't face them."

"You won't have to. Call them."

"I'll e-mail them."

"Too impersonal. You have to *say* you're sorry, not write it."

"A lottery," he grumbled. "What am I, the NBA draft? I won't do it."

"You will, Milton. Ask Moey. Moey is never wrong. He'll tell you I'm right."

"I should ask that nebbish? That pedantic poseur? I can't stand the pompous son of a bitch."

"You shouldn't talk about your own little brother that way, Milton."

"He shouldn't talk to me the way he does. He talks down to me. I may as well be talking to William F. Buckley."

Moey and Milton telephoned each other once a year. Milton's call to his brother was overdue. "Moey's a nudnik," Milton added for good measure.

"Just see what Moey says, Milton. Life is short. At this point in time, what can it hurt?"

Milton knew he'd end up making those humiliating "amends" no matter what Moey said. He was desperate, Baby Ruth was insistent. And in truth he was curious about what his brother's advice would be. Moey usually *was* right, and even when he was wrong he was never in doubt. It was one more reason Milton despised him.

———∿∿∿———

Moses Solomon Kooze, Phd Yeshiva University 1966, was a professor of situational ethics in the philosophy department at Columbia. He had been their mother's favorite; he had been their father's favorite, too; with Milton as his competition, he had been everyone's favorite. Milton had not seen Moey in years. When they talked on the phone, it usually ended in an argument, so he'd have to take care not to insult his brother. Moey was family. You never knew when you might need those people. Milton had not insulted a family member since the night he'd reduced poor obese Aunt Louise to tears, with other family members present, and lived to regret it.

Dutifully, Milton made the call. Moey sounded even more impatient than usual to be rid of him as soon as possible. "Well of *course* your wife is right, Milton," he said irritably. "She is speaking of forgiveness. It's the ultimate, or perhaps penultimate, question our lives come down to. Are we forgiven? Do we forgive? Whether or not there's an afterlife—and I doubt there is—forgiveness is our salvation. Reinhold Niebuhr is clear on this."

"Niebuhr was a theologian. I don't believe in God."

"I'm surprised you know who Niebuhr is."

"So you're getting smart with me, Moey? You think you're smarter than I am because I teach freshman English at City College and you teach Plato and Aristotle at Columbia?"

"I don't teach the Greeks. They're absolutist. They believe in essence before existence. Stick with the subject, please. You asked me what to do and I'm telling you. Make amends! Forgive! Seek forgiveness! You're the poor man's Don Rickles, Milton. Only you're not funny. Your one gift is for insulting people. You're a very sad man."

"It's not a gift. Few of my insults are original. I plagiarize them."

"Which makes you a thief, too. A common *gonif*. I remember the night you insulted Brenda's poor senile mother. It may have been what killed her."

"Old age killed her. She was born during the Civil War."

"She was born during the Great War. You're a misanthrope, Milton. You hate people."

"I love people as a group. I only hate individuals."

"The philosopher Heidegger would call that inauthentic."

"Heidegger was an authentic Nazi."

"In his situation maybe he had to be." Moey sighed. "Make your phone calls, Milton. And don't call me if a ball with my name on it pops out of your blower. I forgive you in advance."

"Forgive me for what? I've never insulted you, Moey."

"When we were kids you never stopped picking on me. It's all right, I could've done worse. I could've gotten Cain for a big brother. I'll say good-bye now."

"Hey, Moey? One more thing?"

"Make it fast."

"Go fuck yourself?"

Milton rang off. Asking your brother to go fuck himself was not the same as insulting him. The conversation had gone well.

⌇

"Moey says I should do what you say," Milton told Baby Ruth that night. "But he was a condescending *schmendrick* about it."

"So what? The important thing is, you make those calls."

"But they're like a blanket amnesty. Blanket amnesties I'm opposed to."

"Do you want a divorce?"

"I'll make the calls, but for five people only. Five lottery balls and that's it."

Her mentioning divorce always frightened him. It was never something she was serious about, or so he hoped, yet it chilled him to the marrow. Milton was terrified of being left alone. If he lost Baby Ruth, how could he replace her? Who else would put up with him? There were days when he thought of his wife as a wise woman; there were days when he thought of her as an idiot savant; there were days when he thought of her as an idiot period. But there was never a day when he thought of her as something he could live without.

"How can you love me?" he asked her once. "Everyone else hates me."

"They don't know you, Milton. Deep down you're as gentle as a lamb and sweet as apple pie."

"I'm sorry I asked."

"But you only show that side of yourself to me. No one else gets to see it. Deep down you're a good person."

That was not how Milton saw himself, and he was flattered. "Baby," he said, mimicking Jackie Gleason, "you're the greatest." He swept her into his arms and kissed her with passionate gratitude.

⸺∿⸺

On Saturday Baby Ruth found a bingo blower at a huge yard sale. She and Milton put thirty ping-pong balls in it. On each he scrawled the initials of an ex-wife or ex-lover or ex-friend he'd grievously insulted and alienated. Old enemies he'd come to miss were included as well.

"I want a ball," she said when they finished. "At this point in time I certainly deserve one."

"Baby Ruth, why? I've never insulted you."

"I feel left out."

"This is not about you, wife. It's about me. May we proceed with this ordeal?"

"Roll 'em, Milton. This should be very in-ter-es-ting."

Milton winced but refrained from comment. He jumbled the balls in the blower and drew one marked "J. K."

"Judy Kolodzney," Baby Ruth murmured. "Don't look so happy."

"Are you kidding? She was a *shkapeh.* A useless moron. Worthless."

"Why do you seem elated?"

"Elated? I'm petrified."

Judy Kolodzney was a vegetarian feminist pothead he'd lived with but lost track of after she kicked him out for insulting her because she'd been seeing another man, whom Milton also insulted, though not to his face. Judy was not bright—her habit had made her spacy. Other than cook a succulent vegetarian *matzah* lasagna and give good fellatio, her only talent had been to roll the tightest joints on the Lower East Side.

Yet Milton had proposed to her. Declining, she'd explained that marriage and a nuclear family were not on her feminist agenda. A week later, she announced that she was marrying a waiter, a starving actor rumored as bisexual. A year later, Milton heard that Judy and her waiter had already managed to produce a son.

When she threw him out, he'd just learned that there was another man in the picture. And the waiter wasn't even Jewish. Making his exit, Milton fired a parting shot: "I always knew you'd end up in bed with a girl." Judy had called him a sexual fascist and a homophobe and shown him the door. She needn't have, because he'd been heading for the door anyway. The goy waiter was on his way over.

"Be careful when you call Judy," Baby Ruth warned. "Don't fall in love with her again."

"I was never in love with that *nafka.* I was in lust with her."

"You wanted to marry her."

"I was bewitched. What a fellatrix."

"That's more information than I want. I wish you didn't have to call her."

"I don't. Toss that ball and we'll do another."

"No. Be strong, husband."

Baby Ruth's jealousy flattered him because it was unwarranted. No woman had given him a second look since his hair had begun to thin and his pot belly to bulge twenty years ago. Few women had given him a first look. People took him for Baby Ruth's father—she'd kept her girlish figure with diet and exercise, disciplines Milton dismissed as narcissistic trends. But he was glad she looked good. A fat dumpy *balabusta* housewife he didn't need.

After six false leads, he managed to track down Judy's unlisted phone number in Teaneck, New Jersey, just across the Hudson River past the George Washington Bridge. Before dialing, he drank two full glasses of Mouton Cadet: it wouldn't do for his voice to shake. Then he sent Baby Ruth out of the room.

About Judy he felt more regret than guilt; they'd had good times, and he'd lied to Baby Ruth that he hadn't loved her. Maybe now he could erase the regret. Have it behind him forever.

The young man who answered the phone sounded like a stoned Tommy Chong on one of his seventies albums. This would be the son, Milton guessed. Like mother, like son: a stoner. Milton had not smoked dope in years.

"May I speak to Judy, please? I'm an old friend."

"Judy? Oh, wow, man. You didn't know? We buried my mother like six months ago."

"O my God!" Milton gasped. "You buried her? I can't believe it."

"Why not? She was dead, man."

Wise punk, Milton thought. No respect for your late mother. He wondered if the boy could be his son. No, the math didn't compute.

"Young man," he said with a grief that was sincere, "I loved your mother. I wanted to marry her, but she wouldn't have me."

"Yeah. Well, she's like gone."

"I am so sorry for your loss. May I ask how she died?"

"I don't know, it was like cancer of the something."

Moron! he thought. *Schlemiel*! "Did she ever mention me? Milton Kooze?"

The boy laughed. "I don't think so. Jeez, is that really your name?"

"Have a good day, *you little asshole*." Milton hung up.

He was short of breath and his mouth dry. Now he had to finish off the bottle of Mouton Cadet just to settle his nerves. The irony of the conversation did not escape him. He had called to apologize for one insult and ended up rendering another. To a stranger. The call had not gone well.

In bed with Baby Ruth that night, he was surprised by the force and duration of his grief. He almost cried, and he'd forgotten how to cry. He hadn't cried since the JFK assassination.

He whimpered, "I missed atoning to Judy by just *six months*."

"Was the boy the son of the man she left you for?"

"I don't know. I couldn't ask the little bastard if his father was a bisexual waiter."

"You shouldn't have called the boy an asshole."

"He was being a wise guy."

"Maybe that's how he's dealing with his grief. He lost his mother, Milton. We each deal with death our own way. They say death is —"

"Just a part of life?"

"I was going to say like taxes. The two things we can count on. I didn't mean to sound callous about Judy. Maybe I'm jealous."

"You're jealous of a dead pothead?"

"You've never grieved over *me*."

"You're not dead."

"That's the only point in time when you cry over someone? When they're dead?"

"I almost cried when they stole the election from Gore."

"We'll draw another ball tomorrow. This time, don't drink wine."

"Can I have a beer?"

"Don't drink alcohol. Be clean and sober when you talk to these people. And be sincere. Because you know what they say."

Milton shut his eyes and braced himself. "What."

"You're never sorry for having said you're sorry. That's from *Love Story*."

—◈—

The second ping-pong ball to pop out of the blower read "P. J. S." Years ago, Milton Caleb Kooze and Peter John Spaulding had been best friends. One night, in a moment of drunken can-

77

dor at McSorley's Old Ale House in Greenwich Village, Peter had divulged to Milton that he'd been unfaithful to his wife, Deirdre, with not one woman but five.

"We had sort of an open marriage," Peter explained. "I never told you."

Milton was incensed. To him marital infidelity was unpardonable. An abomination. He was old-fashioned that way. He'd always thought of Peter as faithful as a St. Bernard. Peter even looked like a St. Bernard. Big sad eyes, droopy eyelids, overweight…Why had he never shared that he had an open marriage? What kind of best friend was that?

Milton was angry for another reason, too. Secretly, he'd lusted after Deirdre, a raven-haired green-eyed colleen with big round breasts like inflated balloons. (Baby Ruth was *zaftig* too, but not like Deirdre.) Only his friendship with Peter had kept him from making a pass at Deirdre even if he did regard adultery in most cases as an abomination. Now, learning that Peter's marriage had been "open," he realized that Deirdre might have let him bury his face in those huge titties had he asked to. He was furious. It was all he could do to keep from flinging his stein of beer into Peter's St. Bernard dog face.

"Deirdre doesn't know about the five women," Peter was saying. "She thinks there were three."

Milton erupted. "Philanderer!" he shouted across the table. "Faithless oyster of phlegm! Marriage vows are sacred!"

"Be *quiet*, Milton. People are staring. What's wrong with you?"

"You are lower than whale shit. Leave this bar. Now."

"What?"

"Get out of here. Take the check with you, I'm broke."

Peter grabbed the check and stormed out. Their friendship was never the same again. They stopped drinking together. They stopped seeing each other. When Milton called to demand that they stop speaking, Peter agreed, even though they hadn't spoken since that night at McSorley's Old Ale House. Milton lost his best friend.

Now, calling Peter to make amends, he was more nervous than he'd been calling Judy Kolodzney. But Peter sounded very glad to hear from him. He and Deirdre were fine, he reported. He'd lost his hair and some of his hearing, and Deirdre had lost a breast to a mastectomy. And their daughter, Judith, had been run over and killed on Bedford Avenue in Brooklyn by a Yemeni cab driver. Otherwise life was good and he was doing well in the market with his Apple stock.

Milton wondered if Peter could be serious. Life was good? The man had more tribulations than Job. Then he remembered, fondly, that Peter had been a guileless simpleton who put a happy face on things. As they talked, reconnecting with his old friend lifted his spirits and eased the burden of guilt he felt about him. Milton was glad he'd called. After more catching up, he said, "Peter, I want to apologize for that night at McSorley's."

"Say again? I didn't hear."

"I want to APOLOGIZE."

"Oh, me too. Let me go first. I guess Baby Ruth told you."

A wary pause. "Told me what," Milton said, apprehensively.

"You know. That I made a pass at her."

Milton felt his blood freeze and his testicles contract. "You what?"

"Your hearing is bad like mine? I made a pass at her. Nothing happened, I swear. But I shouldn't have done it."

"*Damn your eyes*," Milton hissed. "You're still an oyster of phlegm."

"What's that about oysters?"

"I shouldn't have called you."

"Why did you?"

"I don't know. I despise you, you faithless son of a bitch. I never liked you to begin with. Get out of my life."

"Say again?"

Milton slammed the receiver into the cradle. The call had been a mistake.

—◦◦◦—

This making amends business, Milton told his wife, might end up causing him more problems than it solved. He should postulate a theory, an axiom. *Whatever chemistry made you fight with someone in the first place will reactivate and start another fight if you crawl back and try to make up.* It was why marital reconciliations never worked. He should patent it. They could call it Kooze's Law and put it in textbooks.

"How ridiculous," Baby Ruth scoffed at Kooze's Law. "Milton, you're not asking to move in with them. You're having a five-minute conversation. Can't you be civil to someone for five minutes without fighting?"

"Why didn't you tell me Peter tried to shtup you?"

"I didn't want to ruin your friendship."

"For years it was ruined!"

80

"He only tried to kiss me. I called him a Silly Willy and pushed him away. We laughed about it later."

"You saw him again? All this time you're living a lie?"

"I did you a favor. They say what you don't know won't hurt you. I can't imagine why he told you about it."

"The next time a friend of mine sexually harasses you, mention it."

"You don't have any friends, Milton."

"Anybody, then!"

"I promise to tell you if someone as much as looks at me. I should be so lucky. Didn't you have a thing for Deirdre?"

"Excuse me?"

"You heard me. Didn't you?"

"Again you're jealous? First Judy, now Deirdre? What's wrong with you, woman? You're consumed with jealousy. You're sick."

"Answer the question, Milton."

"I did not have a thing for Deirdre. I swear it on my sainted mother's grave."

"Your mother was no saint. You hated your mother. I remember Deirdre's big breasts. You like big breasts."

"Deirdre's I found grotesque. Those bazooms were like basketballs. And now she has just one. That's really grotesque."

Baby Ruth's mouth trembled. She knew when he was lying. "Why don't I believe you?" she asked. "I want to."

"So what can I tell you? I never gave the woman a second look."

She paused. "You know," she said, "this resurrecting women

from your past is giving *me* grief."

"Whose idea was it? We should stop! Right now!"

"No. We agreed to do five balls. We have to finish."

She was right, Milton realized. So far the experiment hadn't succeeded, but making the effort was enabling him to feel a little better about himself. He was doing his part; if the people he made amends to wouldn't cooperate, that was their problem. He had known it wouldn't be easy; he just hadn't expected it to be so hard.

—◦◦◦—

M. M. A., the initials on the third ball to pop out, belonged to another of Milton's ex-best friends. Years ago, as starving writers in the West Village, Morris Mark Abraham and Milton Caleb Kooze had bet five dollars—then a large sum to each—on who'd get published first. Milton won. At a dinner party he threw to celebrate selling a one-page short-short story to *Cavalier* magazine, Milton had stood and lorded his triumph over his unpublished friend before ten seated guests.

"You too have talent for writing, Morris," Milton had slurred, waving his wineglass around. "But you weren't given a full measure. God shouldn't play jokes like that on people."

An embarrassed hush fell. The normally ruddy Morris turned pale.

"Robert Frost," Milton continued, "wrote a poem that goes *'Forgive O Lord my little jokes on thee / And I'll forgive thy great big one on me.'* The Lord played a great big joke on you, Morris Mark."

Morris was a battler. "Getting into *Cavalier* has given you the fat head, Milton," he responded. "It's a third-rate men's magazine. I will still outwrite you."

"I've read your short stories," Milton persisted. "They run the whole gamut of human emotion from A to B."

"And you," Morris replied, "are the first person I've known who can strut while sitting on his fat behind."

"At least I have something to strut about."

Had the repartee been deliciously witty, the dinner guests might have enjoyed it. But it was low-grade stuff, drunken banter. Embarrassing. Milton was too drunk to care. When Morris hit back with "You sound like a writer who's sold one story his whole life," Milton's rejoinder was predictable: "How many stories have you sold, Morris?"

"Will both of you *stop?*" pleaded Brenda, Milton's first wife.

"Your writing," Milton went on, "isn't writing, my friend. It's typing."

"That line worked better when Capote said it about Jack Kerouac!" Morris shouted. "What a *gonif* you are! What a pathetic putz! What a schlemiel!" He sprang up, flung his napkin onto the table, and stormed out.

The other guests soon left too: the party was pooped. "For God's sake, Milton, why did you do that?" Brenda scolded Milton afterwards. "You ruined everyone's evening."

"Morris voted for Nixon. Twice. He told me earlier."

Brenda blinked. "He did? So what?"

"So he's a Republican! A Jewish Republican! A disgrace!"

"Milton, why did I marry you? What a jerk you are. First you can't handle failure and now you can't handle success."

"Take his side against your husband, why don't you?"

Milton had other reasons for insulting Morris. Not only did his friend vote for the anti-Semite Richard Nixon, he'd also confessed to privately being a Yankee fan who hated the Mets. And who thought Neil Diamond was a better songwriter than Leonard Cohen or Randy Newman. Morris's favorite singer was Barry Manilow. Morris revered Ayn Rand's novels, especially *Atlas Shrugged*. Morris didn't deserve to be anyone's best friend.

Later Milton learned that Morris had moved to L. A. and become a chauffeur. Morris was an excellent driver — he would give him that. Milton proudly took credit for his friend's abandoning his dream of becoming a successful writer. But one day, Shoshana Abraham, Morris's yammering yenta of a mother, called to brag that Morris was living next door to Jack Nicholson in Beverly Hills. Could that be true? Were even the chauffeurs there rich? Morris probably rented a garage apartment behind Nicholson's mansion.

The old woman had given him Morris's phone number in Los Angeles. "Oh, he'd just love to hear from you, Milton," she cawed. "Our little Morris is quite the *macher* now, such a big shot he's gotten to be…"

Milton didn't like the sound of it and hadn't ever called. But now he made himself phone Morris, to make amends. Even about Morris he felt some guilt, though not much.

Right away, things got off on the wrong foot. Morris could not remember the dinner party in question. "Sure you can," Milton prompted. "Our gang of twelve was there. Brenda made salmon latkes. For dessert, we had hamantaschen cookies and kosher ice cream."

"I don't remember evenings by what I ate, Milton."

"You left before dessert. You must remember. I can quote you every vile thing I said to you that night."

"Don't bother." Morris laughed. "What difference does it make now? It's water under the bridge, old friend. I forgive you. Let's talk about the present. Did you read my novel?"

Milton hesitated. "Your novel? I thought you became a chauffeur."

"Only for research. I wrote a novel, under the pseudonym Sean Pawnee, about chauffeuring movie stars. Hollywood adapted it for that movie *Driving Mrs. Robinson.* Did you see it?"

"Never heard of it." Milton had seen the movie twice. "Why did you use a pseudonym?"

"Doubleday didn't like my name. They said Morris Mark Abraham sounded like a Talmudic scholar. They needed a Native American name for their fiction list. They suggested Sean Pawnee. That gave them some Irish as well. Even more diversity."

Milton felt sick.

"That's New York publishers for you. Liberals and their ethnic quotas. Doubleday has offered me a six-figure contract to write a sequel about the same chauffeur. *Driving Lauren Bacall.*"

"Morris, I have to go now."

"Wait. What about you? *Vi gaits?* What are you doing these days?"

"Teaching at City College."

"Good. And your novels?"

"Unpublished. I don't write fiction anymore."

"Oops. Sorry."

"Listen, I only called to apologize for insulting you that night."

Morris laughed. "You assume a lot, old friend. But then you always had delusions of grandeur. *You* could never insult *me…*"

⸺༄⸺

Batting oh for three now, Milton was discouraged. Yes, he had assuaged some of his guilt, maybe most of it, but how naïve had he been to hope that apologizing to five victims could earn him forgiveness for a lifetime of victimizing? For him there was no forgiveness. He was the Unforgiven, like Clint Eastwood in that awful Western. Enough was enough already. He wanted to abort the mission.

But Baby Ruth wouldn't let him. "You're overdue," she encouraged. "Nobody loses all the time. Besides —"

"It's not whether you win or lose but how you play the game?"

"I wasn't going to say that."

"Winners never quit and quitters never win?"

"Stop it. Go get the bingo blower."

The fourth ball to pop out was one he should never have put in the blower to begin with. The initials "B. K." belonged to his first wife, Brenda Kooze, nee Kauffmann. Brenda the castrator. Brenda the barracuda. What could he have been thinking when he loaded things up?

"Please, no," he begged. "Her I can't call."

"You can. But be careful. She still loves you. She hates you, but she still loves you."

86

"How would you know that?"

"I'm a woman. They say women have a sixth sense about these things. Now they have a term for it. Women's intuition."

He'd last seen Brenda five years after their divorce. A good while ago. She had put on weight (though her face was gaunt) and started smoking. It was her fiftieth birthday and they'd met for a "no-hard-feelings" drink on the dubious assumption that there were no hard feelings. After a second drink, they picked up where they'd left off in the office of Brenda's divorce attorney cousin Murray Finkel, a *shtunk* and a shyster if there ever was one. Halfway through a third drink, they were shouting at each other and the bartender asked them to leave.

He knew it was going to be bad. This time he made Baby Ruth leave the house. His hand trembled as he dialed the number. But to his relief, Brenda sounded calm and civil, so he got straight to the point:

"I want to take back the insult that caused our divorce and ask your forgiveness, Brenda. I know I don't deserve it, but I ask you to forgive me anyway."

A silence, as though she were waiting for a punch line.

"Brenda?"

She laughed. "What a schmuck you still are, Milton. A thousand things you should apologize for and you apologize for one insult?"

"What else would you like me to apologize for? I will."

"Hah!" she cackled. "Apologize for insulting my mother on her ninetieth birthday! She even disinherited *me* for that. Apologize for wrecking my life! Giving me a nervous breakdown! I tried to kill myself, Milton. A whole bottle of Extra Strength Tylenol I took. I got fat. I started smoking. I gave up on men and became a lesbian. Women were even worse than you. Ten years later I'm still in therapy. You could start with those things."

"All right. I apologize for those things, too."

She was silent again.

"What's this about?" she asked. "Are you doing A. A.?"

"Of course not."

"You should be. What a mean drunk you were. I remember the insult you're talking about. You took a long sympathetic look at me, like I had cancer, and then said, 'Tell me, *when did you die?*'"

"Yes, that's the one. I apologize."

"Do you know why that still hurts? Because I found out it was a line from one of Norman Mailer's movies. Original you never were, Milton. Even your insults you stole. But a recycled insult from a *Norman Mailer* movie?"

"Mailer was a great writer."

"His movies were dreck."

"He won two Pulitzers and should have won the Nobel."

"He stabbed his wife."

"It was just a pen knife."

"You think that didn't *hurt*?"

"It was fifty years ago. Even the wife laughs about it now."

"He had six wives! He was a polygamist!"

"He had one wife at a time. Mailer died recently. Show some respect."

"You haven't changed, Milton. You've intensified. You're worse than ever."

"I have to go now, Brenda."

"Why did you call? Do you want to get together?"

"I told you why. To make amends."

"Because if you want to see me again, you can't."

"I don't want to see you again."

"So you called to reject me? You putz! You insensitive *paskudnyak!* You're *not* forgiven. Fuck you!"

Afterwards, he tried to give the call a positive spin. It could've gone worse, he told himself. At least he hadn't agreed to see her again. Nor did he believe she'd tried to kill herself. She'd tried to kill him, but not herself. Why had he married a *meshugeneh* basket case with a victim complex? Even her smoking she blamed on him! She was a demon—all she needed was talons and a tail. He'd been lucky to escape with his genitals intact. Even Judy Kolodzney would've made a better wife.

Now he gave himself an E for effort. Four attempts to atone had failed, yet he was feeling better about himself. Baby Ruth had predicted that. Maybe the process was fail-safe. It had taught him some lessons. It had taught him that insults are irrevocable: you can take them back, but you can't have them back. People may forgive, but they don't forget. So they don't really forgive, either. And when you asked them, "Was it something I said?" it always was. Words are dangerous weapons.

Milton vowed never to insult another human being for as long as he lived. Better to strike real blows into flesh—the wounds healed faster. Norman Mailer said that. God bless him,

Mailer should have lived longer. But Milton vowed not to strike anyone, either. He was through with hurting people. Thanks to Baby Ruth, he was finding a way out of his torment and guilt. What would he do without his wife?

⟞∿∿⟝

"You're in a good mood," she observed that night. "Any reason?"

"I'm so happy you're my wife and not Brenda."

"She was an easy act to follow. I'm still jealous, by the way."

"Oh, Baby. Why?'

"I don't know. I feel left out. Am I being silly?"

"Left out of what? Stop envying those losers. They're dead to me. They belong in a bone yard. One of them is there already."

On the morning he was to draw his fifth and final ball, the bingo blower looked fuller somehow, as if replenished overnight. Watching him, Baby Ruth seemed jittery, apprehensive, with a strange look on her face. What was up? Milton wondered. Was his imagination working overtime?

He set the blower in motion. On the ball that popped forth was scrawly handwriting and initials he didn't recognize. "Who the hell is B. R. K.?" he asked. "This ball I don't remember."

"It's me," Baby Ruth said. "I put it in after you went to bed. And twenty others like it. I wanted to maximize my chances."

Milton shook his head and tossed the ball aside. "I told you before. I've never insulted you."

"That's what bothers me. It means you haven't been honest

with me."

"You're not making sense, wife."

"I see how much these people mean to you. You still care for them, don't you. Where does that leave me?"

"You're not a player in this game."

"I am now. Give me my insult and make amends."

He didn't like the look on her face. It revealed something he'd never seen there before, something ugly. Something like an accusation. It triggered the dread he'd felt while being pulled over by a traffic cop. All of a sudden, he didn't recognize the woman with whom he'd lived with relative ease for so long. This person was a stranger to him. Perhaps an enemy.

He swallowed. "All right," he said. "I apologize for not insulting you. Are you satisfied?"

"No. I want an insult and I want you to make amends."

"That's *meshuga,* woman! Crazy! Nobody wants to be insulted!"

"I do. You often mention a person's worst fault when you insult them, Milton. I want to know mine. And don't make one up. Be a mensch."

He felt trapped. He would need to be so careful here. Cornered, put to a test he must not fail, he tried to beg his way out. In a whiney voice he pleaded, "I don't want to play this game any more, Baby Ruth. Let's stop, please."

"I am not joking, Milton. God damn it, you drew a ball with my name on it. You can call me later on my cell phone and make amends. Now give me my insult."

He shook his head. "I made a vow to God that I would never insult another human being."

"You don't believe in God. Break the vow."

He felt like a child being bullied into a fight he has no chance of winning. His penis shriveled, he had to pee, he wanted to run. His knees buckled. He needed to sit down.

"Insult me!" she demanded. "Or do you want a divorce?"

She wasn't kidding, Milton realized. Now he had to chance it. He thought for a moment, drew a deep breath, and hoped for the best. He placed a hand on each of her shoulders and peered into her eyes.

"All right," he said. "For practice one day, God or Jehovah or whoever created ten thousand *balabusta* fishwives. They were mindless twats who spouted clichés and old saws and adages and bromides and platitudes and couldn't even get the words right. Then He created His sublime and ultimate masterpiece. *You.*"

Baby Ruth seemed puzzled. Her lips moved as if she were replaying the insult, word for word, in her head. Milton's eyes widened with fear. He feigned a smile and held his breath.

Then she shrugged and laughed. "Jeez, Milton. Is that all you've got?"

He blinked. "Isn't that enough?"

"After all these years, at this point in time I expected more."

His body went limp as a wet dishrag with relief. He'd been afraid he'd gone too far and he hadn't gone far enough. "Baby," he said, sweeping her into an embrace, "you're the greatest." He gave her a long hard kiss like that fat bus driver Ralph Kramden gave his wife Alice at the end of each "Honeymooners" TV segment. He had survived. He was home free.

Or was he? Baby Ruth had pressed her lips together, squinched up her face, shut her eyes tight, and turned her head away from him. Her body was as stiff as a mannequin's. She wasn't satisfied. She wanted more — an insult on the scale of those his other victims had merited. Or a real kiss, a better marriage, a genuinely passionate husband.

He raised her up, let her go, and stepped back. Now he had to make amends. But how, he wondered with a flash of lucidity he might never recover from, could he make amends for all the things she wanted that he could never give her? As in a dream, he saw himself as an old man hobbling after a bus that pulled away as he reached its front door. The door had closed. He yelled for the bus to stop, but the driver, big fat Ralph Kramden, couldn't hear or see him. Milton had missed the bus. There would not be another. He smelled and tasted the noxious fumes of the vehicle's exhaust as it pulled away from him.

He began to whimper like a kicked puppy. His legs collapsed, he sank to his knees. "I'm sorry, Baby Ruth," he blubbered. "I'm so sorry for insulting you."

"Oh, Milton," his wife comforted him. From deep in her ample bosom she plucked a handkerchief, patted his wet cheeks, and cradled his head against her waist. "There, there… don't cry…I forgive you…" With an enigmatic smile she added, "In life we have to take the bitter with the bittersweet."

Milton shuddered. "Oh, we do," he wept. "We do."

ODE TO BILLY JEFF

Many Americans would recall the summer of 1967 with fondness and nostalgia. Tim Kirkland would not. His memories of it were painful and troubling. It had been a season he was fortunate to survive—one of high hopes and crushing disappointments, Pyrrhic victories and little deaths, bitter lessons learned the hard way. A season out of time.

San Franciscans remember it as the "summer of Love" when young people with flowers in their hair flocked to their city to make love or get stoned or drop acid or groove to Joplin and Hendrix and the Grateful Dead—and protest the Vietnam War while they were at it. They recall that summer as an historic "happening," a religious pilgrimage, a spiritual be-in, a neopagan lovefest. But Kirkland's memories of it had nothing to do with communal spirituality or flower power or the romantic City by the Bay. For him the summer of '67 would always be the summer of the Billies. Billy Jack, Billy Joe, Billy Jeff.

—∾—

Ever since his teen years Kirkland had displayed an uncanny knack for picking "sleepers"—obscure offbeat songs, films, and performers destined for success. (He saw himself as a sleeper, in fact, whose talent would illumine the world like an incandescent sunburst any day now.) The first of his Billies, Billy Jack, was the hero of an indie action film, "The Born Losers," released that June. A creature of its decade, it decried social injustice and advocated peace, love, and nonviolence even though Billy Jack was a gun-toting ex-Green Beret and a master in karate-hapkido. Kirkland saw the film five times—not because it was that good (it wasn't) but because he pegged the handsome half-breed Billy Jack, with his blue denim jacket and his black hat worn flat across his forehead, as an action superhero for the sixties. Kirkland went out flacking for the film like a publicist. He arranged for busloads of Native Americans and Vietnam vets to watch and discuss it together. He paid for a color ad touting it to appear in newsletters mailed to rural communes throughout the Southwest like the commune in the movie. Though not an immediate success, "The Born Losers" eventually spawned a skein of Billy Jack sequels that rang box-office cash registers in thirty countries.

In July that summer's second sleeper materialized. Kirkland fixated on the suicide mourned in the Southern Gothic pop hit "Ode to Billy Joe." Its eponymous subject has jumped off the Tallahatchie Bridge. The haunting ballad revealed that Billy Joe and the young female narrator were seen throwing something off the bridge. What they threw was never revealed. A gun? An aborted fetus? A live baby? No one knew but Bobbie Gentry, the raven-haired Mississippi beauty who wrote and sang the ballad, and she wasn't telling. Kirkland flooded radio request lines with demands that the "Ode" be played and discussed every hour. When it topped the charts four consecutive weeks in August, he congratulated himself on having picked another winner.

That month, after championing two fictional sleepers, Kirkland faced a much tougher challenge in Billy Jeff Basehart, a real person. Reversals of fortune had seemed to disqualify this sleeper as a winner. Seven years earlier, at thirty-three, Basehart had sold his novel *A Man of the People* to the prestigious Boston house that published Emerson and Hawthorne in the nineteenth century. Critics compared the book to Robert Penn Warren's *All the King's Men*. Literary samurai Gore Vidal placed it "among the finest political novels ever written." *The New Republic* called it "an American classic that will be on reading lists a hundred years from now."

Though the hardcover edition bore the byline William Jeffrey Basehart, the author insisted that his real name was Billy Jeff. His novel was a *roman á clef* about a populist Southern Governor based on an actual one, Beauford Jackson, who'd since become a U. S. Senator, the Finance Committee chairman, and a Democratic presidential hopeful. Basehart had been Jackson's speechwriter. Despite being portrayed in its pages as the sole visionary in a Lilliput of half-blind yahoos, Jackson publicly trashed Basehart's book because the Senator's wife, Emmylou, was offended by the profanity in its dialogue. It was said that Jackson used his influence to sabotage a Hollywood movie that would've starred Jackie Gleason as himself and Paul

Newman as a lusty young state legislator irresistible to women.

Jackson's treachery took its toll. Few American novels earned so much critical acclaim and then enjoyed so little popular success. *A Man of the People* sold just 1500 copies in hardback before it was remaindered. In paperback it fared no better. Kirkland heard that the crestfallen author could not believe the master he'd immortalized in print had stuck a dagger in his back and given it a twist. He had never recovered from it.

Kirkland saw Basehart as a tragic figure, worthy of Seneca or Shakespeare. This heedless, callous betrayal of a loyal subject by a modern-day Lear grew to obsess him. By the summer of 1967, when he finally met Basehart, he'd read *A Man of the People* three times and could quote by heart its opening passage—a panoramic description, unsurpassed in American letters, of the escarpment where the terrain metamorphoses like a shimmering hallucination from Old South cotton country and marshland to the cattle ranches and oil derricks of the Southwest. Basehart's cascading prose rivaled that of Faulkner and Thomas Wolfe. No previous novel had so nakedly exposed the machinations of state politics. But the book's major achievement was the searchlight it cast on the conflicted soul of a humane Southern politician—a "man of the people"—facing re-election in a state fond of Jim Crow laws, union busting, and corporate avarice.

Having just finished his own first novel, eager to unveil it, Kirkland needed a mentor, a literary star to hitch his wagon to. The one he wanted, William Jeffrey Basehart, had already begun to fade. Demoralized and depressed, Billy Jeff was rumored to be in the throes of alcoholism, drug use, and (having pocketed a hefty advance for a second novel) writer's block. But Kirkland knew that novelists had their ups and downs and mood swings. He saw Basehart's future as not unlike that of the millionaire entrepreneur who loses his fortune, every penny, only to make it back the following year with interest. He was sure this sleeper had another masterpiece in him.

And even if he never wrote it, Basehart could be of use to him—as a resident guide, a teacher, a facilitator. And maybe a "blurber" for Kirkland's book. Tim Kirkland was positive that his future and Billy Jeff Basehart's were linked. That spring, Basehart and his young second wife had left the East Coast and moved back to the state capital where he'd written for Beauford Jackson by day and written about him by night. Kirkland heard that Basehart, having squandered his advance for a second novel, was destitute and living off his wife's meager earnings as a department store model. Seeing Basehart as down if not out, Kirkland dreamt of putting him in his debt by picking him up and helping him in his hour of need. The day would come when that debt would have to be repaid. Until then, there would be lessons to learn from the best writer the state had produced, as well as contacts to be made with agents and publishers and writers whom Basehart knew and Kirkland wanted to know.

But how to put Basehart in his debt? Patrons were wealthy or well stationed, Kirkland was neither. He was just the trade book editor for a regional house near the Capitol that mainly published textbooks. But somehow he would find a way, he told himself.

There was always a way if you kept your eyes and ears open.

—⁓—

Kirkland serendipitously wrangled an introduction to Basehart at the opening of a local art gallery. The dust jacket for *A Man of the People* did not include a photo, and Kirkland had pictured a rugged, bearded, nicotine-stained John Steinbeck sort. Instead the author he met that night looked like Woody Allen. But smaller and uglier.

The person who introduced them, saucy Connie Cummings, was a pasteup artist in the production department of the publisher Kirkland worked for. In the elevator he'd often flirted with this pert blonde divorcée, who was pushing forty but looked twenty-five, and all that stopped him from doing more than flirt was a strictly enforced rule against editors socializing with other house employees. Kirkland worked for a publisher whose departments, competing for budgets, waged petty internecine wars.

That night, strolling from room to room, sipping champagne from plastic cups, he and Connie viewed the op art and pop art together. "Tim?" she whispered at one point. "See that little guy with the leggy redhead?"

Kirkland saw a balding gnome, in black horn-rimmed glasses, talking to a willowy beauty, with waist-long straight auburn hair, who towered over him. "The homunculus?" he laughed. "What about him?"

"Shh. That's Billy Jeff Basehart. The redhead's his new wife."

"You're kidding," Kirkland exclaimed under his breath. "That's Basehart? It can't be."

"I went to TCU with him," Connie said. "He was three years ahead of me."

"Introduce me."

"No. He's bad news and I don't want to talk to him."

"Introduce me, Connie."

She sighed. "All right. But you'll owe me."

Basehart's handshake was limp, Kirkland's vigorous. "I read your novel three times, Billy," Kirkland chortled. "You could call me a fan."

The gnome managed a melancholy smile. "Three times? Why'd you do that?"

"Tim has comprehension problems," Connie jibed. "He's an editor for Hawkes-Prince. I work there too, unfortunately."

There were uncertain chuckles, and Connie asked if she could fetch Basehart and his wife, Sue Anne, some champagne. "Billy doesn't drink anymore," Sue Anne declined. "*Connie.*"

Kirkland's eyes slid from woman to woman. He wondered if Connie and Basehart had been more than college schoolmates. The author seemed to be ignoring her, but his eyes, magnified by his grotesquely thick glasses, didn't appear to focus on anyone. It was like the gaze of a blind man.

"Alcohol," Basehart glumly confirmed, "is no longer my drug of choice. I'm a mean drunk. I throw things."

Sue Anne said, "And I hate champagne. Thanks anyway, Connie."

Kirkland blurted, "So Billy. When will we see a sequel to *A Man of the People*?"

"There won't be one," the gnome replied. "I should've killed off Beauford when I had the chance."

"What a despicable man," Sue Anne said. "Billy should've put him in bed with a teenage bimbo and given him a coronary."

Basehart got serious. "Tim, did Connie say you work for that little publisher downtown?"

"Hawkes-Prince," Kirkland said. "Guilty as charged."

"Could you find me a job there?"

"Oh, honey," Sue Anne said. "Don't embarrass Tim."

Connie scoffed. "Tim doesn't embarrass easily."

Kirkland's pulse quickened. "Billy — are you serious?" He smelled opportunity.

The homunculus nodded. "I need a job. I have newspaper and magazine experience. I'd start for as little as a hundred grand a year."

Everybody laughed again, and Kirkland said, "You could probably buy the company for that. But if you're serious —"

"He's not," Sue Anne said.

"I am," Basehart insisted. "I wouldn't ask for much. Hire me, Tim, and you'll get an autographed first edition of my novel."

"He's got one," Connie said. "He shoplifted it from a bookstore."

Kirkland pretended to mull over the request. "I'll see what I can do, Billy."

"Please," said Basehart.

Later, when they were alone, Connie said, "I wouldn't if I were you."

"Wouldn't what?"

"Get him a job at H-P. You'll regret it."

"You sound bitter, Connie. Did he break your heart?"

"Billy Jeff doesn't think like a normal person. He's unreli-able and irresponsible."

"Nobody's perfect."

"He's a pathological liar. He makes things up."

Kirkland shrugged. "Sounds like a novelist."

"His brain is fried, Tim. He's a druggie and an alky. He lives in a parallel universe."

"Definitely a novelist. How'd he ever write *A Man of the People?*"

"I don't know. He certainly hasn't written anything since. Don't say I didn't warn you."

Kirkland didn't hear. He heard opportunity knocking. If he could finagle it, the author soon would be in his debt. And somehow he would finagle it. There was always a way if you kept your eyes and ears open.

—⁓—

Kirkland didn't love the benighted, politically reactionary state he lived in so much as he loved its liberal, freewheeling, youth-oriented capital city. He'd earned his journalism degree at its football-crazed university. But after graduating, he'd moved on. He'd lived and tried to write for eighteen months in Manhat-tan, aping Thomas Wolfe, but without Wolfe's success, before getting drafted and assigned to the 1st Armored Division ("Old Ironsides") at Fort Hood, Texas, near a town without pity called Killeen.

It was not the best time to get a letter with "Greetings" as a salutation: Old Ironsides was gearing up for Vietnam in 1964. After training as a heavy weapons infantryman, Kirkland maneuvered his way into the orderly room as acting company clerk and processed paperwork that sent other men to Vietnam in his stead. Like *Catch-22's* ex-PFC Wintergreen, he became his unit's most powerful enlisted man. He wrote thrilling accounts of field exercises and war games for the post newspaper, *The Armored Sentinel*. For officers who couldn't write, which was all of them, he wrote grammatically perfect letters and other corre-spondence snappy with military jargon and requiring only their signatures. His evenings and weekends were spent at the post library, writing an Army novel. He quickly rose to the rank of "Buck" Sergeant E-5 (three stripes, no rockers) and become known as the best clerk-typist-journalist at Fort Hood.

Honorably discharged with a certificate of commendation, Kirkland returned not to Manhattan, where the going had been tough, but his college town, where the living was easy. (A good novelist, he rationalized, could write anywhere—look at Faulkner.) An undemanding job in publishing there would leave him the energy to write fiction at night. His editing sinecure at Hawkes-Prince was his second since the Army, his first having been with the university's literary quarterly before it folded from underfunding and a campus-wide lack of inter-est.

Hawkes-Prince was a small but steady regional house, old and venerable, with two departments: Textbook and Trade. Textbook published high school history books for statewide adoption; Trade published nonfiction other than textbooks. Textbook regarded Trade as a vain sideline, a bid for prestige, a waste of money. Trade didn't care. The department had been

Kirkland's idea. He knew the Textbookers resented him for it, but so what? As head of Trade, he made as much money as any of them, more than most, and earned it, too, because his sinecure proved not as easy as he'd expected.

Actually, nobody made a lot of money at Hawkes-Prince, and that included its octogenarian owners R. L. "Doc" Hawkes, a confirmed bachelor, and Millicent Prince, a wealthy dowager. The old house was tight as a snare drum; editors had been fired for comparing salaries; there was no telling how little money Basehart agreed to work for once Kirkland talked the old people into hiring him. As Trade's first "writer-in-residence," Basehart, it was decreed, would rewrite travel guides for young readers. When the Textbook editors learned of his hiring, they were more convinced than ever that what the company needed was a pair of funerals. Or maybe a trio—though Kirkland, in his mid-twenties, was unlikely to die anytime soon. They resented him because they saw him as the owners' pet (he was) and possibly their spy (he wasn't), and because his pay grade was that of a department head in a department heretofore consisting of himself. The chief Textbooker, Jason Clay, a beefy, hirsute Texas A&M alum who pasted NRA stickers on the bumper of his Ford Mustang, didn't even say hello when he passed Kirkland in the hallway.

Making Trade a two-person department by getting Basehart hired had been easy. When Kirkland convinced the owners, vulnerable to flattery in their dotage, that the novelist wanted to work for them, their rheumy eyes widened and gleamed. Basehart was not just a literary lion but a "yellow dog Democrat"; both owners had revered FDR and JFK; both admired *A Man of the People*; both religiously read *The New Republic, The Nation, Mother Jones, The Texas Observer*, and *Ramparts* and routed them to the staff. What feathers would adorn their caps when readers of *Publishers Weekly* learned that the author of *A Man of the People* was now a writer-in-residence for Hawkes-Prince Publishers!

Kirkland realized what an improbable match, or mismatch, he was making. He didn't expect Basehart's career at Hawkes-Prince to last long—it would be like Van Cliburn playing Ferrante & Teicher in the piano bar of a cruise ship. But he did foresee the author's staying put long enough to be of use to him. A mutually profitable friendship could be forged, with everyone temporarily happy but the Textbookers; and Kirkland secretly delighted in making them unhappy. As they looked askance at him, he looked down on them and they knew it. They even hated him for having gone up to "Jew York," as they called it, to live and write and come back with a superior air and a patina of Manhattan chic.

——

"Billy, I'm curious about two things," Kirkland told his department's new writer-in-residence on the eve of Basehart's first day of work at Hawkes-Prince. "Why was there no character in *A Man of the People* based on you?"

Basehart managed a wry grin. "There was," he joked. "The Governor's colored manservant."

"Second question: Why wouldn't your hardback publisher use your real name as your byline?"

105

It was a soft summer evening and the two were sitting outdoors, under the trees at a wooden table in the old German *biergarten* Basehart had described with loving care in *A Man of the People*. He'd asked to meet there because the garden held memories for him. He nursed a stein of iced tea while Kirkland drank Shiner Bock from the bottle. From some speakers in the trees, the plaintive 1940s voice of Eddy Arnold sang of sending his lady love a "big bouquet of roses," one for every time she broke his heart.

Basehart explained, "Boston publishers frown on nicknames. When I told mine that Billy Jeff was the name my parents gave me—the one on my birth certificate—they said, 'It nevertheless doesn't convey the gravitas befitting a serious novel.' Those were their exact words, Tim. They rechristened me William Jeffrey. Hell, they could've renamed me Ralph Waldo Basehart if they'd wanted and I'd've gone along to get my book published. I'm done with that crowd, thank God. Random House has offered me a contract for a biography of Beauford."

"And?" Kirkland asked with concern.

"Obviously I turned them down."

"You did? Why?" It made no sense that Basehart would nix Random House and then work for Hawkes-Prince.

"I'm not a biographer. I'm a novelist. I just heard from Simon and Schuster. They want a second novel."

"It's Simon and Schuster now? Do they want another political novel?"

"Yeah, but they won't get one. I'm through with politics. I don't even vote." Basehart snickered and sipped his iced tea.

Kirkland realized that he was still bitter about Jackson. He wanted to ask about the advance for the second novel, and the rumored writer's block, but held his tongue. Be patient, he thought. Once they start talking about themselves, people will tell you everything. It was the first rule of interviewing.

"I want to write the definitive rock-and-roll novel," Basehart volunteered. "A multivolume Proustian take on the psychedelic rock scene. Ken Kesey and Hunter Thompson are at it already. I hear from those two acid heads all the time. I can do it better and faster than either of them."

"Sounds exciting," Kirkland commented.

Comically magnified by his giant glasses, Basehart's eyes widened in disbelief. "Exciting? Jesus, Tim, our country is undergoing a fucking cultural revolution. Hemingway and Fitzgerald would've loved the sixties. This is a pivotal moment in American history. The summer of love and LSD and free pussy."

Unsure how to respond to that, Kirkland changed the subject. "Do you ever hear from the Senator?"

"Beauford?" Basehart shook his head. "Before he bush-whacked me, he said, *'We tried to read yore book, Billy, but couldn't get past all the dirty words.'* This from a man with the foulest mouth in Christendom."

"What do you think of Millicent and Doc?"

Basehart shrugged. "Two peas in a pod out of one harvest. The last of the red-hot thirties liberals. They used to be an item."

"They had a thing? How do you know that?"

"When they interviewed me, I could tell. She's still in love with that old walrus. She's an East Texas Southern belle and he's an East Texas peckerwood prick."

"Why is he a prick?"

"The old bastard asked me what kind of money I was looking for. I told him I'd consider whatever they felt was appropriate. He laughed and said, *'Boy, you sure must be desperate.'*"

That sounded like Doc, Kirkland thought, closing his eyes and clenching his teeth. "I'm sorry he offended you, Billy. Your being so upfront probably embarrassed him. He's just a tactless old man."

"He's a prick."

Kirkland shrugged and drank his beer. He disliked having to defend the ham-fisted curmudgeon. Doc was gauche and rude, but Kirkland had learned to tolerate him. He greatly preferred Doc to the Textbookers—five former history teachers with Master's Degrees, underpaid then, underpaid now, who believed in states' rights, admired George Wallace, and felt that North Vietnam should be bombed back into the Stone Age.

"Don't get me wrong, Tim. I'm not complaining about my salary. I'm tickled to have this job. We weren't getting by on Sue Anne's modeling. Her daddy, a Dallas Bircher to the right of Goering and Goebbels, mails her twenty-five-dollar checks with sarcastic digs about me. I was about to rob a Seven-Eleven."

"I hope you're being paid enough, Billy. I told the old people to be generous." It was a lie, but Kirkland had wanted to tell them.

Basehart changed the subject. "You'll have to come over for

dinner. We have a log cabin on the lake that belongs to Sue Anne's folks. Everything in there does except my Remington portable typewriter. Sue Anne's a great cook. Down-home food, but that's what I like."

"I suppose I'm available," Kirkland said, hoping Basehart couldn't hear the elation in his voice. "I like down-home food too."

"I'll earn my pay, Tim. I promise I won't embarrass you. I have just one question."

"Fire away."

"Where can I get good speed in this town? I've been gone seven years. I work better on speed."

The light-blue Kleenex-box office building housing Hawkes-Prince Publishers was three blocks from the state Capitol. The firm owned two floors—far more space than its small list and few employees warranted. The editorial offices had eggshell-white walls and blue carpets and a library containing a burnished mahogany conference table. Each editor had an office, hardly bigger than a cubicle, with a small walnut desk, two swivel chairs, a telephone, manual typewriter, and window with a view of the parking lot. Each owner had a spacious office with a large walnut desk, two cushy chairs, a sofa, Intercom, TV, private restroom, and window with a view of the Capitol.

Kirkland dreaded Basehart's first day on the job. As his department head, he would have to orient the new writer-in-residence (actually rewriter-in-residence) by showing him his office, introducing him to the other employees, going over company rules, and assigning his project. He was relieved to see Basehart wearing a coat and tie.

"You'll have to every day," Kirkland told him.

Basehart made a face. "Christ, Tim, I thought the fifties ended when John Foster Dulles died. Can I wear boots and jeans?"

"If you wear a jacket and tie. Even Doc wears boots. Make sure your jeans are pressed and your boots are shined."

Kirkland outlined other retrograde house rules. The hours were eight-thirty to five, with forty-five minutes for lunch and two fifteen-minute coffee breaks. One did not arrive late or leave early without permission. Beverages and snacks at one's desk were tolerated so long as one kept right on working. The owners were known as Mr. Hawkes and Mrs. Prince. First names were verboten; ditto radios, private phone calls, and reading the newspaper, though one was encouraged to read the periodicals the owners routed. Editors could be discharged for fraternizing with members of other departments or dating employees of the opposite sex irrespective of department.

Kirkland added, "That includes lunch dates. The owners frown on office romances. You might call them old-fashioned."

"I'd call them antediluvian. You left out punching the time clock."

Kirkland laughed. "They don't need one. The receptionist records your coming and going."

Basehart looked unhappy. "Tim, if I'm just rewriting manuscripts, couldn't I work at home? I'd make my deadlines."

"Sorry, no. They want you here to show you off. You're a superstar." Kirkland looked around and lowered his voice. "Don't worry, they won't hassle you. Neither of them has touched a manuscript in years. I'll be your boss. There's a staff meeting with art and sales every Wednesday in the library, but since you're not an editor but a writer, I'll get you out of it."

"Please."

Kirkland went over Basehart's project. Stacked atop the new employee's desk were four typewritten manuscripts extolling the marvels of travel in New Zealand, New Guinea, Fiji, and Australia. Atop the stack were yellow boxes of color slides and four-color transparencies. "Our Pacific Travel Series author," Kirkland explained, "whose name, believe it or not, is Douglas MacArthur Madison, owns a Houston travel agency and a Florida cruise ship. His travelogues are part of our Junior World Traveler Series. His photos are okay, but he writes like a pipefitter. You'll rewrite his manuscripts. The series is geared to a tenth grade readership. I'll give you a vocabulary gauge."

Now Basehart's face had a crestfallen look. "What will you be working on?"

"Our Southwest Writers Series. A line of pamphlets like Cliff Notes." Kirkland grinned. "I believe there's a pamphlet on you."

The author brightened. "Could I work on the Southwest Writers Series instead?"

"No. That's my baby. It's all editing, no writing or rewriting. It was my idea."

Basehart gave a shrug. "Well," he said, "I know a little about Australia. Beauford and Emmylou took me to Sydney with them on a junket."He removed his horn-rimmed glasses, whose lenses looked thicker than the bottoms of yesteryear's milk bottles, and held them up to the light; without them, his gaze was serene, his face almost handsome. The change was dramatic. Kirkland could see how some women found him attractive.

"I need cataract surgery," Basehart disclosed. "I'm blinder than James Joyce. Legally blind, can't even drive. Does this job carry health insurance?"

"Believe it or not," Kirkland was happy to say, "it does. The owners are liberals, you know."

"Really. You could've fooled me."

<hr>

Basehart's first three weeks at Hawkes-Prince went smoothly. He wore cowboy boots and jeans to work with a seersucker sport coat, buttoned-down blue Oxford shirt, and black knit tie. He was punctual. He was polite and friendly to the Textbookers, who actually seemed to like him. Every morning at nine-forty-five, he and Kirkland went to coffee, not in the company snack bar but the street-level coffee shop downstairs. That Basehart ordered a "Quickie" Breakfast—three scrambled eggs and biscuit—made Kirkland nervous, but the gnome wolfed it down and they were never late getting back.

Kirkland would have gone to lunch with him too, but the troll brought his lunch to work in a paper bag and ate it in his office with the door closed while he read *Rolling Stone*. On coffee breaks, he became a storyteller who told on himself. Some of his stories required a suspension of disbelief, and Kirkland remembered Connie's calling Basehart a pathological liar; but the raconteur spun entertaining yarns which Kirkland chose to believe. Why would Basehart lie to him?

One story recounted how he'd written *A Man of the People*, all 490 pages, in just three months. "I wrote it at night on speed. It was a tradeoff with a security cop at the Capitol who was stepping out on his pregnant wife. He got me pure crystal meth his precinct had confiscated. I lent him my office near the Capitol for his afternoon trysts. Have you written on speed, Tim? It's fantastic. Better than anything Coleridge ever shot up. It lets you access corners of your unconscious you can't otherwise. I never slept—in the daytime I wrote speeches and letters and press releases for Beauford. I caught a nap on Sundays. Without speed I'd never have written my novel. Back then, I championed civil rights, fair housing, and abolishing the poll tax; now the only issue I care about is drugs. I hate how ridiculous the ignoranti are about harmless stuff like grass and speed. And mushrooms."

Another story had Basehart joyriding with Jackson in the Governor's pink Coupe DeVille convertible: "We were like two teenagers in a stolen Cadillac. Beauford would drive up into the Hill Country. He took me along as a sounding board. We'd break a dozen state rules and regulations. His bodyguards needed to know where he was and they didn't. He wasn't to go anywhere without security. He was supposed to use his driver. He'd chain-smoke even though his heart specialist told him to quit — hell, he'd strike the fabric of my suit coats with kitchen matches to light his Camels. He'd be swigging Cutty Sark from the bottle and going ninety and playing Conway Twitty on the radio louder than a siren. The top was down, people could see. I'd be wired on speed or high on weed. We'd eat fried chicken and toss the bones onto the shoulder. The Highway Patrol never stopped us. And what if they had? They couldn't give the Governor a ticket. He'd rehearse the speeches I'd written for him. When he got to my bleeding-heart stuff about malnourished Negro orphans and twelve-year-old *chicana* mothers, his voice would break and he'd cry. He wasn't faking it, either. Later, when he gave the speeches, he'd leave that stuff out."

Kirkland's favorite story featured Billy Jeff's first wife, Maureen: "The fifties were a wild time in this town, Tim. I'm talking threesomes and wife swapping and key parties. Maureen and I agreed to experiment. It was before our twins Dottie and Melanie arrived, and we saw ourselves as Continental and avant-garde. Celebrities would come to town to see Beauford but end up at our house and party all night. At first it was just pols, but then it was movie stars and pro football players and writers like Bill Styron and Dwight McDonald and Willie Morris, the editor of *Harper's*. Maureen was the town's first groupie, but the term didn't exist yet. At first I was jealous, but then I started getting my kicks from it. I never knew what celebrity she'd bag next. One night I came downstairs after having passed out and she was doing Bob Hope on our living room couch."

—∿—

Before long, Kirkland was so caught up in the daily storytelling that he was forgetting to monitor Basehart's progress on

114

the Pacific Island manuscripts in the Junior World Traveler Series. One afternoon, remembering to with a touch of panic, he rapped on the door to the troll's office and poked his head inside.

"How're you doing on Australia, Billy?"

"Come in, Tim. Have a seat. Did I tell you I was hypoglycemic?"

Basehart was eating white cake frosting out of a plastic tin with a spoon and washing it down with Dr Pepper. He called it his "stay-awake sugar fix." Open on the desktop before him was the latest *Rolling Stone.* On the work surface behind his chair, neatly stacked between typewriter and telephone, the four travel manuscripts did not look to have been touched.

Mildly concerned, Kirkland sat down. "How's it coming on Australia," he repeated with a glance at the manuscripts.

"It's coming. I was reading about Janis and Big Brother and the Holding Company. I love rock, Tim. Can't believe I used to love jazz."

"Talk about Australia, Billy." Now Kirkland's tone was stern.

Behind his comically thick glasses, Basehart's eyes widened in mock alarm. "Okay, Australia. But what's to talk about? I just got off the phone with General Douglas MacArthur in Houston."

"Douglas MacArthur Madison. And he's a retired Air Force Colonel."

"The Colonel gives terrible phone. And he's delusional. Thinks he can write."

"What did you talk about?"

"Him, mostly. And his illiterate manuscripts. I told him I

was rewriting every page and he was insulted. That pompous ass can't write his own name, Tim. I've read better prose on the men's room wall in a bus station. Rewriting his dreck is like squeezing frozen toothpaste. But I'm on top of it. Did you know Australia's land area is exactly the size of the Continental U. S.? Or that Ayers Rock is the most famous rock in the world except for acid rock?"

"I did not know that," Kirkland said, sounding like Johnny Carson even though he didn't want to play along.

"Australia is one-third desert. It's the only continent that's an island. You don't want to go too far into the Outback or you won't come back. Australian Aborigines are not Negroes but an indigenous race called Australoids. I've been to Australia."

"You mentioned that. Did you like it?"

"Loved it. Go in July and beat the heat, because it's the start of winter there. Australians are more civilized than we are, by the way."

"Don't say that in the manuscript."

"They have income ceilings. A few fat cats can't own ninety percent of the wealth like they do here. And the rudest thing you can ask someone is what religion they practice."

"Should we move there?"

"I'd rather move to San Francisco and groove to Richie Havens and Gracie Slick and Jerry Garcia."

"Let's talk about work, Billy."

"About time, isn't it? Why didn't you assign me deadlines for these manuscripts, Tim? I can't write with someone looking over my shoulder like you're doing. My first wife used to do that."

Kirkland resented being put on the defensive, and he wasn't looking over Basehart's shoulder. But the gnome was right about deadlines. "Okay," he said. "I'll give you two weeks to rewrite each manuscript. Starting today."

"That'll work. Also, you never gave me that vocabulary gauge."

"I'll get you one now." Kirkland rose to leave. Pinning this gremlin down, he realized, was like grabbing a fistful of smoke.

—·w·—

Later that day, R. L. "Doc" Hawkes summoned Kirkland to his office.

Basehart's reference to the curmudgeon as an old walrus had been apt. Tall and paunchy, stooped and pear-shaped, with a droopy mustache and leonine head, Doc wore pinstriped three-piece suits and sported a pince-nez like that of his idol Teddy Roosevelt, whom he remembered from his teens. The old man straddled two centuries, having been born during the Chester A. Arthur administration. Kirkland revered him as an antique piece of genuine Americana.

"I expect you know, Mr. Kirkland," the walrus drawled, "what high hopes Miz Prince and I have for your Trade Department. We're real optimistic. We're fixing to start up a pamphlet series on Southern writers to complement your Southwest Writers Series. A Professor Jim Blaylock at SMU will coordinate it. You'll edit. If our Mr. Basehart pans out, I'll have him help you. I expect he'd enjoy that. By the way, how's our literary gent progressin' on our Junior World Traveler Series?"

"He's slow but sure, Mr. Hawkes."

"I'd put it different: He sure is slow. I get the feeling he doesn't cotton to me."

"He respects you, sir."

The old man harrumphed. "Miz Prince took a shine to him, and she's usually right about folks. But stay on top of him, hear? Make sure he earns his keep. We're paying him top dollar."

"Yes, sir." Kirkland wondered how much "top dollar" was by the house's penurious standards.

"One more thing," Doc added with a canny smile as Kirkland was rising from his chair, and the editor sat back down. "In the fifties, on Saturday nights, the Lucky Strike Hit Parade used to play a song called 'Don't Let the Stars Get in Your Eyes.' We have a star working here now. You might want to heed the message of that song, Mr. Kirkland. I expect you know what I'm talking about."

⚬⚬⚬

Kirkland took his time before telling Basehart about his Army novel. The moment had to be just right. It came the evening the troll made good on his promise to have his benefactor over to his house for drinks and dinner.

Since his legal blindness ruled out driving, Basehart's wife picked him up from work, but on this particular day it would be Kirkland, not Sue Anne, who drove him home. The lakeside cabin the author had mentioned lay in the blue-grey hills west of the city in a forest primeval redolent of pine and cedar. On the drive, Kirkland glimpsed young people—college students—water-skiing and splashing on the glistening lake created by damming up the Colorado River. He heard their cries of pleasure. Though it was August, it felt like spring, and Kirkland's spirit took flight as he drove high up into the hills. Life was good, he thought. And getting better.

His passenger said, "You'll meet my two best friends tonight. Couple of dime novelists named Ridgeway and Everson. Unlike me, they make a living by writing. They're rich. I hate 'em."

Kirkland's pulse quickened. "I've read their novels."

"Their old ladies will be there too. Don't hit on 'em. You'll want to."

When they arrived at the cabin, Chip Ridgeway and Buzz Everson, whose names made Kirkland think of astronauts or golfers, were sitting on the front porch drinking beer. In their silk western shirts and snakeskin boots and designer jeans with silver belt buckles, they might have been dressed for a Grand Old Opry concert on a Saturday night in Nashville. Both had attended TCU with Basehart and then worked with him in the sports department of the *Fort Worth Star-Telegram*. When Basehart ventured into politics, the apolitical duo became contributing editors to *Sports Illustrated* and began writing about pro football.

Kirkland knew about them because they were important figures in Billy Jeff's bio. He envied them even as he saw them as interchangeable, like Keats and Shelley or Abbott and Costello. He could never remember which was which. Though opposite in appearance, they mirrored each other. Both were pushing forty. Short, rotund Travis "Chip" Ridgeway had published a best seller with Doubleday about the womanizing quarterback of a team modeled on the Dallas Cowboys. Tyler "Buzz" Everson, tall and lanky, had published a best seller with Viking about the womanizing owner of a team modeled on the Houston Oilers. Both novels were praised by the *New York Times* and peddled to Hollywood by the same agent. Both movies were slated for Christmas 1967 release.

Up close, Chip and Buzz were genuinely likable "good ole boys"—friendly, unassuming, and down to earth, with bow-legged gaits and barbed twangs. Kirkland would not have taken them for novelists. Sportswriters, maybe. But he would not have taken Billy Jeff for a novelist, either. Luminaries, he'd read, were often disappointing in the flesh; writers, always.

Even so, it turned out to be a magical evening, perfect but for a moment that revealed how much Billy Jeff hated working for Hawkes-Prince and how much his friends pitied him for it. The log cabin was rustic but expensively furnished with antique Texana and Southwestern art: Frederic Remington sculptures, Porfirio Salinas paintings, a wood-burning cook stove that must've been a hundred years old, a green-felted poker table from the Long Branch Saloon in Dodge City. Like Billy Jeff, Chip and Buzz had wives ten or fifteen years younger than themselves who looked like fashion models, and Kirkland wondered if they too were second wives.

Otherwise, he scarcely noticed the women; the novelists commanded his attention, though he ranked Everson and Ridgeway rungs below Billy Jeff on his prestige ladder. It didn't seem fair that their football novels should be made into movies when *A Man of the People* hadn't been. A fat joint circulated, and

Sue Anne Basehart dispensed icy sweating longneck beers to everyone but her on-the-wagon husband. Then the women disappeared back into the kitchen to cook dinner. Savory aromas wafted from there as the four men lounged in the Saltillo-tiled living room.

Kirkland let the others chat while he hung on their every word. Mellow from the beer and marijuana, he soon basked in a glow of well-being he wished might never dim. He could not have felt luckier had he been a guest of the Sinatra Rat Pack in their Vegas hotel suite. Surely this camaraderie hinted that his moment had arrived. *I belong here*, he told himself. *I deserve to be here. They like me.*

He sat back, closed his eyes, and smiled approvingly at the casual mentions of "Shel" [Silverstein] and "Frank" [Zappa] and "Jerry" [Garcia] and "Terry" [Southern] and "Benton" [Robert]—celebrities the novelists counted as close friends. When Basehart announced, "Larry's coming in next week," Kirkland knew he meant McMurtry, a Texan whose first novel was made into a movie that won three Oscars. The chance to meet McMurtry, maybe even schmooze with him, made Kirkland's heart flutter.

"We'll take Larry to The Bad Trip," Everson suggested, meaning the local rock emporium.

"The Fugs will be there," Basehart added. "Sanders is crashing here."

"I thought Ed was stuck in the Haight all summer," Ridgeway said.

"He's sneaking out," countered Basehart.

It wasn't that funny, but Kirkland laughed explosively. "So Tim," Ridgeway said, taking notice of him. "Do you write too? Or just edit?"

Kirkland cleared his throat and sat upright. "I wrote a novel when I was in the Army. I haven't shown it to anyone yet. It's not a Vietnam War novel…Call it a Vietnam-era novel…It's about stateside duty, garrison soldiers…"

"Well, sure," said Ridgeway, who seemed interested. "So was *From Here to Eternity*."

"It's called *Requiem for a Lifer*," Kirkland continued, unable to stop. "It's about Regular Army noncoms…enlisted men who keep reenlisting…The Army is a womb to them. They never leave the post. They're scared of life on the outside."

"Hell, Tim," Basehart interrupted. "You never told me you wrote a novel."

"You never asked."

Polite laughter. Someone put a Willie Nelson album on the stereo and the subject changed to what was happening out in San Francisco. And then to the event planned for October in Washington: a nationwide march on the Pentagon to protest the Vietnam War.

"We should go," Everson decided.

"Where?" Basehart asked. "San Fran or D. C.?"

"Both," said Ridgeway. "Buzz and I are driving to the Haight in two weeks. You coming, Billy?" Politely, he added, "You're invited, Tim."

Kirkland knew it was a token invitation, but he was flattered all the same. He took a swig of beer, grinned appreciatively, and gave no response.

Then came the exchange that almost ruined his evening. "Tim and I can't go," Basehart lamented. "We have a job."

"At Hawkes-Prince?" Ridgeway guffawed. "That's not a job. That's slave labor, Billy. You told us it was a sweatshop straight out of Dickens."

A pregnant silence. Instantly embarrassed, the three novelists glanced at Kirkland, who lowered his eyes.

"Open mouth, insert foot," Everson chided Ridgeway. "Tim is Billy's boss, Chip."

"Sorry, Tim," Ridgeway said.

"It's all right." Kirkland shrugged, determined not to let it bother him. "I guess it is a sweatshop."

"Y'all come eat!" Sue Anne called from the adjoining dining room. "Get off your chauvinist butts! Dinner's ready!"

The dinner—pineapple-glazed ham, black-eyed peas, corn on the cob, a salad from the garden, baskets of steaming cornbread—was a feast. Afterwards, Sue Anne brought out the German Chocolate cake she'd baked that afternoon and Everson's wife trailed her with bowls of homemade vanilla ice cream. Grand Marnier was poured into snifters, fresh coffee brewed, and Ridgeway's wife put a Buffy Sainte-Marie album on the stereo. The conversation grew spirited and loud, though Kirkland wouldn't remember much about it later. An after-dinner joint circulated. He lost track of time.

Then it was dark outside: time to go. Still high, full of food, half drunk and loving everyone, Kirkland kissed all three wives goodnight and pumped the hands of their husbands.

"Good luck with your novel, Tim," Ridgeway said a little sheepishly, as if to atone for his earlier faux pas.

Basehart walked Kirkland to his car. "I'd like a look at your novel, Tim," he said. "If you'll let me. Maybe I can help you find a publisher."

Kirkland was so happy he could've kissed Basehart too. He couldn't believe how beautifully things were coming together. Basehart was paying off his debt in a hurry. Kirkland felt like singing. The promise of good fortune rolled and stretched before him like a red carpet. He had picked another winner. Another sleeper. Himself.

—⁓—

Reluctant to seem overeager, Kirkland patiently waited two whole workdays before showing Basehart his novel. He may have waited too long. When he delivered the manuscript bright and early on the third day, the troll could not remember having asked to see it.

Disappointed, dismayed, Kirkland had to explain what it was without seeming angry or offended, and Basehart was apologetic. He'd been reading *Evergreen Review* with a magnifying glass, and now he was embarrassed. "Oh, Jesus, Tim," he said. "Of course. I'm sorry. I was baked the other night. I'll read it today." He accepted the manuscript gingerly, palms up, as though it were a sacred scroll.

Then he remembered something. "Tim, did I tell you my agent is coming to town? I should introduce you."

In a flash Kirkland was feeling better. "Well, yes, Billy," he said, trying to maintain his cool. "I'd like to meet him."

"I'll set it up. Listen, I think I'll skip breakfast this morning. Would you shut the door on your way out?"

Kirkland had noticed that Basehart was keeping his door closed these days, but sometimes he kept his own closed, so that didn't bother him. What did, once he'd returned to his office, was that he'd forgotten to ask about the Australia manuscript. Today was Basehart's deadline. Or was it yesterday? He should go back. Right now.

But he didn't. The manuscript he'd just delivered had priority. Having Basehart read his Army novel was more urgent than having him rewrite pages of juvenilia about kangaroos and koala bears and wombats. He would grant his writer-in-residence an additional day of grace.

Later that morning, his phone buzzed. "Mistuh Kirkland," a doleful bass voice droned. "This is Mastuh Hawkes. I tried to read yore novel but couldn't get past all the porn-yo-graphic words."

Kirkland laughed. "What's up, Billy Jeff?"

"I dig your book, Tim. I'm giving it a rave review."

He wasn't kidding. An hour later, Kirkland's phone buzzed again, and the caller spoke with an accent that gave of Harvard Square and Hyannis Port and Martha's Vineyard. "Tim Kirkland? This is Aaron Glass in Boston. How are you? I'm Billy Basehart's agent."

Omigod, Kirkland thought. He hoped it wasn't Basehart doing another impression.

"Tim? Are you still there? I hope I'm not interrupting your work."

"Not at all, Aaron. What can I do for you?"

"I just spoke to Billy and he's a fan of yours. He sang your praises. I'm looking for new writers, Tim. Fresh blood, if you will. I understand you've written a Vietnam novel."

Kirkland tried to keep his voice steady. "Vietnam-era novel," he corrected. "But yes, Aaron."

"I'll be coming your way on Friday. We could get together when I meet with Billy. I'll be staying at the James Bowie Hotel. Could you overnight-mail me some chapters? Or even your whole manuscript?"

"Be happy to." Kirkland fumbled with a pencil and pad. "Give me your address, Aaron."

It's actually happening, he realized once he'd hung up. Right on schedule. He had read in *Publishers Weekly* that it's harder to interest a topnotch agent in a first novel than to interest a publisher in one. He wondered if Billy Jeff really liked his novel or was just paying off his debt. He had read it suspiciously fast. Maybe he'd just browsed it.

⁓

Billy Jeff didn't show up for work next day. At ten o'clock the receptionist buzzed Kirkland and told him "Mr. Basehart" had "called in sorta sick."

"He said he has the East Texas misery," she added. "Whatever that is. He wanted to talk to you, but you were in the little boy's room."

The East Texas misery! Kirkland remembered the expression from *A Man of the People*, where it meant a summer cold. Basehart didn't show up the next day either, but his name came up at the Wednesday meeting in the library. The Art Department head, a prissy little toad named Smoltz, asked, "When will we have the honor of working with our new 'writer-in-residence'? I declare, we never see him."

"He's home sick," Kirkland muttered.

"He doesn't exist," laughed beefy, hairy Jason Clay, the Textbook Departrment head. "Mr. Basehart is a figment of Mr. Kirkland's imagination. A homoerotic fantasy."

The other Textbookers snickered, and the Sales Department head Doris Karnovsky, a bottle-blonde spinster of a certain age, almost choked on her mirth. Another Textbooker, Cecil Ritter, who'd said he hated the Billy Jack movie, clapped his hands in appreciation. Kirkland realized how much the others disliked him. He had underestimated the extent.

"Y'all settle down," Doc Hawkes growled like a first sergeant, and the library grew quiet. "Get serious."

From his high-backed throne at the head of the mahogany conference table (Millicent Prince sat at his right hand), Doc drawled, "I expect you Art Department folks will get to meet Mr. Basehart soon enough. That travel series he's working on has slides and transparencies that need to be sized and positioned."

"It's time we got started on that," Smoltz said.

"Millions of readers are waiting," wisecracked Jason Clay.

Doc gave Clay a stern look. "You Textbook folks worry about your own department. Worry about getting *Our American Pageant* adopted in Arkansas."

Once the meeting had adjourned, Millicent Prince motioned

Kirkland into her office. The dowager's white hair was bound in a tight bun; her face was a road map of wrinkles; her faded blue eyes were rheumy. Yet he could tell she'd once been beautiful; Connie Cummings said she still shopped at Neiman-Marcus.

"Have a seat, Mr. Kirkland. We have a problem."

Kirkland swallowed. "Yes, ma'am?"

"Did you explain to Mr. Basehart that we frown on personal phone calls?"

Kirkland responded that he had. With both hands the old woman held up a sheet of paper that was clearly a phone bill. "This came today. He's been calling New York City. Long distance costs money, Mr. Kirkland. He's also called Houston. But I expect those calls were to Mr. Douglas MacArthur Madison in reference to our Junior World Traveler Series."

"Yes, ma'am. I'll speak to Mr. Basehart about the New York calls."

"How's he doing on his travel manuscripts?"

"He's still working on Australia. But he's making progress."

"He needs to make it faster. How long's he been out sick now? What ails him? We're mighty proud to have someone like Mr. Basehart on our staff. But like any other editor, he has to make his deadlines. He's been milking the cow close to a month now. It's time he churned the butter."

"Yes, ma'am."

"He's your responsibility — you're his department head. Bear in mind that not everyone here appreciates you like Mr. Hawkes and I do. I'm afraid Mr. Clay and Mr. Ritter and Miz

Karnovsky don't appreciate you at all." She gave a small chuckle. "They'd like to see you gone. They think publishing houses are for making money. We're lucky to have a Trade department. Our board of directors is conservative. Do you catch my drift, Mr. Kirkland?"

—⁓—

How soon sweet things turn sour, Kirkland thought. Yesterday everything was hunky-dory. Now he smelled a storm brewing. Basehart might be putting both their jobs in jeopardy. Why didn't the old people reprimand him themselves? Either they felt it was beneath their dignity or they too were in awe of him. Billy Jeff was becoming a problem. *"He's your responsibility."* What if Connie Cummings had been right about him? *"You'll be sorry, Tim."* He was already a little sorry.

When the writer-in-residence inexplicably missed work a fourth consecutive day, Kirkland called him at home. Sue Anne Basehart answered. Her voice was composed, but she sounded out of sorts.

"Hey, Tim. I figured you'd be phoning. How are you?"

"Not so good. Where's Billy Jeff, Sue Anne?"

"Certainly not here."

"Is he well?"

"I hope so," she sighed. "He's in San Francisco. He drove out there with Chip and Buzz in Chip's V-W Bus."

"San Francisco? Why didn't he say anything? Why didn't you go?"

"It was a guy thing. They talked Billy into it. A paycheck arrived from your company in the mail, and pardon my racism but Billy got to feeling nigger-rich. I hope he doesn't fall off the wagon. Those guys like to party."

Kirkland groaned. Beneath his shirt and coat a trickle of sweat was sliding down his side. "I'm trying to save his job, Sue Anne. I'm trying to save my job. I need to talk to him. Is there a phone number?"

"I don't know who they're staying with. Probably Ken Kesey and the Pranksters. Or else with Tim Leary or Ed Sanders. Billy didn't tell you because he was scared. He said to ask you not to be mad if you called."

"What is he, twelve? I am mad. Is he planning to come back to work?"

"Billy doesn't plan. He told me you guys are meeting with his agent on Friday at the James Bowie. He said he'd see you then."

Kirkland was silent.

Then: "Has he used me, Sue Anne? Is Billy making a fool of me?"

"I don't know. I know he likes you."

"I'm not sure how much longer I can stay in his corner."

"I was thinking the same thing about myself. Take care, Tim."

Kirkland was beside himself. Taking deep breaths, he raked his fingers through his hair. Bathed in perspiration, he was so nervous he couldn't sit still. He was tempted to call Connie, who had a prescription for tranquilizers, and ask for a Xanax. Steady, he told himself. Remember your Hemingway. Grace under pressure. He decided to call Douglas MacArthur Madison, the Houston travel mogul, and ask when he'd last heard from Billy.

"It's been weeks!" Madison barked. "You people ought to know that without having to ask me. What kind of outfit are you running? Where the hell's Bobby Jeff anyway? At first we were on the same page and he seemed honored to work with me. Then he stopped taking or returning my calls. And now he's AWOL? He needs to shape up or ship out. I have some Tasmania slides to send him. I'm thinking of complaining to Doc. Or telling you *all* good-bye."

"No need for that, sir."

"Bobby Jeff has some nerve, Tim. New York publishers call me every day. Why, McGraw-Hill—"

"I'll handle it, Colonel. Go ahead and send your slides. I may take over the project."

"Is this character some kind of fruitcake? Didn't he write a book about Beauford Jackson? I didn't read it—I hate the Democrats. But how can he just ignore me? It's insulting, is what it is. It's insubordinate. He better contact me soon, Tim…"

—⁂—

Kirkland sat massaging his temples, then staring out the window, then tapping his fingers on the desktop. Pondering what to do. He needed to do something fast, but what? He thought of searching Basehart's office, turning it upside down, finding out how much (if anything) the gnome had done on the travel series. He had every right to. But he didn't want to take over Madison's travel project himself. And Billy Jeff would know that his private space had been invaded, his personal effects tampered with, and who had done it. This might end their friendship. And it couldn't end yet, not with that agent flying in from Boston.

Time was short. If the old lady was running out of patience, the old man had run out already. Sure enough, Doc called him onto the carpet that afternoon. Fearful that Madison had already complained, Kirkland braced himself.

"Any word from our esteemed literary gent?" Doc asked as he wiped his pince-nez with a handkerchief the size of a dish-towel.

"He's still down with the East Texas misery, Mr. Hawkes. Respiratory problems." Kirkland smiled wanly, wondering how much longer the walrus would stand for being lied to.

"Horse feathers, Mr. Kirkland. Nobody is out a week with a summer cold." Doc stuffed the handkerchief into his coat pocket. "We'll give Mr. Basehart two more days of sick leave. Then if he's still AWOL, fire him. And take over the travel series yourself."

Kirkland's heart sank. Everything had come undone so fast. He nodded painfully. He squirmed in his chair like a man with hemorrhoids.

The curmudgeon's tone was gruff. "It appears you got hoodwinked, Mr. Kirkland. So did this company. Remember that song I mentioned? 'Don't Let the Stars Get in Your Eyes'? We let it happen. I did, you did, even Miz Prince did. Mr. Basehart has made us look right foolish, and certain folks here will be happy about it."

"I'm sure Mr. Basehart has an explanation, sir."

"He better. By the way, you're flying to Dallas tomorrow."

"Dallas? What for?"

"I want you to meet with Jim Blaylock. Head of the English Department at Southern Methodist. Knows literature professors all over the South. He wants to get going on our Southern Writers Series. Buy him lunch, give him a contract. Schedule the first six subjects and find out who'll write the pamphlets. You've done a good job on our Southwest Writers Series, so I expect you can handle it. You'll come back Thursday."

Grateful still to have the old man's confidence, Kirkland asked, "Will we be involving Mr. Basehart in the project?"

The curmudgeon fixed him with a pitying stare. "Now that's a foolish question, Mr. Kirkland…"

———

Kirkland hoped the quick forty-minute trip to Dallas and back on Southwest Airlines might clear his head. He needed to get away. He liked the SMU campus—its Georgian red-brick buildings, its green grassy quadrangles—and he was glad to learn, when he arrived, that antiwar demonstrations were held there even though the city was still a bastion of superpatriotic jingoism. It had been just four years since the Kennedy assassination, but the city, thank God, had mellowed some.

Professor James Blaylock—a bearded scholar, barely older than Kirkland, with shoulder-length hair—was overbooked and had to cancel on lunch. They met in his office and the meeting was brief. Lists were exchanged, a contract signed, deadlines established. Then the two men, both preoccupied with other matters, shook hands good-bye.

Kirkland dined alone that evening at a locally famous steak house and attended a Dallas Theater Center production of *Look Back in Anger*. He enjoyed neither the Porterhouse nor the play. He couldn't stop thinking about Basehart and Doc Hawkes and Millicent Prince. And the agent Aaron Glass. He'd phoned Glass that afternoon and learned there'd been no word from Basehart. Their meeting was set for ten o'clock Friday.

Before finally drifting off to sleep that night in his king-sized bed at the Love Field Holiday Inn, Kirkland had a painful realization: it didn't matter whether Basehart showed up Friday or not. It might be better if he didn't. Basehart had used him, embarrassed him, but made up for it by interesting Glass in his novel. By Friday the agent would've read *Requiem for a Lifer* and the meeting could just be about that. Basehart's presence would be a distraction.

Life was cruel, he thought. The gnome had served his purpose but then become a liability and signed his own walking papers. Doc had passed sentence, Kirkland had to wield the axe. He had never fired anyone, and the prospect of firing one of his sleepers tied a knot in his stomach and yanked it. He liked Billy Jeff. Everybody liked Billy Jeff. Hadn't the poor little guy been hurt enough already? But Billy had sabotaged himself. Maybe he'd wanted to get fired, to collect unemployment. He was an idler, a slacker, the first loser Kirkland had ever backed. Connie Cummings had been right about him.

Kirkland dreaded taking over the Junior World Traveler Series and working overtime on its Mickey Mouse manuscripts. But it looked as though he'd have to. It was a small price to pay to get his novel published.

—◈—

Five-storied, ornately Romanesque, the James Bowie was the oldest, most beautiful hotel in town. In 1934 young Beauford Jackson had met his future wife, Emmylou Baylor, in its dining room for their first date. Having been the campaign headquarters for his 1964 Senate victory, it was still Jackson's favorite hotel. Earlier, during the 1960 presidential campaign, JFK and Jackie had slept there and breakfasted in the dining room with Beauford and Emmylou and the Governor's speechwriter and special assistant, whose name was Billy Jeff Basehart. Kirkland knew all of this.

The agent's room, on the penthouse floor, was high-ceilinged and quaintly elegant, with plum-colored carpeting and a four-poster bed with a white canopy. In a corner beside a curved window overlooking Congress Avenue was a round Chippendale desk with scrolled legs and clawed feet; the backs of its matching chairs were hand-woven silk. On the desktop lay a manuscript Kirkland recognized as his own. A strong pulse beat in his throat.

Right away a sterling silver coffee service was delivered by a black busboy in a white uniform. Aaron Glass turned out to be a boyishly freckled, red-haired fellow in his thirties. He wore a pale summer suit, a paisley tie, and a worried frown. Kirkland, apprehensive to begin with, took the frown as a bad omen and expected the worst.

He said no to coffee, and the two men sat down at the desk.

At the agent's prodding, Kirkland recapped his experience with Basehart. "So as of today," he concluded it, "Billy's missed seven straight days of work."

Glass sighed. "He won't be joining us, Tim. He left a cryptic phone message with the desk clerk. It offered no explanation."

Good, Kirkland thought. He said, "I guess he's still in San Francisco."

The agent shrugged. "Who knows. He's dodging me. Usually, the agent dodges the writer, not the other way around. He's done this before. It could mean he's come into money. He may have landed another advance on his own."

"That's unlikely, isn't it?"

"For anyone but Billy, yes. Believe it or not, he's still getting offers."

"Which could explain why he no longer needs this job. We just mailed him a month's wages."

Glass managed a smile, but the smile was morose. "He told me your company was more generous than he'd expected. Billy can con anyone. If I were you, I wouldn't count on seeing him again until he comes back for his personal belongings. His drugs and paraphernalia."

Kirkland was silent. He wanted to talk about his novel and not about Basehart. But he needed to be patient.

"Tim, I don't know what to do. I've gotten Billy four advances, and he's bilked three other publishers by himself. Seven victims. He spends the advance, produces zilch, and moves on to a new publisher. He's become a serial scammer. He even ripped off Hugh Hefner—he promised *Playboy* a profile of Jackson. Dial Press threatened legal action against him to retrieve thirteen thousand dollars in unfulfilled advances."

"Why have you stuck with him, Aaron?"

The agent sipped his coffee. "Because I like him. Who doesn't? Billy's a sweet funny little guy who'd give you the shirt off his back. But he'd steal the shirt off yours and sell it to buy drugs. I was his editor on *A Man of the People*. He didn't have an agent. We became friends. I called him when I started my agency and volunteered to represent him. I was sure he had another big book in him."

"So was I."

"I landed him a contract with Random House for a biography of Beauford. He spent the advance in nothing flat and never wrote a word. That's when I should've dropped him."

"He told me he turned down Random House."

"Billy lies, Tim. When I talked to him last month, he said he was working on a rock-and-roll novel he called *Krishna's Head Band*. He mailed me some pages and they weren't bad. I managed to get Simon and Schuster interested."

"Yes. He mentioned Simon and Schuster."

The agent poured more coffee. "They're still interested. What they really want is a novel about Beauford Jackson, because he's running for president. But Billy said no politics. He's had the most amazing shelf life. He promised me six chapters today. Has he been writing anything?"

"Not for Hawkes-Prince. Maybe he's been writing *Krishna's Head Band*. I don't know how he's filled up all these hours. If he'd been writing a novel on the sly, I'd feel a little better. But I think he just read magazines all day."

"And got by with it? Nobody called him on it?"

Kirkland flushed. "Like you, I trusted him, Aaron. I handled him with kid gloves. I'm ransacking his office when I get back. I need to take over his projects anyway. If I find something that looks like a rock-and-roll novel, I'll give you a call."

"Don't be surprised if you just find cake icing tins and a junkie's pharmacy. Billy may not be able to write anymore, Tim. He's fried his brain with crystal meth and acid and mescaline. I hope he's not drinking. His wife made him do A. A."

"His new wife? Sue Anne?"

The agent nodded. "I'm done with him after today. I've had it."

Both men sat glumly silent. There seemed nothing more to say about Billy Jeff. When Kirkland stared at the manuscript on the desk, the agent picked it up and set it down. "I read this," he said. "It's good. It's better than good. But I can't take it on, Tim. It's not what the houses are looking for. There's a term they use: 'reader mood.' Reader mood right now is anti-military, and your book celebrates the career enlisted man. James Jones's noble savage. A grunt. Your patriotic lifer would get laughed out of every house on the Eastern Seaboard."

Kirkland objected: "I wouldn't call my novel pro-military —"

"Maybe not. But publishers want a best seller about Americans burning villages and cutting the ears off corpses. A Vietnam novel. I can't imagine who'd buy a book like yours today. Maybe a regional house in the Midwest. Or maybe the Rocky Mountain Press…"

"I want an East Coast publisher. A prestigious house."

"Fine. But hawkish or dovish, your novel needs to be about Vietnam."

Kirland flared: "I never went to Nam, Aaron! All I knew to write about was Fort Hood!"

"Don't give up, Tim. Sooner or later this war will end. I have a friend named Katharine Plato who's starting her own agency in Gramercy Park and looking for new voices. She's a screaming pacifist who hates the military and calls our soldiers baby killers and war criminals. But I could send her your novel if you want."

"Would you? What would be my chances?"

"About one in a hundred."

Kirkland closed his eyes. "Send it, Aaron. What have we got to lose."

<hr>

Outside in the noonday heat, Congress Avenue was noisy and bustling. Kirkland pounded the pavement so hard his heels clattered on the sidewalk. He had never been so angry and so dejected at the same time. He swung his arms in a headlong rush, bumping into other pedestrians, shouldering them aside. I'd like to deck that fucking Basehart, he thought. Lay him out, clean his clock. He knew Billy Jeff wasn't to blame for the agent's rejecting his novel, but the gremlin was a jinx who'd brought him bad luck. A black cat.

Now he felt like a fool, a dupe, a loser. He had written an untimely novel that nobody wanted to read. It would never mean anything to anyone. All he had to look forward to was a dull job at which he'd embarrassed himself by hiring a loafer. A malingerer. The Textbookers were probably laughing at him. Soon he'd have to face them and they would not be kind. They'd conspire to get him fired.

He stormed into the editorial offices, marched past the startled receptionist, and headed for Basehart's office. The floor was hushed—it was lunchtime and everyone was gone, even the owners. Basehart's office door was closed but unlocked. Kirkland barged in and switched on the light, leaving the door open.

The lower shelf behind Basehart's desk was haphazardly crammed with newspapers, magazines, tabloids (*Rolling Stone, Evergreen Review, Ramparts, The Texas Observer, The New York Review of Books*) and stacks of typing paper. On the middle shelf were what he recognized as the travel manuscripts. But first Kirkland sat down at the desk and rifled through the drawers. You could learn a lot about a man from the contents of his desk. His heart was beating richly—he wondered if this was the adrenaline high a burglar enjoyed.

From the large sliding drawer on the lower right he carefully removed a green paperback entitled *Sex-Starved Slut*; a sealed can of Betty Crocker cake icing; a Wyamine nasal inhaler; a tin of Dexedrine; a two-pack of Twinkies, wrapped in cellophane; a yellow vial of RUSH amyl nitrate; a sheaf of folded articles clipped from *Rolling Stone*; three empty green bottles with prescription labels for pills he'd never heard of; a white bottle labeled "Black Mollies"; and an unopened half-pint of Jim Beam. There was junkie paraphernalia, too—a silver spoon, book of matches, thin rubber hose, and a boxful of the hypodermic syringes drugstores sold over the counter to insulin users. He did not find methedrine, but why would he? Billy Jeff would have his speed with him.

The other drawers yielded little of interest. He was making a terrible mess, but so what? It felt good, and he was still in a rage. He would slide all the trash into Basehart's wastebasket and haul it out but keep the travel material separate. He grabbed the stack of manuscripts from the lower shelf. He removed the Australia manuscript, thumbed through it, and found red-penciled editing marks on the first five pages but none thereafter. The other manuscripts were unmarked, untouched, immaculate.

Jesus, he thought. *The bastard never hit a lick.*

He glimpsed on the high shelf behind the desk a yellow legal pad tucked between a Merriam-Webster dictionary and Roget's Thesaurus. The pad was thin—ten or twelve pages of longhand, in black ink, with large looping letters: the handwriting of a man half blind. The first page bore a title scrawled in caps: KRISHNA'S HEAD BAND. These would be the opening pages of the rock-and-roll novel, he thought. He would keep them, read them, and call the agent when he felt like it.

Then he noticed an object on a far corner of the desk that must have been there since Basehart's first day on the job: a gold-framed 5 X 7 color snapshot of twin girls, four or five years old, in pigtails; both were smiling impishly; each held an index and middle finger in a V behind the head of the other. Billy's daughters—what were their names? Dottie and

Melanie? He picked up the picture and held it in his hands. He had forgotten that Billy was a dad; it was hard to imagine. The longer he held the photograph, the heavier it seemed, and soon he saw himself as an intruder, an interloper who's gone too far. His cheeks burned with shame.

"What the *fucker* you doin' with that?"

In the doorway Basehart slumped against the jamb as though standing upright were impossible for him. He wore jeans, a Western shirt with piping, a black cowboy hat too big for his head, and a squint-eyed scowl meant to strike fear. It was funny and sad instead. When he spoke, he slurred his words, and Kirkland knew he was drunk.

"Put that fuckin' *picksher* down! Those are my kids!"

"Billy Jeff?" Kirkland piped. "I thought you were in San Francisco."

Basehart lurched forward, grabbed a metal stapler off the desk, and threw it. Kirkland dropped the picture but ducked too late. In its seven-or-eight-foot trajectory the stapler only nicked his left temple but stung like a bumblebee. Basehart wobbled forward and kicked aside a chair. He threw a round-house punch, but Kirkland, Army trained in hand-to-hand combat, slipped inside it, got both hands on his shirt front, and tore him down like a crumpled puppet. Basehart's cowboy hat and glasses flew off. He shielded his face with his elbows as Kirkland—the bigger man and sober—crouched over him, knees bent, with a clenched fist poised to strike.

"Stop!" a thunderous bass voice commanded. "That's enough!"

Both combatants froze. A glaring R. L. "Doc" Hawkes loomed

in the doorway with feet widespread and arms folded like a policeman's. Behind him, utterly appalled, stood Millicent Prince, and peering over her shoulder stood the grinning head of the Textbook Department, big hairy Jason Clay. Other people were approaching.

Mouth dry, head buzzing, Kirkland stepped aside. Basehart was crawling around on all fours, groping for his spectacles. Kirkland picked them up from the blue carpet along with the photograph, whose glass had cracked, and handed them to the wobbly drunk once he'd struggled to his feet.

"Both of you get out," Doc ordered. "This is a publishing house. You're fired."

Basehart giggled drunkenly. "I want severance pay."

"I'm sorry," whimpered Kirkland. "I'm sorry." He staggered off.

Out in the corridor, stumbling toward the elevator, he ducked into the men's room. He looked in the mirror. There was a trickle of blood where the stapler had cut the skin of his temple. His tie was askew, his hair tousled. He doused his face with warm water and dabbed at the cut with a paper towel. He wondered if this could be a nightmare.

He descended in the empty elevator with his back against the rear wall. As luck would have it, the person who got on one floor below was the person he least wanted to see right now in all the world.

Connie Cummings appraised him with alarm. "Jesus, Tim—you're bleeding!"

"Just a scratch. You should see the other guy."

"I can guess who it is."

"Please don't say you told me so."

"We should get you to a doctor."

"I'm fine." Kirkland grinned with effort. "Hey, Connie, guess what? You and I can go out now. I just got fired."

—◦◦◦—

The singer Scott McKenzie would immortalize the summer of 1967 with his breezy hit song "Be Sure to Wear Some Flowers in Your Hair." But for Tim Kirkland the so-called summer of Love was ending on a sour note. At that point, having hit bottom, he assumed that things couldn't get any worse for him. He was right. They got better.

He never saw Billy Jeff again, but he got his job back. One morning two weeks later, with all the moxie he could muster, he strode into the editorial offices, apologized to Doc Hawkes and Millicent Prince for brawling with Billy Jeff, and for hiring him in the first place, and asked to be forgiven. To his surprise (and later that morning, the fury of the Textbookers), they said yes. The old people had missed having a liberal Democrat in the office and wanted him back.

A one-man department again, Kirkland soon found himself editing the Southwest Writers Series and the Southern Writers Series and rewriting the Junior World Traveler Series. None of them would earn a penny of profit, but each did find a marginal readership that enhanced the prestige of Hawkes-Prince Publishers. Kirkland's brave side had hoped the old people wouldn't take him back and he'd have to start over with a clean

144

slate. But his craven side had checked the want ads and found the job market tight. For all its faults, Hawkes-Prince had been as much a womb to him as Fort Hood was to the lifers in his Army novel; he too was afraid of the outside. He was a coward, Kirkland realized.

Then lightning struck. His luck turned around. Aaron Glass sent *Requiem for a Lifer* to his New York colleague Katharine Plato. She read it and reluctantly—despite its military subject matter—consented to represent its author. Even more surprisingly, a month later, she placed the novel with a reputable New York publisher, St. Martin's Press. Kirkland pocketed a $2,000 advance. Fortune had smiled on him. Sometimes a sleeper has to give up on something before he gets it.

But his luck didn't last long. A year later, after tepid reviews, *Requiem* was remaindered and faded into oblivion. There was no paperback edition or talk of movie rights. Glass had been right about "reader mood." Nevertheless, publishing a novel earned Kirkland the fifteen minutes of fame he'd been willing to kill for. When he signed copies and gave readings at a local bookstore, the turnout was surprising; the local PBS channel and NPR radio station interviewed him; three starstruck co-eds—and Connie Cummings—crawled into his bed. As Hawkes-Prince's second ever writer-in-residence, he got a raise and a mention in *Publishers Weekly*. For a while, he saw himself as a winner. Then reality set in.

Kirkland never wrote a second novel. He tried, but one wasn't in him. He discovered that he hadn't wanted to write so much as to have written—and now he had. With the new decade, the seventies, he returned to Manhattan, as he should've when he got out of the Army. He was hired as a junior fiction editor at Farrar, Straus and Giroux. He realized that he'd no more belonged at Hawkes-Prince than Basehart had. He'd never belonged there. He saw the house for the sad old dinosaur it was. Yet part of him still loved and revered it.

Millicent Prince and R. L. "Doc" Hawkes both died within a year after his departure. Doc went first. Their obituaries were posted in *Publishers Weekly*. The Textbookers took over the company, changed its name, and discontinued the Trade Department.

———

Postscript: a flashback.

In October 1967, the month of the historic March on the Pentagon, Kirkland had come across an AP news photo of Billy Jeff shuffling behind Norman Mailer, linguist Noam Chomsky, poet Robert Lowell, and pediatrician Benjamin Spock as the five were being herded into a paddy wagon for breaking police lines at the protest. Kirkland gave a whoop. On impulse he called Sue Anne Basehart, who was busy divorcing Billy Jeff, and learned the gnome's phone number in the hometown to which he'd returned: Fort Worth.

Kirkland called Basehart. Their chat was cordial. Billy Jeff was teaching journalism at TCU, whose university press wanted him to write a book about state politics.

"Don't ask for an advance," Kirkland could not forgo saying.

Basehart laughed. "I already did. They said no."

"You went to that march in Washington and got arrested? I thought you'd sworn off politics."

"Buzz and Chip wanted to go. We got in a scuffle with some neo-Nazis. We were separated and I got thrown together with Mailer and Spock and Chomsky. The pigs frisked me, but I was clean. I'm not a junkie anymore, Tim. I live life at its own speed now. And I love teaching."

"Great, Billy. Listen, I want to apologize for that day in your office."

"I told you I was a mean drunk. I throw things."

"About that picture of your daughters —"

"Forget it. By the way, I bought your novel. It's up on my shelf."

"Aaron found me an agent for it. I never got a chance to thank you."

"It was the least I could do. Take care, Tim."

That might've made for a happy ending had it been the ending. But it wasn't. Living in Manhattan, Kirkland heard rumors he hoped weren't true: that Billy Jeff was fired from his teaching post at TCU; that as a writer-in-residence at the University of Iowa Workshop, he was busted by campus police for drug possession; that having failed as the manager of a heavy metal rock band in New Orleans, he'd declared bankruptcy and taken a job as assistant hors d'oeuvres chef at a Canal Street restaurant; that he was going blind from glaucoma. Kirkland chose to ignore the rumors.

Then, in the summer of 1977, ten years after the summer of Love, he read in the *New York Times* that Billy Jeff had died of cardiac arrest from a drug overdose. Kirkland and many other mourners flocked to the funeral in Fort Worth; Senator Beauford Jackson and Emmylou could not attend, but they wired flowers.

At the grave site, lurking in the background like a Zelig behind Buzz Everson, Chip Ridgeway, Larry McMurtry, Basehart's two ex-wives, and both his teenage daughters, Kirkland felt his eyes blurring with tears. He didn't mourn Billy Jeff the man, since he'd barely known him, but he did mourn Billy Jeff the novelist. What a waste, he thought. Had *he* been given this man's talent, he would not have wasted it as a chronic suicide, a junkie with a bad work ethic.

Ultimately, however, the nation would remember Basehart as a winner and not just a tragic figure. In 1978 *A Man of the People* was republished in hardcover under the author's real name: Billy Jeff Basehart. Four paperback editions would follow. In 2000 the literary establishment officially proclaimed it the finest novel yet written about American politics.

Time was kind to the other sleepers Kirkland backed in 1967 as well. The three Billy Jack sequels netted millions of dollars at the box office, and a fourth, *Billy Jack for President*, was rumored as in production. In 2011 a seventy-year-old Tim Kirkland purchased the boxed "Billy Jack Ultimate Collection" on high-definition three-dimensional Blue-Ray Disc with THX Surround Sound.

In 2004 Bobbie Gentry's "Ode to Billy Joe" made *Rolling Stone*'s list of the 500 Greatest Songs of All Time. In 2012 Billy Joe cultists were still arguing about what was thrown off the Tallahatchie Bridge that sleepy, dusty, delta day the third of June.

Billy Jack, Billy Joe, Billy Jeff. Each a sleeper who left his footprints in the concrete of American culture. Kirkland had been right about all three that summer of '67. The only sleeper he'd been wrong about, the only one who'd fallen short of expectations, the only one who'd let him down was himself. Yet he was comforted by the knowledge that (as a famous writer named John Milton might've put it) they also serve who only stand and cheer.

The Lap Dancer

This is a story about a writer who falls in love with a dancer. The dancer's name is April, though she has various stage names, and the writer's name is Phil. I'm Phil.

The story is set in the early nineteen-eighties, the golden age of city magazines. I don't mean the skinny kind of city magazine published by Chambers of Commerce, which nobody read. I mean the fat kind—filled with four-color ads, oily with perfume, and bankrolled by Reagan-era millionaires or their trophy wives—which a certain type of reader read every month from cover to cover, hoping to find himself or herself mentioned, and maybe even photographed, inside. I wrote for city magazines during that era, and for two or three years I loved it.

I was good at it, too. In my mid-twenties but greener than St. Paddy's Day in Dublin, I'd stopped trying to write novels. It took too long, and I had nothing to say in a novel anyway. I hadn't lived enough. Instead I'd started writing for slicks with names like *D* (Dallas) and *SA* (San Antonio) and *Houston City*. When someone at a party asked, "What do you do?" I was proud to answer, "I'm a city magazine journalist." Such pride would not survive what happened with April; after that, something more like shame would take its place and make me question whether I deserved to call myself a journalist. But I can't lay the blame on city mags, or even April herself. I have only myself to blame.

I'll call my favorite slick *New Americaville Monthly*. It was the magazine of the city I lived in, but I was partial to it because I was its star writer, the sole freelancer listed on its masthead as a Contributing Editor. For "Monthly," as we called it, I could pick my subjects, write as long or short (within reason) as I wanted, and get paid on acceptance rather than publication. No other magazine treated me that well. For a 3000-word feature I commanded $500. It paid my rent and my utilities.

The only thing I didn't like about Monthly was the way its editor, Ronnie Dubonnet, smelled. Behind his back we called Ronnie "Stinker" because he wore the same black turtleneck every day, hot or cold, rain or shine, like a uniform, and it reeked of his goatish body odor. Ronnie called himself a "gonzo journalist," sported a bushy beard like Alan Ginsberg's, and rode the kind of Harley police motorcycle Peter Fonda and Dennis Hopper did in *Easy Rider*. His personal hygiene caused more than one anonymous note ("Wash That Sweater!") and jumbo can of Right Guard to be left on his desk. To no avail.

Otherwise, I didn't mind Ronnie as my editor. In the sixties, he'd published a feisty underground newspaper called *The Gadfly*. He had sound editorial instincts and what Hemingway called a "built-in shockproof shit detector." Ronnie couldn't write, but he could rewrite a mediocre story and make it a reasonably good one. He was a sucker for story ideas that went against the grain of conventional wisdom. "The Case for Concealed Handguns." "Why New Americaville's Restaurants Shouldn't Ban Smoking." "A Few Kind Words for the Local Klan." Argue that down was actually up, bad good, or jet-black snow-white and he'd buy your story in a nanosecond.

He'd summoned me to the Monthly office one Sunday morning when normal people were asleep or in church by claiming it was an emergency. I sat at a safe olfactory remove—he was wearing that black turtleneck—as he began his pitch: "Phil, have I got a story idea for *you*."

"I pick my subjects, Ronnie."

"Help me out this once. I've got a five-page hole in my November dummy. I need a feature about the new titty bars springing up around town."

"Gentlemen's clubs, I believe they're called."

"Whatever. They've gone upscale. The clientele's not just beer-bellied plumbers in gimme caps anymore. It's also yuppies in three-piece suits, sipping martinis and flashing plastic. These clubs make money hand over fist. They even have valet parking."

I was underwhelmed. "Where's the spin, Ronnie?"

He flashed a smile like a shark's. "Everyone assumes the dancers are victimized and exploited. Junkies and hookers. But I hear those babes do pretty well for themselves. I want a story about a stripper who loves her work and feels she's benefited from it. And not just financially. Physically and emotionally, too. Maybe even spiritually."

"Spiritually? As in 'From G-Strings to Jesus?'"

Stinker was not amused. "It's a sweet gig, Harkin. You'll get paid to watch beautiful girls dance naked. Most heterosexual writers would kill for it. I assume that might include you?"

"I've seen a naked woman, Ronnie."

Actually, I hadn't seen many. Despite my having grown up during the Sexual Revolution, there were few notches on my belt. Like many young men who wanted to write, I was shy with women, especially beautiful ones.

"Listen, Harkin," Dubonnet ordered, all business now. "Remember the Happy Hooker? I want you to interview the Happy Stripper. Really get to know her." He stroked his bushy beard. "Explore the pole-dancer industry from the inside out. Get those coozes to open up for you." He leered. "I'll give you some cash for expenses."

The assignment should've sounded good. Why didn't it? Something smelled, and it wasn't just Ronnie Dubonnet's turtleneck. "I don't know," I waffled. "I have a bad vibe about this. Give it to Chester the Molester."

"Rainey? That degenerate is too close to the subject matter. I need a fresh take. Besides, he'd spend a fortune. Go downtown to that big new club called Sugar Britches. If they like the story, they'll advertise with us."

It being the Reagan era, this former counterculturalist didn't mind that his livelihood depended on something as crassly capitalistic as advertising. Or that topless bars objectified and exploited women worse than Hugh Hefner or Bob Guccione did. We had outlived the Age of Aquarius. Greed was good again, money made the world go round.

"But don't let the club know what you're doing," he added. "Have your dancer keep her piehole shut. Help me out, Harkin."

"All right," I relented. "But I'm not wild about this gig. Sleaze can be depressing."

"How would you know? Weren't you an altar boy?"

"I was. Incense, cassock, surplice, everything."

"Well, say a fucking *dominus vobiscum* and get on it. We go to camera in five days."

"A rush job? I want six hundred." I was a capitalist again too.

"Five-fifty. And I'll need a draft in three days."

"Six hundred and rising, Ronnie."

"All right, six hundred. But it better be good."

Something told me I would earn every penny.

—~~—

Before tackling any story, I did my homework. For this one, though I dreaded it, I had to phone Chester Rainey. Fellow bachelor, fellow failed novelist, fellow city magazine freelancer, Chester called me "young man" even though he was just two or three years my senior. He resented my being a Contributing Editor while he was just a contributor. He'd written for magazines longer, he knew the city better, but his prose lacked spark. Chester wrote like a suburban newspaper hack with a hangover.

"What it *is*, young man. What can I do you for?" Freshly minted phrases were not his forte either.

"How much do you know about strip clubs, Chester?"

154

"Need you ask? I know everything."

Chester the Molester, as we called him, took pride in his unsavory reputation. He claimed to own every issue of *Hustler* ever published and revered Larry Flynt as a journalistic hero, a messiah in that genre of magazines to be read, as Chester put it, with one hand. Chester played the lowlife as hard as Ronnie Dubonnet played the gonzo journalist.

"Why didn't Stinker give me this?" he carped when I'd explained my assignment. "Why send a boy to do a man's job?"

"You'd have to ask him."

"I don't go near that gamy bastard without a gas mask. All right, listen up. Sugar Britches is classy but pricey. They'll stick you for a cover charge at High Noon. They cater to suits and plastic and BMWs. A beer costs four bucks, a cocktail five, a table dance ten."

"Is a table dance the same as a lap dance?"

He sighed. "Jesus, Harkin. Have you been to a topless bar?"

I hadn't. But I knew that a fool and his money were soon parted in those places. Chester explained how the "Go-Go" bars of the sixties, with caged-up girls in bikinis and white Courreges boots dancing the Frug or Swim or Watusi, evolved into the topless "titty bar" of the seventies and then the nude or seminude "Gentlemen's Club" of the eighties. Even further back had been burlesque and striptease, and the new clubs paid homage to those genres. But today's dancers, Chester emphasized, were less into stripping for you than pairing off with you in a dark corner and pleasuring you as much as the law allowed and you could afford while they humped your lap.

Every club had an ATM machine.

"There are still rules," Chester cautioned. "Just one-way physical contact is allowed. You can't touch the merchandise, but it can touch you. Don't have them dance on your table or the bar. Ask for a lap dance in the V. I. P. room. It'll cost an extra twenty, but it's worth it. Be sure to tip—the skank will be grateful and tell you more about herself than you want to know."

"How much should I tip? Five dollars a dance?"

He sighed again, deeply. "*Jesus*, Harkin. A song lasts two minutes. You'd go broke. I'd better come along."

"I'll manage."

"Don't fall for their sob stories. They're all single mothers with brats to raise. They'll hustle you. Don't buy them drinks— it'll be iced tea disguised as Crown Royal. And whatever you do, don't lend them money. You'll never get it back."

"Are you speaking from experience?"

"Tell Stinker I'm pissed he didn't give me this story. I know my sleaze, young man. You wouldn't know a pussy from a pussy willow. Call me if you need help."

"Thanks, Chester, I will." I meant it.

———⁓———

Gentlemen's clubs were said to dislike Mondays because hedonists tend to stay home that day, recuperating from their weekend. A small house on a Monday afternoon might allow my interviewees time to talk to me. As I slunk in from the bright sunshine, a three-hundred-pound bouncer waved me by without a cover charge. Monday was bargain day.

Sugar Britches was cavernous. The music—New Wave racket shouted rather than sung—was the loudest I'd heard outside a live rock concert. The interior was so dark I had to grope my way to a table. Once I got seated, things took shape. I saw a main stage and three satellite stages whirling with multicolored strobes lights, each with a metal pole in the center. I saw thirty or more tables dressed in white linen, four or five occupied. In the back, a long bar. Off to one side, half visible through a beaded curtain, a shadowy room, with couches and plush armchairs, that looked empty.

Salome couldn't have seduced Herod by stripping to the music that was playing; maybe that's why no dancer was dancing. I had to shout "Heineken with a cold glass!" to be heard by the fishnet-hosed cocktail waitress who materialized at my table. My beer cost $4.50; I gave her a five and said keep the change. She walked off in a huff.

The New Wave noise ended, and an amplified voice like an old-time carnival barker's boomed from a perch behind the bar: "Now let's give it up for MISTY, guys, on the MAIN stage! And make some NOISE!"

The D. J. played a Cyndi Lauper number, "Girls Just Wanna Have Fun." Misty was black and topless, high-heeled and heavy breasted, with shapely long legs like Tina Turner's and a spangled red-white-and-blue bikini bottom. She looked all of eighteen. Her dancing was professional, but her attitude said she wouldn't do as the subject of my article. Misty was not enjoying her work. She looked bored.

Before long, as customers trickled in, every stage had a

dancer. There wasn't much stripping—the girls, lean and buff as Olympic athletes, started out with little to take off and kept that on. Several displayed tattoos on their lower backs and buttocks as they crawled along the floor in simulations of doggie-style sex with some invisible male lover. Contortionistic splits and gymnastic gyrations had replaced the bumps and grinds of old. The dancing was mechanical and without soul, dancing by the numbers. The girls used the metal pole as a giant phallus, stroking it, kissing it, rubbing their faces against it, wrapping their arms and legs around it. They used it for balance, too— their spike-heels must've measured six inches.

Not even the toned blonde who could've doubled for Kim Basinger or the sultry *Latina* who resembled a young Sophia Loren was a subject possibility. Their gazes were blank and vacuous. I was looking for a face belonging to someone who might put together a sentence without using the word "like" more than twice. I watched a lanky cowboy with a concave face mosey up to a stage, stick a tightly rolled green bill into a G-string, and receive a kiss on the forehead from a squatting goddess. I resisted going up and wouldn't have to; during the next five minutes, one by one, three bare-breasted nymphs plopped down at my table to ask if I wanted company. But "Brandy" and "Raven" and "Destiny" were airheads with nasal twangs that set my teeth on edge. I didn't offer to buy them drinks, and when I said No to a table dance, each left without saying good-bye.

I was enough of a male feminist (or liberal snob) to pity those girls. I even pitied the ogling patrons. What deprivation lured grown men into a dark cavern on a sunny afternoon to squander their hard-earned cash or unemployment benefits? Some, as Ronnie predicted, wore tailored three-piece business suits, and I wondered why they weren't out earning commissions or playing the stock market. I had not come to Sugar Britches to feel sorry for people to whom I probably looked like an undercover cop. I ordered another beer and decided Chester the Molester Rainey should've gotten the gig after all.

But I needed the six hundred dollars. And I'd never walked out on an assignment. I had to make something happen, because the place was not working for me and I was getting more discouraged by the second. "LET'S HEAR IT NOW FOR THE *LOVELY,* LOVABLE, LUSCIOUS *AMAZON!*" the D. J. was thundering as I crept over to a table beneath the main stage. Maybe a front-row seat would change my luck.

It did. Right away, I could tell that leggy "Amazon"—in a snug white evening gown, long white gloves, and red spike-heels—was enjoying her work. I felt the house sit up and take notice. While the other dancers communicated a sullen resentment, good-natured Amazon, like Gypsy Rose Lee, wanted to entertain you. Make you smile. She wanted your spirit to climb. Mine was already climbing.

Even without heels, Amazon might've stood six feet tall. The woman was like some heroic statue of a goddess, magically come to life. She looked at least thirty-five—today they'd call her a "cougar"—but the soft champagne light was flattering to her. I wondered if she was house *materfamilias,* a den mother for the younger girls, though her costume argued her as the feature attraction. Like the Dolly Partonesque hostess who greets you with a red velvet menu in a rural steak house, Amazon wore her blonde hair piled high atop her head in swirls. Her face was pretty but coarse—pouty mouthed and snub-nosed, with squinty country-girl eyes bluely shadowed. I took her for a refugee from a town where civic decisions got made over coffee at the Dairy Queen.

She was performing a slow, sultry Madonna number, "Justify My Love." Her movements verged on the awkward, yet their very gracelessness was endearing, like a housewife's dancing for her husband on his birthday. Wasting no movement, she swayed her hips but seldom moved her feet, and when she did it was to strut in those spike-heels like a model on a runway. Her stripping was expert. By the end of the set, without using the pole, she'd shed her long gloves (twirling each before flinging it aside) and shimmied out of the snug white evening gown. She was down to her black panties, red pumps, and good-natured grin.

Her breasts, small but firm, had big brown areolae like ginger snaps. And the grin? It was all for me. And not just because I had that front-row seat. She was favoring me with eye contact as if I were the only man in the room. How many other fools had flattered themselves with such conceit? Hundreds, probably, yet something complicit in her grin said she knew we were the only two people in the club with an IQ in three figures. "*Slip a five into her panties,*" an inner voice urged as the set was ending. Instead, while the crowd cheered and she was gathering up her costume, I rose and motioned her to my table.

She blew me a kiss, as though I were an old boyfriend. "Five minutes!" she promised. "Find a table near the bar!" And then, shoulders back, head high, costume bundled in her arms, Amazon regally strutted off into the wings.

—⁂—

I waited longer than five minutes, I must have waited fifteen. Slowly but surely, Monday afternoon or not, the club was filling up. I was surprised how many men—suits and boots alike—arrived with women. When Amazon (in heels and black panties and a red velvet jacket) joined me, it was at a table in the rear where we'd have privacy. Nervous but hoping to appear suave, I stood, executed a courtly bow, and kissed her hand instead of shaking it.

"Greetings, Amazon," I said, seating her. "I'm Phil. I really like your dancing. Your act is terrific. You're terrific."

She smiled and thanked me. "Call me April," she said in a voice husky but melodious. "Amazon's my stage name."

I got down to business: "I need to ask you something, April. Tell me the truth now."

"I always tell the truth."

"Do you like what you're doing? Being a pole dancer, I mean. Do you enjoy it?"

She seemed taken aback. "Why would you want to know that?"

I swore her to secrecy and asked if she'd like to be written up in a swanky magazine.

She arched an eyebrow and shrugged. "Maybe," she said. "If the price is right…"

"There'd be no money for you. But it would make me happy." Instinct told me that might work.

"Would it," she said. She moved close enough for me to smell marijuana on her breath. "Then I'll do it. But why me?"

"Because you're the star of the show. The main event. The class act."

She drew back. "You couldn't use my real name or my picture. Or the club's name. I'd get fired."

"No real names, no pictures. I'll invent names for you and the club. Will you answer my question?"

"Will you buy me a drink?"

"If you'll answer my question."

She gave her squint-eyed grin. "Do I like what I'm doing? Of course I do. It pays the rent and buys my groceries and helps me support my son."

The single mother strapped for cash, I thought. Chester knew his stuff.

"How old is your son, April?"

"Eighteen."

She was even older than I thought. Reading my mind, she said, "Yep, I'm no spring chicken. At my age who else would pay me to take off my clothes? I want to be a manager. Maybe have my own club someday."

"So you do it for the money."

Her eyes flashed blue in the semidark. "Not just the money. It's good exercise. It makes me watch my diet and my figure. It's given me self-esteem."

I had my subject. I could've kissed her.

She went on: "It's made me like my body. Do you know how many women don't like their bodies, Phil?"

I told her I hadn't given it much thought. "A lot," she said. "And my customers get something so valuable in return."

"What's that?"

"Human contact. Lots of guys come in just to talk. I'm a good listener, Phil. They tell me about their wives and ex-wives and girlfriends and jobs. Nobody walks into a bar without a problem. We all crave contact. Even eye contact." She giggled. "I used eye contact on you."

"I know. It worked."

"Don't laugh, but I do good here. The Bible says to do good works. I do mine by listening to people. And caring about them."

The spiritual fringe benefit, I thought. Stinker's gonna love you.

"Can you hear me okay, Phil?"

We were having to shout above the music. It was useless to start my tape recorder—I was reading her lips. "Barely," I yelled back. "Will you tell me about yourself?"

"Sure you won't pay for it?"

"No, but my story will tell your story. Think of it as doing good works. I'll write whatever you want to say."

She was tempted. She glanced toward the curtained room with the sofas and plush armchairs. In a coy voice she asked, "Wanna move to the V. I. P. room?"

"Can we hear each other in there?"

"Much better. I'll give you a lap dance."

"That's not necessary."

"I like you, Phil. It's a comp."

"I can pay."

"You won't have to. Grab your beer."

———❧———

En route I saw her flash the D. J. a signal by forming a cross with her index fingers. The V. I. P. room that had looked empty wasn't. Slowly now, dark shapes came alive and began to writhe on the furniture, as if we'd entered some orgiastic netherworld. Three cushy armchairs were in use: in each sat a man, and on his lap, squirming to the music with her back to his face, a dancer. As the men were pelvically stimulated, their hands were free for drinking and smoking, allowing them to enjoy three sensual pleasures at once. No wonder these joints made money.

"What was with the cross?" I spoke into April's ear. "Were you warding off a vampire?"

"It signaled what I want him to play. Enigma."

"What?"

"Enigma. They're a Euro rock group. I requested it for your lap dance."

She had me sink down into one of the sofas. A cocktail wait-ress appeared. "Can I have my drink now?" April asked me, and I was happy to break one of Chester's rules. She ordered a rum and Coke, I stayed with beer, and she sank down beside me. As we waited for our drinks, she lit a cigarette and we lis-tened to the music.

And what music. It conjured up a Satanic sex mass. The or-chestra was electronic, with an erotic percussive beat and eerie melodies. A choir of monks chanted what I recognized as Church Latin in the Gregorian mode. A woman's voice spoke of "the principles of lust" and "the principles of love." A young girl whispered French phrases I couldn't translate, and another sighed "Mea culpa" and panted in the throes of an imminent orgasm. I heard water burble, a horse whinny, a mezzo-soprano's voice operatically soar. The heavy breather repeated the name "Sade" like a mantra.

"My God," I said. "This is bizarre."

April laughed, crushed out her cigarette, and shed her red velvet jacket. Bare-breasted, in black panties and red heels, she mounted my lap with her back to me. Her perfume was intoxicating. She turned her head over her shoulder and kissed me on the mouth. Unable to check myself, I nuzzled her neck and pressed my lips to her ear. Too late, it occurred to me that I was breaking quite a few rules of traditional journalistic protocol. *But you're just doing your job,* an inner voice rationalized as April moved her buttocks back and forth on my lap. For all her girth and length, she was amazingly light, as if her bones were made of balsa wood. My response was swift and firm.

"*Mea culpa,*" the Enigma girl's voice confessed. Her panting grew heavier.

With a 180-degree shift of upraised legs and high heels, April swiveled in my lap to face me without rising. She arched her back and pressed her breasts against my face. Her nipples, first the left, then the right, found their way between my lips and teeth. She ground her crotch against my groin.

"*Mea culpa!*

The singer was about to come and so was I. "We'd better stop," I groaned. "Please."

Getting me off may have been part of the V.I.P. treatment. But I was wearing khaki trousers and didn't want to be embarrassed when I walked out into the sunlight. With a laugh, she dismounted. Our drinks arrived—I gave the waitress a ten and a wave. The song ended. April lit another cigarette and nestled against me on the sofa. Her drink wasn't iced tea—I could smell the booze in it. Chester wasn't right all the time.

"Whew," I said. "So that's a lap dance. You're amazingly lightweight."

"For a big broad, you mean?" She laughed like the best of sports. "You should've let me finish you off."

"That's a mortal sin," I joked, lamely. When I tried to slip a twenty into the elastic of her panties, she slapped my hand. "I told you this was on me," she said. "And so you'll know—just walking into this room costs thirty bucks."

Chester had said twenty. "Is what we did against the law?"

"Sort of. You're not allowed to touch me. But V. I. P. rooms get a wink from the V-squad. It's stricter out on the floor. Listen, baby, I have tips to declare. Thanks for the drink."

"Wait! When and where can I interview you?"

"Not here, it's too loud. Nowhere in public. We can't make dates with the customers."

"Why not?"

"Safety. And management doesn't want us free-lancing outside the club. But I do like you. I get off at ten. Come by my apartment."

Something told me that was a bad idea. She read my mind. "Unless you're scared," she taunted. "Some guys are scared of older women." A sexy pout cushioned the taunt. "I'm the one who should be scared, Phil. What if you're a stalker? A serial killer? Write down my address."

I took out a notepad and pen and handed them to her. "I'm breaking the rules for you," she reminded me as she scribbled.

"Thanks. I just broke a few myself."

"I really like you, Phil. You're sweet and gentle. My kind of man."

"I'll bet you say that to all the guys."

She frowned. "Don't tease me. Don't you like me?"

"Is the Pope a Catholic?" I was so lightheaded that I wondered if my beer were doped. Half an hour earlier, I'd wanted out of Sugar Britches. Now I wanted to stay all night, here in the V. I. P. room, with April the contortionist Amazon. I began to understand how a lesser man could get addicted to the place.

"Seriously, Phil. Do you like me?"

I kissed the tip of her nose. "Lady," I said, quoting e. e. cummings, "I swear by all the flowers…"

⸻⟊⸻

She lived in a ramshackle complex that looked like a jumble of cheap motels converted to apartments as an afterthought. Any dun-colored two-story building might have been any other. The grounds were so badly lit I could've gotten lost. Yet I managed to find her unit—a one-bedroomer that probably rented for $325 a month, with free cable. I wondered if the son she'd mentioned would be there. Should I interview him too? Probably not.

Letting me in, she seemed guarded, cautious, as if I were a door-to-door salesman. This was a different persona from the coquette at the club. She even looked different. Having let down her hair and washed off her makeup, she looked older and tired. She'd just worked a nine-hour shift. Barefoot, she wore loose jeans and an orange tank top with no bra. Yet her bearing was still regal. Even without shoes, she stood taller than I. Over six feet tall.

"Is your son here too?" I asked.

"He doesn't live with me, Phil. I don't know where he lives. I just pay his rent."

I was relieved. I preferred to interview tête-à-tête, with nobody else around. She offered me a beer. I declined, and we sat down on the living room couch. Her décor was minimalist—generic grey carpet, low ceiling, a small Walmart TV with a built-in VCR, the ficus at the window, the formica coffee table. Watching me size things up, she said, "Okay, it's not the Ritz. I'm gone most of the time anyway. I'm fixing to move."

"No offense, but I assumed you made good money."

"People always think that about exotic dancers. The clubs don't pay us. We pay them for the use of their space. Our money comes from stage tips and table dances and the V. I. P. room. They skim off a fat percentage. Monitors watch us. We declare tips every four hours."

I wondered whether I should mention such negative things in a piece with a positive spin. The litany of complaints continued:

"The clubs get rich, we don't. They also get rich because customers buy us drinks at full price, with no employee discount, and some drinks aren't real. You bought me a real drink."

"I know. I smelled it."

"I signaled the waitress I wanted rum in it. The clubs should treat us better, Phil."

"You should unionize."

"Don't laugh. I hear the Department of Labor plans to make clubs pay their dancers. But I'm not holding my breath. The Mob owns too many clubs."

I wondered if she thought the Mob owned the Department of Labor too. On the faux mantelpiece I noticed a gold-framed photograph of someone I assumed was a boy because he wore a black cowboy hat and an angry smile. But the fair hair that hung to his shoulders shone with feminine luster.

"That's Keith," she said. "My son. He's older now."

"He's a beautiful kid."

"He's a handful."

We began the interview. When I asked who her best customers were, she said, "suits on expense accounts entertaining fat cats from out of town." The girls called big spenders "jackpotters." Pro athletes on the road were jackpotters, and black jackpotters were generous but too demanding. "Early birds" and "daily regs" and "codgers" were stingy; they liked to come early, for special attention, and they watched every dollar.

She paused. "Are you getting all this?"

I held up a silver cassette recorder the size of a cigarette pack. "April," I said, "your job doesn't sound so great. Yet you love it?"

She wrinkled her nose. "It's complicated." She reached into her jeans and pulled out a small wooden pipe. She lit the bowl, took a hit, and offered the pipe to me.

"No, thanks."

"Please. I'm nervous and it relaxes me. I can't get high if the other person's not. I get paranoid."

Reluctantly, I took a toke, made a face, and handed the pipe back. It had been a while, and her stuff was harsh.

After another hit, she lay back, gazed up at the ceiling, and began to ramble like a patient in analysis. "I had an unhappy childhood, Phil. I was an ugly duckling. Tall and skinny and real gawky, with big hands and feet?" She raised a bare foot and wiggled her toes. "My parents adored my sister, Bobbie Jean. 'Bobbie Jean the Homecoming Queen.' Me they called Olive Oyl. Boys ignored me. I didn't have a date till I was seventeen."

"But baby," I muttered, already stoned, "look at you now."

"If I use bad grammar, will you clean it up?"

"Your grammar's fine."

"Our town was a mean town. One May, the senior boys threw a 'Moose Hop.' Those motherfuckers invited the homeliest girls they could find. The girls didn't catch on till they saw each other. The ugliest girl got crowned Queen. For my first date I was taken to a Moose Hop. I swallowed a bottle of Bufferin when I got home."

I wanted to reach out and hold her in my arms. I had to stop myself.

"After high school I moved to the city. I started to fill out and look better. I went blonde. I jumped in bed with the first guy who asked—a junkie in an acid rock band he called Coitus Interruptus."

"Nice name for a band."

"He was a mainliner. Careless with needles. I was careless too. He knocked me up. He told me he couldn't marry me 'cause his band required a total commitment."

"What bullshit," I said. I was cooked.

"When the baby came, he paid my hospital expenses and split for Nashville. He sent money for three months and then we stopped hearing from him. His mom told me he'd jacked up with an infected needle and died of AIDS."

"Jesus…" I sympathized. But wondered if "Mom" could be trusted.

"There I was—twenty-two and without a job or skills. And a kid to raise. I almost put Keith up for adoption."

I did the math. April was forty.

"I waitressed, I bused tables, worked at McDonald's and typed. I type real fast: ninety words a minute. But day care was eating up my salary. I went on food stamps. Sure you don't want a beer?"

The weed had left my mouth dry—a beer sounded good. She went to the kitchen and I flipped the tape. She returned with a gold can of Coors for me and a tumbler of rum for herself.

"I'd always loved to dance. I'd dance by myself to records and the radio and TV shows like 'Hullabaloo' and 'Shindig.' I found this ad for a go-go dancer, no experience required, and thought, 'What the hell, what have I got to lose?'"

Her guard down now, she was on a roll. The club, a beer joint on the wrong side of town, called itself The Losers Lounge. She auditioned and got hired. One of the strippers gave her lessons and named her Amazon. "They wanted Long Tall Sally, but I'd been called that in high school and didn't like it. For once in my life, my height worked to my advantage. Submissive guys like tall women. Hey — are you hungry?"

"Not really." I didn't want her to stop.

"Let me know if you get the munchies."

"I like tall women," I said. "And I'm not a submissive guy."

She smiled and sipped her rum. "For the first time in my life, I was doing something that made me feel good about myself. The Losers Lounge lived up to its name. You wouldn't believe how many losers never get closer to a woman than they do to us. We're those guys' sex life. So what if they leave the club and go beat off? It keeps them from raping some little girl."

It was an argument I'd heard for prostitution, but I had to agree. She rambled on: "My favorite customer was this quadriplegic Vietnam vet who came to the club every Saturday from the V. A. hospital with a medic that wheeled him around. They didn't call it a lap dance then, but that's what he wanted. I did the best I could, considering he didn't have a lap. Later he told me I was the only thing that kept him alive. I guess he died, 'cause he quit coming round."

I asked whether dancing in the nude aroused her. "Not really," she said. "But it gives me a feeling of power to have sex-starved men desire me. I'll tell you what does turn me on. Watching another girl strip."

That piqued my interest, and she noticed. "Some night," she promised, "me and my girlfriend Jasmine will give you a private dance here. That's what jackpotters like. *Two* girls. One jackpotter I know hires one girl to strip for another girl and give her a lap dance while he watches from a separate chair without touching either of them."

"Kinky," I commented. "Or avant-garde."

"The girls are my family, Phil. We share lipstick and mascara and perfume and blow-dryers and costumes and jackpotters. We also share our problems with men and kids and money."

"Do you share drugs?"

"Just grass. The V-Squad frowns on hard stuff. Ditto the club."

I had enough material now. Any more and the story might sag from overweight. And it bothered me that I was liking April so much. I was feeling protective, a little smitten; I wanted to hug her and thank her. And do more.

She was studying me. "Baby, you look uptight. What's wrong? I'm the one who should be scared, with a strange man in my apartment."

"I'm not uptight, I'm not scared, and I'm not strange."

"It's my turn to ask the questions. Why do *you* do what you do?"

"You mean write for magazines?" I had to think about it. "I guess I like to learn the truth. And then tell it."

"Me too," she said. "I hate lies and liars." She yawned prettily, reached behind her, and switched off the lamp. We were in the dark. "So listen, Mister truth teller. Tell me more about you. You seem shy. Are you one of those losers that never get close to a woman?"

I was a tad insulted. Before I could frame a comeback, she leaned over and planted a wet kiss on my mouth. It tasted of rum and marijuana and something sweet, like bubble gum. When she kissed me again, filling my mouth with her tongue, I knew why it had been a bad idea to come over here. If April was the patient, I was the analyst, so ethics and scruples were in order. She was vulnerable and asking to be taken advantage of.

"Grass makes me affectionate," she purred into my ear, and then licked it. "Hope you don't mind…"

Ethics and scruples would have to wait. I don't know how long we necked like teenagers on that couch in the dark. Her mouth was soft and sweet and luscious as a ripe peach. The pot warped my sense of time and place, and soon I was back in the V. I. P. room and she was giving me another lap dance. All we needed was "Enigma." Again I tried to rationalize it as research; again I failed.

It may have been too late, but I had to try. "Listen, April, maybe we should stop."

There was a rap at the door. We both stopped.

We waited, frozen in silence. The doorbell chimed. A male voice barked "Mom!"

"O God," April whispered. "It's Keith. My son."

<hr>

The rapping grew louder. "Well," I said, switching on the lamp, "you'd better let him in."

She sprang up and headed for the door. Frustrated but also

relieved, I stood up to tuck in my shirttail. Saved by the door-bell, I thought. Was it divine providence or low comedy? Respected journalists did not screw their subjects. Yet I hoped she could deal with the boy in the foyer and get rid of him in a hurry. In my tumescent state, I would not make a good first impression.

I overheard them talking: "*Jesus,* baby. I gave you a hundred last *week.*"

"That was for my Seroquel, Mom. This is for my Lithium. Forget it. I'll do without."

"No. I'll get you three hundred tomorrow when the bank opens. Don't snort it."

"You should talk. You're drunk and stoned. Who's in there?"

"A magazine reporter."

"A *what?*"

I groaned. My arousal wilted, and that was a good thing.

"You heard me. Come in and meet him."

I took a deep breath. He was the kid in the picture all right, still wearing that defiant smile. And taller than either of us. He must've stood six-four. In his designer jeans, snakeskin boots, and denim jacket, this cowpoke looked old enough to vote but not to drink. Beneath his black cowboy hat, his long hair — silver-white, almost platinum — grew to his shoulders. He had the face of some lesser angel lurking in the corner of a Renaissance painting. But his eyes and mouth were April's.

His handshake was indifferent. He gave me the once-over. "So you're a magazine writer? What magazine?"

"*New Americaville Monthly.*"

"No shit. I thought maybe you were one of my uncles. I used to have lots of uncles."

"Keith, don't," April warned.

"And you're gonna write up the old lady. Any bread in it for her?"

I shook my head. "I'm afraid it doesn't work that way."

"Why not? Never mind. But listen, Hemingway. Aren't we working late tonight?" He sniffed the air. "Do you always turn on with people you interview?"

I was being lectured on journalistic ethics by a cosmic cowboy right out of "Austin City Limits" and had no defense. I swallowed with difficulty. This kid gave off a whiff of menace. Even in a normal state I would have found him spooky. I was in an altered state.

"Stop it, Keith," April warned him again.

"Mom, it's cool. I'm outa here. I'm late for my bipolar lessons anyway. Be gentle, Ernest."

"I'll call you tomorrow," April told him. "I'll go by the bank when it opens."

"I'll pay you next month."

"Don't worry about it. Go home, baby. Get some sleep."

Once he was gone, she seemed flustered and embarrassed. "I'm sorry he was rude to you," she said, nervously sliding her hands up and down her hips. "He's basically a real good kid."

"He was being protective."

"He was being jealous and possessive. And he is bipolar. I'll tell you about that. But maybe you should go now. We can finish the interview tomorrow. Meet me at the club at noon. No one will be there but the cleanup crew."

I was at loose ends. "Listen, April…"

"Tomorrow, Phil. Have your questions ready."

At the door she gave me a hug. "You're my kind of guy. I'm sorry we got interrupted. I'll make it up to you. I like you so much…"

⁓

Half past noon the next day found me sitting at a table in Sugar Britches waiting for her. A genial old janitor who looked like Uncle Remus had let me in. The club didn't open till one, he chortled, but I was welcome to come in and watch him mop up.

A 3000-word story isn't long — a dozen pages double-spaced — and I already had material enough for a bigger story. Yet I felt I was missing some piece that would complete the picture. I hoped that piece wasn't the albino drugstore cowboy, because Keith made purple birds beat their wings within the walls of my viscera. When April finally showed, she rushed past me with a wave on her way to the dressing rooms. She wore last night's jeans, a man's white shirt with the tail out, and a bulging backpack. Her flaxen hair was wrapped in a towel, as if she'd just stepped out of the shower.

Twenty minutes later, she was sitting at my table dressed as a teenaged Catholic schoolgirl. Her hair was braided in two plaits, looped at the ends, and tied with pink ribbons. She wore a short-sleeved white blouse, plaid skirt, and knee-high green socks. For a forty-year-old mother, she looked ridiculous. I asked, "Is that what you wear when you dance to Enigma?"

"Of course not," she said irritably. "That calls for a nun's costume. A lot of men like this schoolgirl look."

"Sorry. It's very nice."

"Listen, I'll have to go on if our Marilyn Monroe doesn't show. I'll get you a drink."

"I don't need a drink. Tell me about your son."

"Don't write about him." She fumbled for a cigarette. "He'd get mad and take it out on me. He's jealous of you already."

"I'll just mention you're a single mother."

"Fine." In a hushed tone, as she smoked, she told me that during her pregnancy she'd done drugs with Keith's father that might have injured the fetus. "Maybe Coitus Interruptus and I are to blame for Keith's bipolarism," she confessed. "But lots of creative people are bipolar. Van Gogh was bipolar. Van Gogh the painter?"

I let that go, and she continued: "Keith is musical, like his father. Only with talent. The kid's a genius, Phil. His electronic rock band plays progressive country he composes with a computer and a synthesizer."

I doubted that. Even mothers of the criminally insane were prone to brag and exaggerate. She went on: "He uses calculus when he composes. For harmony and tonalism? Where he learned calculus I don't know, 'cause he got kicked out of high school for dealing. He's almost nineteen and never had a job. He's a crackhead. He pulled a gun on me once. I don't think it was loaded." She tried to laugh but she couldn't.

I was liking Keith less with every word she spoke. "He scares me," she said. I wanted to say that he scared me, too.

"When did he show signs of being bipolar?" I asked.

She made a face. "One day when he was ten I found him in the back yard eating dirt and washing it down with liquid detergent. I rushed him to the hospital. I've had every diagnostic test performed on him. I had to borrow money from the bank and my tightfisted parents. No two specialists agreed. One said Keith was schizo from a chemical imbalance in his brain. Another said his hypomania was hereditary. Keith must've like gotten the hyper from me, 'cause his father slept all day."

"You've paid for his bipolar medications since he was ten?"

She nodded. "They keep me broke. Mood stabilizers, anti-depressants, anti-manic sleep hormones…Lithium, Zyprexa, Seroquel, Geodon…Do you know how much that shit costs, Phil? We don't have health insurance. Who'd insure a kid so fucked up? I'm always behind in my rent."

It was getting depressing. I didn't want to hear any more about the bipolar boy genius. I asked about her plans for the future. She shrugged and said she couldn't dance much longer and it was unlikely that she'd ever marry. Jackpotters weren't "real good husband prospects" and she wasn't interested in being a housewife anyway. She dreamed of owning her own club, but that was a pipe dream. "Men produce and direct the T-and-A show, women just star in it," she said, giving me a quote for my story. And after adding, "I'll face tomorrow one day at a time" she gave me my close: "And you ask if I like my job? Christ, Phil, it changed my life. It saved my life. It's my fucking lifeline."

I was out of questions, she was out of time, and it was show time. "Stay and watch my set," she urged. "But try not to laugh."

"I need to get home, April."

"Give me your phone number in case I remember something."

Without thinking, I scribbled it on a paper napkin. She drew close and kissed my cheek and whispered, "You're the first person I've told this much to. I want to see you again." She hurried off to the dressing rooms.

I was tempted to stay and watch her routine. Her last sentence relit a fire in my groin. What I really wanted, I realized with shame, was another lap dance. Then we might go somewhere—my place this time—and finish what we'd started last night, before the cosmic albino arrived in his space ship from the Planet Zyborg. But what I needed to do was to go home and begin my story.

I tried to rise but couldn't—a powerful hand clamped my shoulder and held me down. I turned and looked up into a grinning face like a Halloween mask. In the semidark, beneath his black hat, Keith's platinum hair shone like a halo. "Easy, Ernest," he laughed. "It's only me. I saw you talking to the old lady."

I'd had enough of the Hemingway routine. "The name's Phil."

"Whatever." He sat down. "You don't seem glad to see me, Phil. I'm sorry about last night."

"Don't worry about it."

I shouldn't have lowered my guard—he sucker-punched me: "In your fucking story you are not to use the old lady's name or the name of this club. Or mention me. You got that?"

How I was learning to hate this kid. Like a polecat, like the Devil, he gave off a mephitic air that turned my stomach.

He grinned again. "I guess she told you I'm crazy?"

"I don't think she used that word."

"Okay, bipolar. They used to call it manic-depressive. Plus I have a drug problem. I like blow. But, hey —" he shrugged—"I'm a rock star, right?" He fished a card from his denim jacket and handed it to me. "I jam at a club called Positively Sixth Street every Friday night. My band is Coitus Interruptus."

His father's band, I thought. I tucked the card into my shirt pocket. "I'll catch your act," I lied.

"You sure there's no bread in your article for us?"

I caught the plural pronoun. "I'm sure."

"You've never heard of a consultant's fee? Because that's what you're doing with my mother. Besides trying to fuck her."

"Watch your mouth."

"You're consulting her to learn about pole dancers for your book."

"It's not a book. It's two or three pages in a magazine. There's not much money involved."

"And you get what money there is. She needs money, but why should you care? Fine, I'm outa here. The old lady's coming on and I don't want to watch her make a fool of herself. You really should fuck her if you haven't. She's fantastic."

I felt as if he'd punched me in the stomach. Had he said what I thought he'd said? I couldn't breathe. The whole room went into a spin like a board game on a swivel.

"I don't like you, Keith," I managed to say. "I don't like talking to you. Suppose you leave me alone."

He held up both palms. "I'm outa here. You take care, you hear? Don't get yourself hurt. See you around, Ernest…"

"Don't get yourself hurt." Was that a warning? A threat? As you can guess, it didn't inspire me to write much that evening. I needed to transcribe my tapes, but I couldn't get started. I felt like taking a hot bath, as if I'd spent the afternoon in a flophouse. I took a cold shower and watched a black-and-white horror movie on TV and kept seeing Keith's leering mask of a face and hearing him say "She's fantastic."

Questions hounded me and demanded answers. Why would Keith slander his own mother? Being a teenage paranoid-schizophrenic bipolar crackhead might have something to do with it, but why did I care? I'd already learned more about April than I had to for the story. All I'd needed to know was why exposing her body to a roomful of strange men made her feel like Mother Teresa feeding the starving in Calcutta. Now I knew enough about her for a book. *"The skank will tell you more about herself than you want to know."* But how much did I want to know? I couldn't trust Keith. Could I trust her? *"You're the first person I've told this much to."* Was I really? Why me?

I was afraid I'd dream about Keith that night, but I didn't. I dreamed about April. In her snug white evening gown she danced in my dreams, and the next morning, after I'd jumpstarted my nervous system with caffeine, her voice on my tape recorder made me want her more than before. I forced myself to concentrate. By mid-afternoon I'd made my phone calls to the library (Googling was still a few years up the road) and transcribed my tapes onto my word processor. In my mind's eye, I saw every paragraph of the story I would write later that day.

It would begin with April's unhappy girlhood as a skinny gawky wallflower and end with her inspiring triumph as an exotic dancer who gave sexual cripples reason to live. In between I would take the reader inside a strip club and explain how archetypal male fantasies were recycled there to make grease monkeys and floor managers feel like sultans and pashas. I would encapsulate the history of dancing girls since biblical times and striptease since World War II. I would cite industry $ figures. By then, no space would remain to moralize about victimizing the dancers or public lewdness or lax law enforcement, but that was fine, because I had promised Stinker—and April—a positive spin.

Ordinarily, visualizing a story that thoroughly was tantamount to having written it. But when I tried to write this one, I hit the wall. I hit it hard. Abruptly I was the nervous kid at the piano recital who sits down and can't play a note. I had to rewrite my first paragraph twenty times and couldn't finish my second.

I shouldn't have taken on this story to begin with, I realized. I was too conflicted and ambivalent about the subject matter, too involved with the subject herself. I had never been in love and wondered if I might be now. In my panic and frustration, I had the urge to hammer the keyboard with my fist. I wanted to bellow curses, to howl from my window.

The phone rang. I grabbed the receiver, hoping it was April.

It was Chester Rainey. "How's our story coming, young man?"

"It's not," I said angrily. "And it's not our story. It's my story."

"You sound like you're in a state. Need help?"

"I said I'd call you if I did."

"Skin bars are just like I told you, right?"

"I don't know. I've only been to one."

"Did you find your happy hooker?"

"I found a subject, yes."

"Why can't you write about her?"

"For Christ's sake, Chester, I'm just having trouble getting started." Why was I talking to this ass?

"I have to go," I said.

"Has she hit you up for money?"

"No, she hasn't."

"Give her time."

—⁓—

I quit for the day and took in a movie. Things went better the next morning. Around noon, April called to ask how it was going (I'd finished five pages) and whether I needed more info (I didn't). Her sunny mood and husky melodious voice were balm for my morale. I did not mention my confrontation with Keith, or the bombshell he'd dropped at the club. Or yesterday's writer's block.

"I gave you a new name," I told her. "Scheherazade."

"That's pretty. It sure beats Amazon. I hate Amazon. I can't wait to read our story, baby. We'll celebrate when it's done. Remember what I promised."

"Remind me."

"A private dance. Me and Jasmine. A night you'll never forget."

"We don't need Jasmine. You're my muse, April."

"I'm not sure what that means, but thanks. I have to go, baby.

I love you."

That left me with an erection. Somehow I got back to work. By the next morning, the story was finished, but that's the best I could say for it. It was too long, too diffuse. I'd tried to do too much. I'd gone over the top glorifying April as a working-class heroine, a modern-day Moll Flanders, without deploring the sordid workplace in which she chose to make her living. But I'd promised Ronnie a draft in three days and never missed a deadline. "When you're up against a deadline," Chester once told me, "it's more important to get the story in than to get it right." Besides, I was exhausted. Ronnie Dubonnet could cut or rewrite whatever he wanted; I had written the bones, he could flesh them out. I was done.

I had no fax or e-mail then—I had to deliver hard copy. When I got to the Monthly office, Ronnie was gone to lunch. I left the story with the receptionist and realized I was hungry. I hoofed it to a deli up the street renowned for Philly Cheesesteaks and Belgian ales. After a hearty meal, I drove home and crashed. I would pick up my check tomorrow.

At dusk the phone woke me from a deep sleep. "Harkin!" a male voice barked. "What the hell is this?"

"Ronnie?" I was still half-asleep.

"Are you porking this old broad?"

"What are you talking about."

"I can't believe you wrote this dreck. You're in love with this cooze."

"You don't have to call her that. You said to make it positive."

"I didn't say make it a valentine. It's not even your style."

"I'm sorry." I yawned. "If it needs work, rewrite it."

"I'm in deadline. You rewrite it if you want to get paid. I should have given this to Rainey. He said you were having trouble."

Now I was awake. "He said what?"

"You told him you couldn't piss a drop. He asked me to give him the story and let him rewrite it."

Chester the Molester and I were through.

"I may give it to him, Harkin."

"He is not to touch my story. Is that clear?"

"I picked you because he was too close to the material. Apparently you got even closer. I thought if I could trust anyone, it would be you."

That hurt. I had no defense.

"Okay, Harkin. Listen. Rewrite it in the first person. Have the stripper tell her story. Get your mooning ass out of the picture. Lose the X-rated purple passages. It's not a Harlequin Romance."

"It wasn't meant to be. Anything else?"

"It reads too much like a pitch for the titty bar industry. I want an ad, yes. But not that bad."

Now he'd crossed the line. "I don't give a rat's ass if you get an ad or not, Ronnie. I didn't want this gig, remember? I took it as a favor to you. You said it was an emergency."

"A rush job doesn't mean a mush job. You're running out of time, altar boy. Make your deadline or I give this to the Molester."

⌇

He'd also had the nerve to hang up on me. I hated being hung up on.

I went back to sleep and woke two hours later feeling like a new man with a new attitude. Stinker's dressing down had been a reality check, a slap in the face. The kick in the pants I'd needed. It was as though I'd been drunk for three days and now I was sober.

I took a long hard look at myself in the bathroom mirror. What did I want more than anything else? It was to be a tough, hardboiled journalist, pardon the cliché, who lived by the code and went by the book and could not be compromised. I had played the good cop and now it was time to play the tough cop. I had turned in work I knew was mediocre and sentimental. I'd thought I'd written a paean for April, but as I reread it, the paean had more the squishiness of a puff piece. Stinker had been right about it.

Something weird had happened to me in that club. I'd been introduced to a self I didn't really want to know. I'd gotten bewitched by a hoochie-coocher almost old enough to be my mother who'd humped my lap in the dark to some Eurotrash music. And thought she had to tell me Van Gogh was a painter. And had more problems than Madame Bovary or Blanche DuBois. But I wasn't Flaubert or Tennessee Williams, I was just Phil Harkin, failed novelist, wannabe journalist, and way out of my element, my comfort zone, with such a woman.

I microwaved a TV dinner, wolfed it down, and boiled a pot of strong tea. Then I sat down at my word processor to rewrite the story. I hardly rose from my desk until, many hours later, I had rewritten, edited, proofread, and polished it. Scanned and spell-checked it. Read it again. Finally, I congratulated myself that it was good. Not a prizewinner, maybe, but a damned sight better than what Ronnie Dubonnet had seen. It was at least work I didn't need to be ashamed of.

Retitled "Dancing in the Dark," April's story in her own words began: *"I am long-legged, tall and beautiful, and an exhibitionist. My name doesn't matter, because every night, when I go to work in what some people think of as a gutter, it changes to Scheherazade. I make my living by climbing up on a stage in a dark club called Dream Weavers, taking off my clothes, and dancing naked in front of people I don't even know. I'd like to say I don't enjoy it, but I do. I'd like to say I just do it for the money, but I don't. I do it because it makes me feel good about my body. I do it because I love people, especially men, and it allows me to give them pleasure. I do it because it saved my life. Let me tell you how."*

At some point, I must've fallen asleep at my desk. When I woke, sunshine rimmed the room and sparkled along the floor. My agenda was to shower, shave, and dress; drive downtown, drop off the story with Stinker, and pick up my check; and then deposit it at the bank. The rest of the day I would play by ear.

The phone rang. Ronnie or Chester, I assumed, calling to hassle me. But it was April, and she was crying.

"Phil? Oh, baby, thank God you're home. I have to see you."

"April, I finished the story. I'm handing it in."

"Keith's had a seizure. He went off his meds. He's in the hospital."

My mind refused to process that.

"I don't mean the emergency ward," she sobbed. "A real hospital. The doctor wants to keep him under observation. He's prescribing some expensive miracle drug, and I'm so broke I can't pay my rent."

"Calm down," I said. "It's going to be okay. You can work out something with the doctor and the hospital and the pharmacy."

"I *can't*, Phil. Could you loan me five hundred dollars?"

There it was. Chester's prophecy. *"Give her time."*

"Please help me, Phil," she begged. "I have no one else to turn to. I'll pay you back."

"Jesus, April —"

"Or we could…you know. Work something out."

"What does that mean?" I asked. But of course I knew.

She was crying again. "I don't know. I'm going crazy. The club said they'd advance me a little money, but I need more. Jasmine and the girls are taking up a collection."

I felt myself weaken. I had a few hundred in savings and a small CD.

"I helped *you*, Phil. I told you all about myself and my job. I risked getting fired by seeing you outside the club."

Playing the obligation card is always a mistake. "I'm sorry, April. I can't."

Silence.

"You mean you won't."

"I don't even know you. I just met you three days ago. I'm not one of your jackpotters."

Her gasp was audible, and I wanted the words back. "That's a lousy thing to say to me, Phil."

"I'm sorry."

She was quiet for so long I thought she was gone. "Well," she sighed. "At least think about it. If you change your mind, come by the apartment tonight."

"Not the club?"

"The apartment. Tonight. After ten."

"I'll think about it. I have to go now. I'm sorry about Keith."

"Please help me, Phil. I love you."

I lumbered out to the back porch and sat and rocked for a while on my wooden swing; it was a habit of mine when I needed to think. The morning was cool but sunny, the sky that deep blue almost purple: the sky in an Impressionist painting. I closed my eyes, listened to some birds sing, inhaled the pure sugar of the air, and prayed for a revelation.

I wondered if Mike Wallace or Dan Rather or Bob Woodward or Carl Bernstein ever faced such a choice. What would they do? I knew what Ronnie Dubonnet or Chester Rainey would do. But none of those men would be in my position to begin with. I was beholden to a forty-year-old pole dancer who'd just offered me her body for five hundred dollars and may have committed incest with her son. How had I gotten myself in such a fix? Was character really destiny?

Whatever I decided, I was sure to hate myself in the morning. If I wanted to see April again, my choice was clear: I'd have to give her the money. But if I respected my profession, I had to refuse her. Maybe I was no more cut out to be a journalist than to be a novelist. What was I cut out to be? A perpetual wannabe? A dreamer? A regular at the strip clubs? I opened my eyes and stared at the purple sky and waited for that epiphany.

———

It never came. But by noon, I had decided.

The story was a go—at least I could be sure of that. I dressed, printed out a copy, and drove to the Monthly offices. Ronnie was there, reading proofs in his black turtleneck. His cluttered little office smelled like a goat pen. I tossed the copy onto his desk.

He seemed surprised. "Already? Is it tight and bright?"

"Read it."

He was a speed reader, so it didn't take him long. He raised both thumbs in approval. "Bravo, Harkin. *Very* nice. And you beat the deadline by a day."

"I need to get paid, Ronnie."

"Right now?"

"Right now."

With a grunt of exasperation, he rose from his chair. "Got a date with an angel named Scheherazade? Watch out for that Arabian herpes, I hear it's painful."

"My check, Ronnie."

He led me down a corridor to a cubicle where he directed an annoyed robotic prune of a man in wire-rimmed glasses—his comptroller—to cut me a check for $600. Then he walked me to the elevator. "Give some thought to your next story," he said.

"I'm taking a sabbatical. Use Rainey."

"I may. He's less trouble than you."

"And wash that sweater while you're at it."

In the drive-thru at my bank, I cashed the check and asked for a legal-sized envelope. I inserted all six crisp hundred-dollar bills and sealed it. Then I drove to Sugar Britches. To hell with prudence, protocol, professionalism—I would do what my heart said to. Whether I could honestly think of myself as a serious journalist again was another question. Obviously, I wasn't that staunch, tough, hardboiled journalist who couldn't be compromised. I was some other kind. I'd never heard of pro bono journalism, but maybe this qualified, because I'd just put in five days of hard labor without a penny of compensation.

April had made a point of telling me to come to her apartment that night if I changed my mind. I wondered why there and not the club. The obvious reason was titillating. *"Maybe we could, you know, work something out."* Payment in trade. But I dared not go over there. I should never have gone there in the first place. I'd already behaved inappropriately—I would not make her a whore. I'd slip her the cash at Sugar Britches like a sugar daddy jackpotter and tell her good-bye. She was either at work or at the hospital with Keith. I headed for the club.

Today was Friday, payday, and soon the joint would be jumping. I may have arrived during a break; the place was quiet as I wandered in. April was sitting at a table with two younger girls I took for dancers; fully dressed, smoking and drinking, they looked like any three women off the street. As I approached, she saw me and said something to the others. Both rose and left with their drinks.

I sat down, heavily. "Hey, Amazon."

"The name's April. But you can call me Scheherazade."

She tried to smile, but the smile was frayed. I'd expected her to be happier to see me. She seemed unhappy. It was the fourth time I'd been with her, and each time she'd looked older. Today she looked middle-aged and haggard. She wore no makeup; dark circles of fatigue ringed her eyes; her blonde tresses had a brassy sheen; she looked worried.

She took a sip of her Bloody Mary. "You didn't want to come by the apartment?"

"Ten is past my curfew."

She took a pull off her cigarette and nodded toward the envelope in my hands. "Is that our story?"

"No. Our story hits the stands in two weeks. How's Keith?"

Her fingers shook as she stubbed out her cigarette in the ashtray. "Better," she said.

"How much better?"

"I fed him his lunch at the hospital. I haven't gotten his medicine. He'll be under observation so long it'll cost a fortune. Are you going to help us?"

I handed her the envelope. "Keith thinks you deserve part of my fee. So do I. Your share's in there. It's more than you asked for."

She looked around and tucked the envelope into her purse. "I'll pay you back. I promise."

We both knew she wouldn't. "It's not a loan, April. It's a thank you."

"You're the one who deserves a thank you. You're the greatest, you know that?" She took a deep breath. "But listen, baby.

Maybe we shouldn't see each other for a while. It's causing problems."

I was relieved—I had come to say good-bye and she was saying it for me. But I was heartsick as well, because now I knew I would never have her.

"What kind of problems?" I said.

"My manager has asked about you. He knows you're not a customer. I said you were just an early bird with a thing for me. He's not a nice man, Phil. And Keith hates you. In his condition, I can't afford to upset him. Please try to understand."

She was a mama lion protecting her cub. Also a professional dancer protecting her job. I had never belonged in her picture. I could only wish her well. Maybe one day I would write about her again.

"I do understand," I said. "It's okay, April."

"Maybe someday up the road, when it's convenient. Just not now."

"Right."

She looked around again. I wondered if her manager was watching us.

"You're very nervous," I said.

"I'm up next. I'm doing the whole Enigma set. I need to dress."

"Go. I'll stay for it."

"No. You'd better not."

"Just for one song."

"All right." But she wasn't happy.

"Break a leg, Scheherazade."

She reached out and squeezed my hand. Her touch was cold. "Thanks, baby," she said with a regret that had to be real. "You're still my kind of guy."

Then she was gone. Gone to the dressing rooms and out of my life. I nursed a beer while I waited. Ten minutes passed, twenty — April time always crept by.

I felt empty. But I'd done the right thing, hadn't I? The right thing is not always the smart thing, but I'd done what my heart dictated. High-heeled nymphs with thongs and bare breasts sashayed by and I barely noticed them. The club was filling up and my mood heading south.

At last the D. J.'s amplified voice boomed. *"Okay, guys — let's give it up for SISTER MARY AMAZON on the MAIN stage! Performing her scintillating DANCE OF THE SEVEN VEILS!"*

There was applause, the house went dark, and then April was kneeling in the spotlight dressed as a nun, staring at the ceiling, hands folded in prayer. She wore an old-fashioned habit—long black gown, black veils, white headpiece and collar—and an angelic smile. It was like a Madonna video. Patrons whistled and hooted and stamped their feet.

"Good evening," one of Enigma's enchantresses welcomed. *"In the next hour we will take you with us to another world."* The slow percussive beat began. The kneeling nun rose to her full height and shrugged off the first of her black veils. Then a second. This time I had no illusion that she was stripping for me. Sister Mary Amazon was working the house. My heart was grinding. I was jealous of every man in the club.

Then it happened. It was as if April's routine set off an alarm in my head. I felt a malevolence in the air, a presence hostile as a lethal gas. Everything was askew, out of joint. I scanned the crowd, but all I saw were dozens of avid, leering faces, some female, mesmerized by the naughty nun in the spotlight. Slowly, seductively, April removed her remaining black veils and white headgear and collar; shed her black gown and stepped out of it; shook loose her long blonde hair. She was down to a white Victoria's Secret teddy and black bikini panties. The crowd howled and demanded she take it all off.

Enigma was approaching her musical climax with a *"Mea culpa!"* I checked the crowd again. Nothing. But now my sense of a pestilence was overwhelming. I had to get out of there. I rose and stumbled toward the exit, weaving my way through a maze of tables, praying April wouldn't see me.

And then, turning back for one last look, I spotted him. Sitting alone at a table ten feet from the stage (how had I missed him?), platinum hair shining, ghostly face aglow, he was swigging beer from a bottle and clearly enjoying himself. He did not look like a convalescent fresh out of the hospital. I would never know the whole truth about this boy or his mother. Nor did I want to. What did it matter now? In that moment I knew I would never trust anyone again and understood how people are driven to murder. Keith must have felt the bolt of hatred I loosed his way, because he turned toward me. Our eyes met. He grinned and politely tipped his black cowboy hat.

Carpooling with Strangers

Prices at the pump hit an all-time high that spring, soaring over four dollars a gallon and prompting even affluent families to modify their driving habits. Summer auto excursions were postponed or cancelled. Shoppers began pricing electric cars and hybrids. Able-bodied Americans began walking to places they'd always driven to. A few motorists resorted to an option all but forgotten. The Davidsons, Liz and Michael, a childless two-car couple in their late forties, were among them. They'd tried using just their smaller car whenever possible, but Michael found it uncomfortable over a long haul. So they started to think about carpooling.

The Davidsons were new to Blue Panther Creek, a gated subdivision, twenty-five miles from Michael's office downtown, where $365,000 bought a smartly designed ranch-style house with a deck, swimming pool, and twice the square footage (with five times the backyard area) of their former house inside the city limits. With gas prices spurting through the roof, Michael's fifty-mile round trip five times a week (six, counting his habitual Saturday) was putting a squeeze on the Davidsons' discretionary budget. The couple was not poor—Michael was regional testing coordinator for a national textbook publisher—but neither were they rich, and only one of them brought home a paycheck.

Michael took pride in being the breadwinner. He knew how retro-macho that was, but the embarrassing fact that he and Liz were childless because he was sterile (his sperm count was low) drove his need to bring home the bacon. "My mother never worked," he liked to boast, "so why should my wife?" Actually, Liz had taken an occasional part-time paying job during their twenty-three years of marriage, but now she was volunteering as a junior assistant curator at the Museum of Fine Arts downtown.

When Michael first thought of carpooling, Toyota ruled the automobile kingdom and the Davidsons were loyal subjects. Michael's Toyota was a black six-passenger sedan, a 2006 Avalon XLS; Liz's Toyota was a two-door 2000 Celica convertible, white with a black top. Since Liz's car was more fuel-efficient than Michael's, she suggested he drive it to work and leave the Avalon at home for her grocery store runs and other neighborhood errands. On days when she went downtown, to the museum, they could take the Celica together.

Though far from happy about it, Michael acquiesced. He didn't like anyone, not even his wife, to drive his car; he compared it to another person's using his toothbrush. And soon he'd discover that he didn't like driving someone else's car, either. He felt like an accordion in Liz's convertible, which was too snug and low-slung for his long legs and 245-pound bulk. Liz called him "Big Fella" when she was in a good mood, which wasn't often lately, and indeed he was a big man. But big men had their own set of problems.

"I love you, but I hate your kiddie car," he would complain to Liz. "If someone hit me, I'd be spam in a can."

Playing the safety card wasn't wise. "You've never worried about *my* being spam in a can," she pointed out. "You're acting like a wuss, as usual. Drive the Celica for a while." When he asked how long a while might be, she said, "How should I know? Obviously, until gas prices drop."

"What if they never do?"

"They always do."

"It's different this time. Two oilmen run the country."

"If prices don't drop within six months I'll sell my car and we'll buy a Prius and you can stop whining."

Michael was not comforted. She'd promised to sell the Celica before and reneged. For her it was the child who'd been denied them, or so he theorized like an amateur psychologist, and he predicted they wouldn't get rid of the damned thing until it was an antique. If then. Who drove convertibles nowadays anyway?

Two months later, in June, when gas prices rose again, he found a list in *Consumer Reports* of ways thrifty motorists were cutting down on gas consumption. At the top of the list was carpooling. His mind was made up.

"Goddam straight you should carpool," said his balding next-door neighbor Sid Cameron. An even bigger man than Michael but soft and paunchy and pear-shaped, Sid worked for a downtown law firm that catered to wealthy seniors, mainly widows and widowers. "Listen, Mike," he went on. "Jayne and I have had this conversation. Carpooling makes sense. It's not about the money, it's about the principle. Those goddam Arabs! Why should the greatest country in the world be held hostage by a bunch of sand niggers who hate us?"

Michael winced at the racial epithet, and he knew that when someone said, "It's not about the money," it was about the money. But he welcomed Sid's encouragement.

He and Liz barely knew their neighbors. The Camerons were older—in their fifties. A high brick wall separated their property from the Davidsons'. "Our privacy fence," Sid called it that hot Saturday afternoon he'd had Michael over for a beer. "I had it built after researching the Great Wall of China. Good fences make good neighbors. The man who said that knew what he was talking about."

"Robert Frost said it."

Sid smiled. Sid was often smiling, even when his faded blue eyes weren't. "Right, you are, Mike. Actually, Frost wasn't sure good fences make good neighbors. One neighbor says that to another in one of Frost's poems."

Having minored in English at Rice, Michael assumed he knew more about Frost than a probate lawyer did. "The poem," he said, "was called 'Mending Wall.'"

"Right again. Blank verse, written in nineteen-fourteen. Frost was a good poet, maybe our best, but contrary to his warm fuzzy image he was a rotten husband and father. Son of a bitch was mean as a snake. I did a lot of Internet research on him."

Michael was impressed. How many probate lawyers knew what blank verse was even if they did know who Robert Frost was? Michael would learn that his heavyset next-door neighbor was a repository of trivia—particularly the sensational kind that tarnished the luster of the high and mighty. Sid, he assumed, was an iconoclast. More power to him.

Having a beer with Sid that Saturday, he also learned that the silver-blue SUV parked in the Camerons' garage was a 2006 Volvo Xc90 with a V-8 engine, and that the champagne-colored sedan beside it, belonging to Sid's wife, was a Mazda RX-8. "Her heap is previously owned," Sid disclosed *sotto voce* out of the corner of his mouth, as if they could be overheard. "My wife drives a used car, Mike. Don't tell anyone."

"Don't worry," Michael reassured him. "My wife's car is eight years old." He concluded that the Camerons weren't as well off as he'd supposed. Blue Panther Creek was full of aging couples, soon to retire, whose financial reach exceeded their grasp. He and Liz didn't fit the demographic, but the Camerons might.

Sid poured more beer. "Jayne and I have no kids and no pets," he proudly boasted. "And nobody lives with us. So if you're wondering why I drive a big old gas-guzzling SUV, the answer is simple. *I have no idea.*"

He laughed explosively and raised his foamy stein of beer. Michael grinned and clinked his against it. The man was pure *bonhomie*. Yet there was something about him that Michael didn't like. And it wasn't just Sid's calling him "Mike," a name he hated because he associated it with microphones.

"So when do we start, Mike?" Sid wiped his mouth with the back of his hand and raised his eyebrows in expectation.

"Start what, Sid?"

"Carpooling, what else? Let's discuss it over dinner. What are you and the missus doing tonight? Come by around six. We're having Italian, and Jayne cooks a mean veal scallopini."

"Sounds good. I'll ask Liz if it's okay."

"Don't ask her. Tell her."

⸺〰⸺

"Tonight?" Liz said disbelievingly. "And you said yes? That's not much notice."

"We weren't doing anything. And it's casual—just the four of us. He wants us to carpool with them."

"Carpool. The man doesn't waste time. Does he want to swap wives too?"

Michael laughed. "He definitely wants to get to know us. I get the feeling they're lonesome."

"I suppose it can't hurt. Good neighbors are good to have."

They were sunning themselves on the deck, in their bathing suits, on teak chaise lounges and about to go into the pool. Liz was applying to her shapely tanned legs an Anthelios XL sunscreen, squeezing it like toothpaste onto her hand from a green plastic container. Having retained her girlish figure in middle age, she still looked great in a bikini. Michael gave thanks for that, because time had not been kind to his marriage in other ways. They had not made love this year, and it was almost July.

"What a small world," she mused, rubbing the sunblock into her left shoulder. "I can't believe I'm living next door to Jayne Cameron."

"You know her?"

"I know of her. Jayne's name came up at our staff meeting last week. She runs an art gallery downtown with a sister who lives on the River. They lend sculpture and ceramics for exhibits at the museum. My boss Marge Whitlow, our bitch curator, bows and scrapes to Jayne Cameron."

"I can't wait to see how Jayne decorates her house," Liz added as an afterthought.

"We may not want to carpool with them," Michael warned. "Sid's a know-it-all and probably a staunch Republican."

"And that's two strikes where you're concerned? Don't prejudge people so quickly, Michael. It makes you seem intolerant."

Michael grunted to himself. There were days when Liz made him wonder if he'd ever say anything right again. During their courtship and early years of marriage, his way with people, especially difficult people, would earn him admiring gazes from her. Now he was more apt to get a pitying stare. Time was surely to blame, but had time changed him or changed her? He wondered if sooner or later every husband turned into the Dagwood Bumstead of the Blondie comics, just as every wife was said to turn into her own mother.

"I'm not prejudging him," he protested. "I'm just telling you he uses expressions like 'sand nigger.' He hates the Arab oil sheiks."

"And you don't? I've heard you call them camel jockeys."

She'd nailed him again. He had called them worse when she hadn't been within earshot. He still suspected that the Saudis were behind Nine-Eleven; hadn't the terrorists come from Saudi Arabia?

"Try to get along with him even if we don't carpool," Liz said as she bounded up from her chaise. "I'd like to get to know Jayne. And that big SUV of theirs looks comfy. Maybe we should carpool with them."

"Sweetie," he said, "I'd carpool with Moamar Khadafi and his wives if it meant not having to drive your Celica."

He was proud of the zinger, but Liz hadn't heard it. With a loud splash and the perfect form of an Olympic swimmer, she had dived into the deep end of the pool.

—◦◦◦—

Jayne Cameron turned out to be a short, buxom strawberry blonde whose smooth-skinned face and wrinkled neck hinted that she'd had work done. Michael tabbed her as the old-school subservient kind of wife who'd crawl a mile over broken glass for her husband. He was married to the other kind. Right away, Jayne confessed that even though she owned a gallery, she was no art expert.

"I gallery with my sister for the fun of it," she said. "I'm so impressed that you work with Marge Whitlow, Liz. Pooh Bear —that's what I call Sid—Pooh Bear knows more about art than I do."

Sid grinned and shook his head. "Don't listen to her."

"It's true. Pooh Bear knows more about everything than I

do. He has his law degree from the University of Chicago."

Big deal, Michael thought. There had been no sarcasm or facetiousness in Jayne's voice, and he wondered how bright she might be. The Camerons' living room, minimalist and postmodern, had little furniture, lots of bare hardwood floorspace, and vaults of natural light. There were ceramic sculptures and a huge Armani Xavira glass coffee table. One wall displayed Braque and Rothko and Paul Klee prints, miniatures in a diagonal row; another wall bore a watercolor landscape and self-portrait, both signed by Jayne. Her work was Impressionist pastiche—milky-hued and hazy, with thick brush strokes. Michael found it imitative. Amateurish.

"I'm not very good," Jayne apologized as the Davidsons looked at it.

"Yes, you are," Liz assured her. "I wish I were as good. I only do collage. I can't paint at all."

Michael was surprised that his wife so obviously liked Jayne Cameron; normally, Liz was tough on women. After pouring them two full wineglasses of Pinot Grigio, Jayne took Liz on a tour of the house and garden and studio. Sid and Michael settled into cushy leather armchairs in the den and sipped a single-malt Scotch Michael knew was a bargain because he often bought it himself.

Michael soon felt a buzz—the Scotch tasted better than usual. He and the lawyer discussed the NBA playoffs, and it was obvious that Sid knew more about his Chicago Bulls than Michael did about his Dallas Mavericks. Then Sid picked up the remote, and they watched the closing moments of "Jeopardy" on a high-definition TV with a giant flat screen. Sid blurted out the questions to both remaining answers (Michael learned that the USS *Enterprise* was the very first nuclear-powered aircraft carrier and that *Gone With the Wind*'s Rhett Butler and Scarlett O'Hara named their daughter Bonnie Blue), and then came Final Jeopardy, the moment of truth.

The category was baseball. Michael had played in high school and resolved not to be stumped a third time. THIS SLUGGER LED THE NATIONAL LEAGUE IN HOME RUNS EVERY YEAR FROM 1946 TO 1952 read the white print on the blue screen.

"Take it, Mike," Sid prompted.

"*Damn*," Michael said, scrunching up his face as the tantalizing Jeopardy theme played. "It's either Willie Mays or Duke Snider." But he was guessing. The span of years was before his time.

All three Jeopardy contestants drew a blank. With a forbearing smile, as though it were common knowledge, Sid said, "Who is Ralph Kiner, for Pete's sake." Alex Trebec verified Sid's answer and Michael felt his good mood head south.

"Kiner played for the Pirates, Cubs, and Indians," Sid added. "He was the White Sox announcer when we lived in Chicago. Also, the first TV announcer for the Mets."

"I should have warned you, Mike—Sid knows *every*thing," Jayne called from the dining room as she set a tray of chilled salads on the table.

Yes, he does. Michael thought. He's a fucking know-it-all.

Over dinner—Caesar salads, pastas al dente, eggplant parmigiana and a tender milk-fed veal Marsala—the small talk flowed. As did three expensive bottles of Ruffino Chianti. When everyone seemed mellow and receptive, Sid broached the subject of carpooling.

"Let's try it for a month, guys," he urged. "If we like it, we'll try another month. I'll drive for two weeks and then you drive. Mike, since the ladies don't go downtown every day, it'll usually be you and me. Can you stand me early in the morning?"

Quizzically Michael glanced at Liz, who nodded. "Let's carpool, Sid," he said without enthusiasm.

Details were then discussed: departure and return times, drop off and pickup sites, half days vs. full, what cars driven when. "We'll take our Avalon when we drive," Michael was quick to stipulate. "There's no way four people can ride comfortably in our Celica." He could not resist adding, "There's no way two people can."

"Very funny," Liz said. "Michael hates my car."

"And when I drive," Sid said, "we'll take our big old gas-guzzling SUV. The fact we're saving on gas doesn't mean we can't be comfortable."

"Pooh Bear, my Mazda is not uncomfortable," Jayne objected with a faux pout.

Sid laughed. "It's not, Jayne-O. Truth is, guys, she won't let me drive her Mazda."

"Michael hates for *any*one to drive his car," Liz said, twirling pasta from a spoon onto her fork. "Even me."

Sid suggested the husbands do the driving and the wives do the back-seat driving. It was politically incorrect, but the women admitted that they liked being chauffeured. "And ain't it grand," Sid added, "that we have no kids? Kids would really complicate things."

"You didn't have children either?" Jayne asked Liz.

"No," Liz said. "And now it's too late. We tried to adopt. But things didn't…work out."

Michael was watching his wife. Her voice was composed, but he saw the tremor in her chin. Jesus, he thought. It still hurts her to talk about it.

"We wanted to adopt a biracial child," he said. "And we encountered obstacles you wouldn't believe. The pregnant mother, who was white, was a teenage airhead, a goddam *flake*. She'd been in some kind of Rastafarian cult and may have been a druggie. She changed her mind repeatedly. Her mother wanted a grandchild, even one who was half-black, and tried to talk her out of the adoption. Then a Catholic priest tried to horn in."

"How awful for you," Jayne sympathized.

"Just a typical adoption snafu," muttered Sid.

Michael went on: "I wondered if the kid would even be healthy. Finally our attorney suggested we deal with another unwed mother directly, one on one, and bypass the adoption agency."

"I hope you didn't," Sid said.

"We thought about it," Michael told him.

"As a lawyer, I can tell you that's illegal and expensive. Fire your attorney if you haven't and count your blessings. Also, if that teenage mother was in a cult, the fetus could've been a drug addict. Rastafarians smoke ganja as soon as they wake up in the morning."

"I was willing to chance it," Liz said testily.

"In my opinion," stated Sid, "adoption is a crapshoot. Forrest Gump's box of chocolates. You never know what you're gonna get."

"Liz wanted to start over with another adoption agency," Michael said. "But I was worn out. We're talking months. I couldn't take any more. One day I threw a tantrum, came apart and blew my stack. That was the end of it."

The Camerons were tactfully silent. One look at Liz, who was glaring at him, told Michael he'd said too much and would hear about it later. He had trotted out the worst setback of their marriage for a pair of strangers to render judgment on. He just couldn't stop talking once he'd started drinking.

"Like I said, count your blessings," Sid consoled. "We don't like kids, if you want to know the truth."

"Oh, Pooh Bear," Jayne reproved.

"Usually we don't like people," Sid chuckled. "But we like you people." He raised his wineglass for a toast. "Here's to our next-door neighbors, good eggs we like enough to carpool with. Let's hear it for the Davidsons!"

"Hear, hear!" Jayne seconded. "For the Davidsons!"

Liz raised her glass and smiled uncertainly. This could be a mistake, Michael thought, raising his.

—⁓—

Over dessert—cannolis topped with ricotta cheese and Grand Marnier—the subject of politics arose. The Davidsons were relieved that the Camerons hadn't voted for the White House incumbent, whose days in office, thank God, were numbered. Nor did it bother them that the Camerons styled themselves Libertarians. What bothered Michael was the Camerons' opinion of the candidate to whose campaign he and Liz had just donated $300.

"We supported him too before Sid did his research," Jayne said. "But holy moley, the things he found out. When Pooh Bear does his research, he finds out *every*thing."

"And what did the great Pooh Bear find out," Michael droned. He was drunk and his tone was unfriendly. Liz warned him with an angry glance.

Sid said, "That Obama was brainwashed with radical Islam as a child. The man is not an African American. He's neither African nor American. He's an Australoid."

"Australoid?" Liz's smile was incredulous. "You mean, like the Australian Aborigines?"

"Australoid tribes are nomadic," Sid explained. "They wandered into Indonesia. Obama was born in Hawaii but grew up in Indonesia. The Muslim who raised him, Lolo Soetoro, was Australoid. We're told Soetoro was his stepfather, but really he was his birth father."

"Why would Obama lie about his race?" Liz asked. "If he was born in Hawaii, he's still an American citizen."

Sid smiled as if the question came from a child. "Votes, darlin'," he said. "American blacks and liberals can't wait for an African

American president."

Michael scoffed. "Why should we care about this Australoid stuff, Sid?"

"Because," the host patiently replied, "the Islam practiced by Indonesian Australoids is murderously anti-American. It's no reflection on the man's character. He was indoctrinated at school."

Michael shook his head. "Obama went to Catholic schools in Indonesia."

"In the late sixties, yes. But he switched to a public school in the seventies. The *Basuki* School. Muslim kids spent one hour a day learning about Islam while Christian kids spent two hours a week learning about Christianity. Because Soetoro was Muslim, Barack didn't learn about Christianity. Soetoro took him to a mosque every Friday night. And then to a madrassa, where the brainwashing occurred."

Michael felt his temper rising. "That's all apocryphal, Sid," he said tightly.

"No. Barack had to chant 'Death to America!' like a mantra at the madrassa. He probably still does it in his sleep. They taught him how to make jihadist bombs with gunpowder and bottles and gasoline."

Jayne said, "I'll bet he mixes a mean Molotov Cocktail."

Michael had heard enough. "No offense, folks," he said, shaking his head and showing the palms of his hands, "but this business of Obama's childhood is a tempest in a pisspot. I've read about it, and no two sources agree. It's horseshit."

"Mike, don't kill the messenger," Sid implored, widening his eyes in mock alarm. "I'm not saying it disqualifies him for office.

I'm just saying if he was taught to hate America, it's something we should know about before we elect him president."

An awkward silence followed. "Well," Jayne said, "I still like him. I think he's clean-cut and articulate and absolutely precious."

"I'm curious, Sid," Michael persisted. "What were the sources for your information?"

Sid's smile never wavered. "I have friends in high places."

"Like Denver?" Michael asked "Or Mount Olympus?"

"Stop it, Michael," Liz cautioned.

"Pooh Bear has his law degree from the University of Chicago," Jayne reiterated. "Obama taught there. Sid knows some of his former colleagues."

"But if I told you their names," Sid said, "I'd have to kill you."

After a pause, he burst into laughter. Jayne joined in, and then Liz, and even Michael had to laugh. The situation was defused. More wine was poured. Jayne served up fresh coffee and a different liqueur. No further politics were discussed. Michael was relieved not to have exploded and ruined everyone's evening. When pushed and provoked, he had a short fuse and wasn't afraid to fight. It was the trouble with being a big man.

<hr>

As the Davidsons made ready for bed that night, Michael said, "We might be making a mistake."

"Why do you say that?" Liz asked.

"I don't like him."

She was sitting at the bedroom dresser in her nightgown, rubbing her L'Oreal cream onto her forehead in front of the mirror. "And why not," she said. "Because he beat you at Jeopardy? Or because he doesn't like kids or Barack Obama?"

"It's not what he says. It's how he says it. All magisterial, like some judge whose opinion is settled law."

"He was just speaking his mind."

"He said more than he knew."

"Don't we all? He was probably repeating things he's read on the Internet. Millions of people read those blogs every day and believe them. For all we know, some of what Sid said may be true."

"I don't know if I can take him every morning on the way to work."

She moved from her dresser, turned down the sheets, and slipped into bed. "Well, try," she said. "I want us to get along with them. We have to live next door to them. We've had worse neighbors."

"You're playing Devil's Advocate?"

"They're not so bad. Nobody's perfect but you."

Michael scowled but said nothing. She switched off the bedside lamp and turned her back to him. Before long she murmured into her pillow, "Don't you want to know why?"

"I'm sorry. Why what?"

"Why I want you to get along with them."

"Wasn't it because they're our neighbors?"

"Jayne showed me some authentic Pre-Columbian art in her studio tonight. It was willed to her by a rich uncle. Thirteen Moche ceramic vessels that depict gods and animals and monsters and demons fighting in an Apocalypse. They date back to eight hundred C. E."

"Meaning?"

"The Common Era. Like what we call A. D. I told her the collection could be worth something. Maybe a lot. But she doesn't like that kind of art and neither does her sister. They find it ugly and frightening. They can't market the pieces at their gallery."

Michael saw where this was heading. Ever since they'd given up on adopting, Liz had devoted herself to an art museum in each city they'd lived in. Docent, developmental officer, capital-campaign coordinator, assistant curator…she'd volunteered for every post. In the city where they lived now, at its well-endowed museum, she yearned to be head curator. It actually paid a good salary. Marge Whitlow, the current curator, was moving to the Dallas Museum of Fine Art and the Board had to elect her replacement. Landing the museum a valuable collection of donor art could mean Liz's election.

"Let me guess," he said. "You suggested she donate the ceramic vases to your museum."

He could feel her bristle. "It's either that or sell them, Michael. I told her if the collection is as valuable as I suspect, it could mean a wing of the museum getting named for her."

Michael smirked. Every philanthropist's dream, he thought. Having your name, or even your face, carved in stone on some public building. "I'm surprised Sid hasn't made her sell the collection," he said. "I mean, if he's willing to carpool to save money on gas —"

"He wants to carpool because he hates OPEC. She told me.

He's fiercely pro-Israel and loves Bibi Netanyahu. The Camerons aren't hurting for money."

"Would the museum name a wing after Jayne for thirteen lousy vases?"

Liz sighed. "All right, maybe just a room in the new wing they're building. All I ask is that you get along with them until she decides about the ceramics. Be nice to someone for a change. Is that asking too much?"

Chastised, he snuggled against her and nuzzled the back of her neck. "I'm sorry, sweetie. I'll try to make nice."

"Don't try. Do it. You almost lost it tonight. You had too much to drink and you babbled about things we don't talk about."

Marriage, he thought. The Number One cause of divorce.

At 7:45 a.m. the following Monday, a big silver-blue Volvo SUV carrying four carpoolers zipped through rush hour traffic along the Interstate that connected Blue Panther Creek to the downtown business district. The trip was longer than twenty-five miles if you counted the mixmaster of expressways to be negotiated once the city skyline came into view. That added fifteen minutes before Sid's shiny gas-guzzler could begin, like a shuttle bus, to unload its passengers.

After some cursory chitchat, the carpoolers had lapsed into silence, and Sid turned on the FM classical station. His stereo system had a throbbing bass subwoofer, and the resonance of a symphony orchestra sounded majestic. Michael recognized the final movement of Beethoven's "Emperor" Concerto, and the carpoolers listened in reverent silence. When the music ended, a female disc jockey with an Irish brogue said, "That was the great Dmitri Silverstone at the piano. Critics consider Silverstone a virtuoso equal to Vladimir Horowitz or Artur Rubinstein."

Sid sneered. "Dmitri the candy man. Lock up the kids."

Michael frowned. He had no idea what that meant and he was afraid to ask.

But his wife wasn't afraid. "Why do you say that, Sid?"

"Dmitri Silverstone is a pedophile who likes little black boys. They have to be at least twelve years old, though."

The passengers recoiled. From the back seat Jayne murmured, "And he seems like such a *kindly* old gentleman. Isn't he in his eighties?"

Michael asked, "How do you know that about him, Sid?"

"When we lived in Chicago, I probated a million-dollar will endowing the Chicago Symphony. I heard it from a board member."

"You heard it," Michael said. "So it's hearsay."

"I heard it from more than one source, Mike. In every city Silverstone toured, he'd request Beluga caviar, Stolichnaya vodka, and two little black boys. His entourage would procure them in advance."

"That's disgusting," Liz said from the back seat. "I'll never enjoy that man's playing again."

"Me neither," Jayne concurred. "Of course, concert pianists can't grow up normal. Child prodigies have no childhoods. They're probably abused by their teachers when they're kids."

Michael pressed it. "Sid, I'd question that rumor. For the

past few years in this country we've been finding child molesters under every bed. They're coming out of the woodwork. Someone as famous as Silverstone couldn't get away with a felony that brazen for long."

Sid smiled. "Money will buy anything, Mike."

"And where," Michael continued, "would he get the little black boys? A little-black-boy rental? An inner-city orphanage? An antebellum slave plantation? Whoever procured them would be risking jail time. When I worked in New York, which is a little bigger than Chicago, I used to hear scurrilous tales about singers and conductors and pianists and even *cellists*, for Christ's sake. I'm surprised you'd swallow such crap, Sid."

No one spoke. Michael's heart was hammering and his mouth was dry.

In a tiny voice Jayne said, "When Pooh Bear tells you something, it's usually true, Michael."

"Usually is not always," Michael retorted.

"Could we change the subject?" Liz implored. "I don't *care* about some dirty old man's sexual perversion."

"Three words in my defense," Sid requested. "Don't kill the messenger. Oops, that's four. Sorry."

The carpoolers fell silent. Soon the downtown skyline loomed ahead like a smoggy hallucination. Michael remembered his promise to get along with the Camerons. He was not off to a good start. He knew his wife was displeased. He'd hear about it later and dreaded that. Why does this pompous ass need to talk so much? he wondered. And why do I have to contradict him? Because we're both Alpha males showing off in front of our wives?

The ride back to Blue Panther Creek that evening was free from incident. All four carpoolers were tired. There was little conversation and no reference to the morning's unpleasantness. On FM radio Sid chose NPR over the classical station. The news was humdrum.

Michael knew what to expect when they got home. Liz managed to hold off until they'd finished supper and were comfortably settled, on their new $3000 leather sofa, in the TV den to watch the nightly news on MSNBC. During a commercial, she turned to him with a tight smile and said, "You really don't like him, do you."

"Who, sweetie?"

"You know who."

"I spared his life. I usually kill people who call me Mike."

"You didn't have to upbraid him. *'I'm surprised you'd swallow such crap, Sid.'* You dressed him down in front of his wife."

"He was slandering a great artist."

"Your getting so angry was inappropriate. Jayne had to come to his defense."

"She'd come to his defense if he blew up St. Peter's Basilica. *'Well, Pooh Bear said it would create construction jobs in Rome.'*"

"He could've been right about that pianist, you know. It was probably an exaggeration, but it might've happened once or twice. And for your information, the crackdown on child molesters is *not* a witch hunt."

"I know. But I had to say something."

"You promised to get along with him."

"I'm sorry. I won't open my mouth again if he says Mother Teresa got it on with the Blessed Virgin. Anything to make sure your museum acquires some Common Era vases."

As if to herself, she murmured, "I married a prick...a contentious prick..."

They watched the nightly news in stony silence.

———∿∿———

On Tuesday there were three carpoolers; Liz was not due at the museum till Thursday. Sid proved capable that day, and the next as well, of driving Michael and Jayne and himself to town and back without attacking the reputation of a single famous person. On Thursday Michael was uncomfortably aware of Liz's presence in the back seat, as if she were recording everything he said. Yet the trip went well. The wives discussed the Andy Warhol and Robert Rauschenberg exhibits coming to the Kimbell Museum in Fort Worth. Sid seemed preoccupied and distant. Michael was happy to leave him that way.

On Friday, with everyone aboard and the Volvo's radio tuned to NPR, a newscaster reported that a California assemblyman was reopening an investigation into the 1962 death of Marilyn Monroe. "It's about time," Sid commented. "Everybody knows the Kennedys had Marilyn whacked. They had to. She knew too much after banging Jack and Bobby. Or all three brothers, because I heard Teddy got a little too."

Michael managed to hold his tongue.

"Please, Sid," Liz implored. "Don't start."

"Pooh Bear's right about this," Jayne assured her.

"When we lived in Chicago," Sid continued, "I met a speechwriter who'd worked for Bobby. He told me he'd been in the room with both brothers when Jack ordered Marilyn iced. After that, having in effect become a material witness, he'd feared for his life."

The passengers were silent. Sid gave Michael a sidelong glance to gauge his response. Silently, slowly, with his eyes shut, Michael was counting to ten and gritting his teeth. He had admired Jack and Bobby. But except for that new business about Teddy, it was just the embellishment of a rumor he'd heard before.

"Goddam, fella," Michael finally jibed good-naturedly. "After the speechwriter told you that, you should've been afraid for your own ass. You knew too much yourself."

Sid hesitated, then threw back his head and guffawed. "That's a good one, Mike. Seriously, though. Our presidents must play by different rules. Occasionally people have to go for the good of the country. Marilyn was one of them. Can you imagine how many troublemakers the CIA's had to terminate with extreme prejudice over the past fifty years?"

"Oh, a lot," Michael said. "A whole lot. The agency did what it had to."

The lawyer may have sensed that he was being patronized, but he dropped the subject. Michael's eyes met his wife's eyes in the rearview mirror. With a smile and a nod, she signaled her approval. He winked at her.

—⁓—

Even in Blue Panther Creek life could still delight and surprise. The Davidsons' dinner together that night at home was an unplanned pleasure. Since re-watching *Citizen Kane* a week earlier, and just for the fun of it, Michael and Liz had taken to dining by candlelight, a la Charles Foster Kane and wife, at opposite ends of their long mahogany dining room table. Tonight, as they were finishing their *salades nicoise*, Liz said, "I knew you could do it, Big Fella, even though you loved the Kennedys. You were so cool. All it took was a sense of humor."

A sense of humor, Michael reflected. Yes, that was the ticket. It kept molehills from becoming mountains. It kept comedians on the stage and out of mental wards. It could get a man through a week of carpooling with a boorish gossip and his Stepford Wife. Maybe it could work some miracle for a marriage that needed one.

He was blessed with a sudden inspiration. That evening, and every evening that week, Michael entertained Liz over dinner with a new impression of Sid Cameron. Word for word, mimicking the man's facial expressions, gestures, and vocal inflections, he repeated one of Sid's lurid exposés. It didn't matter whether Liz had heard the originals, or that Michael made a few of them up.

Some were urban legends familiar to the Davidsons—like the one about the leggy androgynous Oscar winner born as an hermaphrodite to her movie star parents. But even those, Sid had recycled with smutty new details to make them seem original. Michael furnished his own embellishments as well, some of them even more outrageous than Sid's.

Michael was a gifted impersonator, and with each performance he got funnier. Before long, Liz confessed to him that during the day she'd caught herself laughing and looking forward to the evening's entertainment. Eventually she moved from her chair at the end of the table to one next to the performer. And soon she'd be giggling deliriously while Michael mimicked Sid's revelation about the blue-eyed, golden-haired, girl-next-door starlet who as a high school cheerleader had fellated the football team and had to have her stomach pumped; or the former President who'd seduce female staffers by having them watch his trained stallion mount the mares on his ranch when he honked the horn of his Cadillac; or the former First Lady so addicted to sleeping pills that she'd sleepwalk through the White House halls in a sheer nightie, a la Lady Macbeth, followed by tiptoeing Secret Servicemen loath to wake her up.

"And I have that on *very* sound authority," Michael would stress. Liz would laugh helplessly ("No, please, tell me he didn't really say that"), and Michael would plead, "Hey, lady, don't kill the messenger!" Or Liz would get into the act by imitating Jayne's mousy voice ("*Listen, Pooh Bear has his law degree from the University of* Chicago"), and it would be Michael who cracked up.

During those minutes of shared delight, those nightly rituals of silly lighthearted play, Michael felt close to his wife again. The Camerons finally served a purpose. "But seriously, sweetie," he said one night as they were gathering up the dinner plates. "What bothers me is the verification Sid provides. He says he fact-checks his stories like an investigative reporter. If that's true, it's disturbing."

"He's disturbed," Liz said. "I feel sorry for *Jayne*."

"Maybe we're complicit. I should tell Sid to knock it off. No more stories. But you know what, sweetie? There are days when I enjoy them."

"Oh, me too. And not just because I know what fun you'll have with them later. It's like eating greasy junk food."

"By the way," Michael added, "you like Jayne. Admit it."

"I do like her. She's basically a sweet person. I enjoy doing lunch with her and shopping with her and talking about art. Do you mind?"

"Of course not."

"When Sid's not around, she's a different person."

One with a brain, he wanted to say, but "I'm sure that's true," he said. "I just question her taste in husbands."

"Well," Liz said, "we all make mistakes."

Ouch, Michael thought.

———⁂———

By the end of another week of improvised dinner theater at their Citizen Kane table, Michael's nightly routines had begun to wear thin. But they'd had a good run, and he was out of material anyway. Midway through some obscene Sid Cameron scuttlebutt about Elizabeth Taylor and Debbie Reynolds and Eddie Fisher in a motel ménage à trois, Liz cut him off. "No, more, Big Fella. Please. I've enjoyed as much as I can stand. But bravo, darling."

Michael took the hook good-naturedly. The shtick had served its purpose and now it was time to move on. Like the caring, attentive husband he'd resolved to be, he asked about her last few days at home alone in Blue Panther Creek, which he should've inquired about earlier. He was less than happy (though he didn't show it) to learn that she and Jayne had gotten chummier. They'd attended art lectures, jogged together, and had Marge Whitlow out to the Camerons' house with a Pre-Columbian art expert to authenticate the Moche ceramics in Jayne's studio.

"They're the real thing," Liz said. "They're worth big money. Marge went so far as to offer Jayne a permanent corner in the new wing. The Jayne Cameron Collection."

"I thought you said they'd name a whole room for her."

"I never said that. You always exaggerate."

She had said that, but he was willing to drop it. "Anyway," Liz resumed, "Jayne promised me she'll donate the collection to the museum."

"Fabulous, sweetie. And then we're through with the Camerons?"

Liz blinked and furrowed her brows. "What do you mean, 'through with them?' Jayne and I are friends. You think I'm just using her? She's a good person and a talented artist."

"And a Stepford Wife."

"That's not fair. Who are you to judge? Do you think you're an ideal husband?"

"I didn't know we were discussing husbands."

Liz was fuming. "Tell me, Michael, do you want me to get the curatorship or not? Maybe I should quit the museum and sell real estate."

"Come on, sweetie. You know I want you to get it."

"Then stop being ugly about Jayne."

Michael promised he'd stop. But he foresaw a problem. His turn at the carpooling wheel was approaching. He'd already begun rehearsing the speech he'd deliver next Monday morning, assuming he had Sid alone, about why the experiment should end (*"not that we haven't enjoyed it, guy"*) once the month was over. Michael wanted the man out of his daily life. Sid was not the H. L. Menckenish iconoclast he'd taken him for. He was a filthy-minded smut monger who probably thumbed through tabloids in the supermarket line, hungry for the latest scandal. He was a gossip, a cesspool, a sewer.

It was the trouble with being married, Michael thought. You were no longer independent or autonomous. You became a hybrid person, an androgyn. Choices and decisions about friends had to be made jointly, as though you were buying a house or a car. Or adopting a child. He accepted all this as rules of the game. But Liz was not playing by the rules. She was becoming close to a woman he could barely stand and was not allowed to criticize. A gross man's ditzy wife and his own wife were getting to be best friends, and there was nothing he could do about it. He felt trapped in his ranch-stye house in Blue Panther Creek, Far Outer Suburbia, the sterile zeitgeist of his existence, and there was no escape, no exit.

—⚘—

On Monday morning, Michael woke in a blue funk of apprehension and dread. He skipped breakfast while Liz slept in. She was staying home to phone the museum docents and board members about Jayne Cameron's Pre-Columbian collection. And in the process, to campaign for the chairmanship. The election was this week.

Michael revved up his black six-passenger Avalon XLS and prepared to take his turn behind the wheel. Jayne was staying home too. It was a golden opportunity to end the carpooling.

The time was right, but the attorney didn't seem in the mood for a man-to-man talk. Or any talk. After praising the Avalon as one of Toyota's best-engineered models ("You've got to hand it to those sneaky little Japs, Mike"), Sid buried himself in a legal brief. He may as well have hung a DO NOT DISTURB sign around his neck. And on the ride home that evening, he studied another brief with even greater absorption. The golden opportunity had been wasted.

Well, he would lower the boom the next time they were alone together, Michael resolved. Plenty of time remained. He just wanted to get it over with.

That night, Liz seemed sullen and distant, as if sulking or pouting about something. He wondered what he'd done now. Or hadn't done. "What," he finally said in the verbal shorthand of couples married for a while.

"What do you mean 'what?'"

"What's wrong, sweetie. Are you worried about the election at the museum?"

"Don't be ridiculous." But there was that tremor in her chin.

"What then?"

"Nothing. I'm tired. I'm going to bed."

On Tuesday all four carpoolers piled into Michael's Avalon. Sid was quiet for the second consecutive day, and Michael thought he sensed a tension between Liz and Jayne, who weren't conversing, in the back seat. He wondered if the budding sisterhood had run amuck. Could he be that lucky? But why was Sid quiet? Usually you couldn't shut him up. It was as if the three of them knew something Michael didn't.

That evening, returning from a last-minute errand to the convenience store before supper, Michael smelled cigarette smoke in the house. He knew what that meant. Liz had quit smoking years ago — they had quit together. The last time she'd lit up on the sly had been the day they'd given up on adopting the biracial child she'd set her heart on. Michael braced himself. He didn't mention the smoke smell. But after dinner, in the kitchen, as she was rinsing plates to put in the dishwasher, he said, "Okay, sweetie, let's have it. What's happened."

"I don't want to talk about it."

"Maybe I can help. Let's talk."

She sighed, whirled away from the sink, and faced him squarely. She wiped her wet hands on her apron front. "All right," she said, her mouth trembling. "Jayne changed her mind. She's going to sell the Moche vases to a collector Sid knows in Houston. He laid down the law. And the museum board voted this afternoon. I didn't get the curatorship. Marge Whitlow's niece did."

It took Michael a while to process all that. "I thought the board was going to vote on Friday," he said. "What happened?"

"They held an emergency meeting. I don't know why."

"Damn! I'm so sorry, sweetie."

After a long pause, he had to say it: "I told you Jayne was a

Stepford Wife."

"Don't do that. Please." Liz was fighting back tears. "Jayne had the right to change her mind. I'm not sure I would've won the election anyway. I don't want Jayne to think I was using her."

"I'm still pissed off at her."

"Fine. Be pissed off. Can we drop it? I rented us a movie for tonight. Let's watch it. I chain-smoked three cigarettes while you were at the store. They made me dizzy, so I quit again. You needn't worry."

Sitting far apart on the sofa like an old couple, they watched the DVD: a Merchant Ivory period film starring Vanessa Redgrave. Michael could neither get into it nor talk to Liz. It was clear that she didn't want to talk. Now he understood her strange mood the night before and the tension he'd felt between her and Jayne in the car this morning.

"Maybe we should move," he said as Liz and he undressed for bed that night.

"Tell me you're not serious."

"No. But the thought did occur."

"Promise you won't pick a fight with Sid. I know you're spoiling for one. I don't need that."

"All right, I promise. But I won't make nice with him either. Did you say a collector in *Houston*?"

"There's a lot of art in Houston. Be civil until we're through carpooling. I still like Jayne, even if I don't like him. I feel sorry for Jayne. Bear in mind that we live next door to them."

How could I forget it, he thought. "I'll be civil," he promised. But he was furious with the Camerons. Furious with Marge

Whitlow and the museum board. Furious with Blue Panther Creek Subdivision, where he'd come to feel like an ineffectual suburban husband in a TV sitcom rather than the forceful, decisive, make-things-happen husband he longed to be.

—∿—

His sleep that night was fitful. His mother had taught him never to go to bed angry, and she'd been right. The next morning, Liz didn't go into town, to the museum, as planned. She didn't even get up for breakfast. Michael let her be. He ate his breakfast alone and left the house in a foul mood, dreading the drive that lay ahead with both Camerons as passengers.

It hadn't helped that over his cereal and coffee he'd read in the newspaper that T. K. Rappaport had died of kidney failure at ninety. When he and Liz were in college, Rappaport had been their favorite writer. He'd been everybody's favorite. His novel *Rose in Spanish Harlem*, about a little Puerto Rican girl with telepathic powers, had found a cult readership, then become a best seller. He was that rare author who really could, as the blurbs claimed, make a reader laugh and cry at the same time.

For ten years, Rappaport's *New Yorker* stories about adult children and childlike adults found their way into anthologies. But during the Vietnam War he'd gone into hiding. He'd moved to Nova Scotia—Camp Breton Island—like an expatriate and become a recluse. He refused to sell the film rights to his novel or grant interviews. In 1996 there were rumors of a second novel, but it never materialized. And now he was dead. Michael felt he'd lost an old friend he'd been meaning to write or call but hadn't found the time to.

"What's eating you, Mike?" Sid asked, riding shotgun on their drive into the city. "Things okay at home?"

"Peachy keen," Michael said, swerving into the fast lane.

"How's Liz?" Jayne asked from the back seat.

"She didn't get the curatorship."

"Holy moley," Jayne moaned. "The poor baby. I should call her."

Michael said nothing.

Sid asked, "Did you hear about T. K. Rappaport?"

"I read about it."

"I loved *Rose in Spanish Harlem*," Jayne said. "Rappaport used to be my favorite writer."

"Ours too," Michael admitted — and then the alarm bell rang in his head. "Actually, I'd rather not talk —"

But it was too late. "I found Rappaport overrated," Sid said. "Did you know he had a thing for prepubescent girls?"

In his whole life Michael had never wanted to smash another man's face as much. A backhanded swing of his right fist would break this fool's nose while he steered with his left hand. He settled for "Are you hung up on pedophilia, Sid? I thought you didn't like kids."

"Seriously, Mike. Did you know that about Rappaport?"

Michael almost lost control of the wheel. He gave Sid a look, but the lawyer was staring straight ahead.

"Yeah," Sid went on, "it's sad, is what it is. That's why the poor devil ran off to Canada. They were about to arrest him here. You could see the sickness in his writing. All those cute little chickadees? Those wise pretty little Alices? He was hotter for them than Lewis Carroll."

Michael filled his lungs with air and clenched his teeth and gripped the wheel hard enough to bend it. His right foot pressed the pedal to the metal. In a voice that shook he said, "Sid, I need to tell you something man to man."

"Pretend I'm not here," Jayne chirped.

Sid said, "Mike, do you know you're speeding?"

"Listen to me. In the short while I've known you, you've ruined my image of a dozen people I admired. I've had enough. For the days we have left to ride together, and I wish there weren't any, just keep your fucking mouth shut and let me drive."

He heard Jayne gasp. Sid was speechless.

Jayne spoke first. "Michael, I don't think that's fair. We all feel badly about Rappaport. But don't take it out on Pooh Bear."

"It's cool, Jayne-O," Sid said, turning back to smile at her. "Mike, I plead guilty. *Nolo contendere*. I talk too much. I'm a debunker. But in my defense, let me tell you why."

"I don't care why."

"You probably call it gossiping. I'm no gossip, Mike. I'm a watchdog. A whistle blower."

"I don't give a shit what you are." Michael's knuckles were white. The speedometer read eighty-five.

"Hear me out, Mike."

"Shove it," Michael warned, speeding faster.

"Allow me a closing statement."

"Pooh Bear, it's all *right*," cautioned Jayne. "Now is not the time—"

"Mike," Sid bravely persisted, throwing caution and self-preservation to the wind, "it's natural for us to celebrate outstanding members of our tribe and make demigods of them. That's why we call them celebrities: we celebrate them. It's also our nature to tear them down when they let us down. That's why we keep abreast of scandals. When our gods turn out to be false gods, we turn on them."

"Go to hell."

"Both of you stop," Jayne pleaded.

Sid wouldn't stop. "We seek the truth even if it disillusions us. Muckraking has been legitimate journalism since nineteen-ten, when the term was coined. If I hadn't been a lawyer, I'd've been a muckraking yellow journalist."

"And written for what!" Michael erupted. "*Confidential? National Enquirer? Midnight?* You'd've been right at home in those sewers, Sid."

Jayne hissed, "Michael, how dare you!"

Sid's mask of a smile had fallen off. He looked frightened. "Slow *down,*" he said. "Right now you're an angry driver."

"Michael, please slow down," Jayne implored.

"I've had it with you, Sid!"

"Okay, but slow down. Why are you so angry? Are you a hero worshipper? A camp follower?"

"I warn you, Sid —"

"A star fucker?"

Jayne shouted, "I think you are that, Michael! You want to kill the messenger! You'll kill us all if you don't slow down!"

Without signaling, Michael swerved full speed into an exit and veered screeching into an Exxon Car Care center adjoining a

Food Mart convenience store. There were angry honks from the cars behind him.

"What are you *doing?*" Jayne cried out.

"Slow down, Mike!" Sid yelled again.

Spraying gravel, Michael brought the Avalon to a lurching halt alongside the curb fronting the store entrance. "Get out," he said. "Both of you. Get out of my car."

"Mike, you can't be serious," Sid protested.

"Don't call me Mike. Get out."

Jayne asked, "But how will we get to town?"

"Call a cab. Hitchhike. Go."

Stubbornly, neither passenger would budge. Thirty seconds passed. Michael's heart was pounding so hard he couldn't breathe. He could see the three of them sitting there all morning, in a comic Mexican standoff, illegally parked while highway traffic whizzed by thirty yards away. He still wanted to punch Sid in the nose. He was dying to.

"All right," he said finally. "I'm going to count to three."

Muttering to himself, Sid clambered out the front passenger door. Jayne slipped out the back. Michael burned rubber as he sped off, leaving the Camerons behind in a cloud of dust and gravel. In his rearview mirror he saw Jayne thrusting up the middle finger of her right hand and Sid brushing off his suit coat with both hands.

Michael had not felt this good since he was twelve and just won a game for his Little League team with a homer.

—⁓—

His triumphant mood was short lived. At the office he remained in battle mode, and the very idea of doing any work seemed like an anticlimax. Too pumped up to sit at his desk, too revved up to concentrate on his correspondence, he locked his office door. Then he shuffled papers, flipped through test brochures, watched the clock, answered his e-mail, paced his carpet, and shuffled papers again. He didn't go to lunch, though he could've used a drink to unwind. After sitting through an endless staff meeting about some new test for underachieving teenagers in Melbourne, Australia, he left work early with no word to anyone.

He still felt like fighting, but not with his wife—he dreaded the prospect of that. They had not spoken since yesterday evening, and she'd been in a bad mood then. Today she'd be awful. He'd promised to control his temper, so how would he explain the road-rage tantrum he'd thrown on a superhighway, at rush hour, to defend a writer who hadn't written since Lyndon Johnson was president? Liz had loved T. K. Rappaport too. But not that much.

He had thrown Sid and Jayne out of his car and out of his life. The Camerons were history. That was fine with him, but it would mean Liz and Jayne could no longer be friends if they wanted to. Being next-door neighbors would be hard enough. He could apologize to the Camerons, of course, but by God he wouldn't do it. Not even to appease Liz. Having finally taken a stand, he would not back down. Nor would he accept Sid's apology were it offered, which seemed unlikely when he replayed the image of Sid in his rearview mirror indignantly beating dust off his expensive suit while his wife shot the bird.

With every mile on the drive home, Michael felt gloomier. The carpooling experiment, whether Sid's idea or his own, had failed spectacularly. By breaking his word to Liz, he'd failed again as a husband and damaged a marriage that could not absorb any more damage. It was his fault that they couldn't have kids and had failed to adopt one. No wonder his wife had turned into a bitch.

It was only mid-afternoon, but by now she'd have heard about his blowup. Bad news traveled fast. He felt his road rage returning. For the second time that day, he floored the accelerator. The cars he passed appeared to be going thirty or forty, cruising in slow motion. The trip was taking forever, yet he made it home in record time. Finally, with a loud sigh of relief, he was easing through the security gate into Blue Panther Creek. He pulled into his driveway, got out of the car, tried to square his shoulders—but slouched toward the house like a disgraced private reporting for his court martial.

But to his astonishment, Liz greeted him at the front door wearing a cocktail waitress's apron, her best black silk dress, and a shy coquettish smile. She had never looked sexier or lovelier. He recognized the scent of a Chanel perfume he'd given her years ago. In one hand she held a long-stemmed glass containing a chilled martini and an olive with a toothpick.

"My hero," she said, handing him the drink.

<center>~~~</center>

As he went inside, the savory scent of seafood cooking wafted from the kitchen. "What's going on?" he asked, trying to smile. He pulled off his coat and yanked off his tie. "Is that shrimp I smell?"

"Your favorite dish. We're having a very early dinner. But a happy hour first." She poured herself a martini from a metal pitcher, and he followed her from the living room through the library into the den.

"Cheers, darling," she said once she was comfortably settled near him on the couch. She still wore the shy smile, but now it had a gleam of wonderment. "I heard what you did this morning."

"You heard?" He took a gulp. The ice-cold martini was dry and bitter and possibly the best drink he'd ever tasted in his life. He felt himself relax.

"Jayne called me on her cell phone. I had to pick them up where you let them off. Or should I say, threw them out?" Liz giggled delightedly.

Michael wondered if she'd had a few martinis already. He closed his eyes and wearily massaged his forehead with his thumb and fingers. "I'm sorry sweetie," he groaned. "I just lost it. I have no excuse."

"Thank God you didn't have a wreck."

"Thank God. I am so sorry."

"They think you're dangerous now."

"I am. Or was."

Her smile had a hint of amusement. "I didn't know you cared *that* much about Rappaport."

"He was our favorite writer. It was the straw that broke the camel's back."

Gently she patted his knee. "I drove them downtown. I had to, Michael. We were committed for the week. I could tell they hated the Celica." She giggled again. "Sid barely fit into the front seat. They said they'd find some other ride home."

"We're not still carpooling, are we?"

"No. They said it hadn't worked for them and they were shopping for a Prius anyway. We're done."

"There really is a God."

"I don't think they want to be our friends anymore."

"Are you okay with that? You're not mad? You're not divorcing me?"

"Not unless you keep apologizing. They couldn't believe you almost killed them because of what Sid said about Rappaport. I took up for you. I told them it was disgusting and I didn't blame you. Jayne said, *'Well, Pooh Bear — looks like this isn't our day.'*"

"I can't believe you're not upset."

"I might be if they'd slandered Mailer or Hemingway or some macho misogynist. But sweet little T. K. Rappaport?"

"What about your friendship with Jayne?"

"It ended. We had it out. She's a liar and a two-face. A passive-aggressive bitch. She denied ever saying she'd donate the Moche ceramics to the museum. She accused me of manipulating her to win an election. And maybe I did. But she was hissing like a *viper*, Michael. She and Sid are selling the vases for a small fortune, and you know what? I really can't blame them."

"Wow," he said, overwhelmed. "But still."

"I didn't want to be curator anyway."

"Yes, you did."

"Well, maybe a little. But I'm glad it's over. Stay here and have another martini, darling. I'll find us some music. I feel like dancing. But first I need to start the rice for your Shrimp Newburg."

"Our Shrimp Newburg," he corrected. "And yes—let's dance."

⁓

They slow-danced to a Sarah Vaughan CD. Their dinner by candlelight at the Citizen Kane table was romantic, sumptuous, a feast. They sat beside each other, in the center, rather than at opposite ends. Dmitri Silverstone softly serenaded with Chopin nocturnes from speakers in the den. Having gone without lunch, Michael was ravenously hungry. He ate and ate. Liz ate heartily too. They had to forgo dessert, a crème brulee, but they had coffee and a cognac.

Throughout the meal, almost comically, each took pains not to contradict the other. Neither dared risk ruining the mood. They were of one mind on every subject. Michael wondered how long that would last. At least until bedtime, he hoped. It was unreal, of course, but wonderful.

An even nicer surprise lay in store. At Liz's suggestion, once their meal was digested, she and Michael did something they hadn't done in months. They made love. Twice, in fact. Afterwards, as they nestled luxuriously naked beneath silk sheets bathed in Blue Panther Creek moonlight that shone through the bedroom slider, Liz purred contentedly before murmuring, "How can we be next-door neighbors with them now?"

Michael chuckled. "That's a pretty high brick wall out there.

238

Sid says good fences make good neighbors."

Liz played along. "Did he research that? Does he have it on sound authority?"

"It's settled law. Pooh Bear has his law degree from the University of Chicago."

"I'm sorry for being a bitch lately. Everything was going wrong for me. I took it out on you."

"I've been a wuss. I should've dealt with the Camerons earlier. I held back longer than I should've."

"I'm surprised you didn't sock him in the jaw."

"I could've stopped those stories long ago and I didn't. I should've said we were offended and didn't want to hear any more."

"I made you humor him."

"I overdid it."

"You couldn't have stopped him. He's obsessive-compulsive. And Jayne really is a Stepford Wife. I'm glad they're out of our lives. If they are."

They kissed and nuzzled some more. They were sated, limp with exhaustion, but Michael would've tried to make love a third time had Liz been game. What a day this had been. They cuddled spoon-fashion, her arms around his waist.

"Hey, Big Fella," she whispered. "I love you all over again."

"Me too…" He grinned in grateful disbelief. If God exists, he thought, He sure has a sense of humor. The neighbors from hell had resuscitated his comatose marriage. The Lord did work in mysterious ways. Tomorrow he and Liz would still have their problems, but tonight had been heavenly, even if heaven did carry a Blue Panther Creek address.

Dozing off, he heard Liz's drowsy voice as from afar. "Darling, are you asleep?"

"Almost, sweetie."

"How many of Sid's stories do you suppose were true?"

He thought about it. "Impossible to say. A few may have been true. Most of them, no."

"I think it frightened us that some of them might be true. Or all of them."

"Maybe we really are hero worshippers. They called me a star fucker."

"He's just a gross sad man and she's a sad silly woman. Don't you think we overreacted?"

"I know I did."

"You won't believe this, but when I dropped them off this morning on Martin Luther King Boulevard, Sid mentioned a rumor about Coretta Scott King having cheated on M.L.K. with Harry Belafonte for years. And Jayne verified it."

"You threw them out of the Celica, I hope."

"They were already climbing out."

Michael yawned. "If I weren't so sleepy, I'd go over there and kick his ass."

Liz laughed. "I think Jayne might be as crazy as he is. Maybe we should've listened to our mothers when they said don't get into cars with strangers."

Had he heard, Michael would have agreed. But he hadn't heard. He was fast asleep, blissfully snoring in the arms of (for the time being) a loving wife. He dreamt that he was flying, soaring like Superman through an ethereal sky of pure azure with gossamer white clouds, happier than he'd ever been. But then a familiar face—bodiless and simpering and chubby, with faded blue eyes—came floating through the sky toward him like a meteorite in slow motion. That ruined his dream. Michael came awake with a start. His heart was pounding like a bass drum. He was fighting mad again.

Going Down with the Ship

Even before those hellish torments, real or imagined, began, Patrick Brendan O'Connell, Capt. USN ret. and Professor Emeritus U. S. Naval Academy, could not forgive his wife of twenty-six years for dying. He was supposed to go first. Tacitly, they'd agreed on that. "I'll not leave you till the day you die, Paddy," Kathleen had vowed. And then left him forever.

And why? It wasn't right, it made absolutely no sense. Barely fifty, seventeen years his junior, Kathleen had been the clean liver with the sensible, healthy habits. She'd made him quit smoking and limit himself to one highball before dinner; she'd made him jog with her every morning; a stern look from her could make him forgo that second slice of pie or scoop of ice cream. Lithe and slender and sinewy, it was Kathleen who'd been the dietician, the runner, the swimmer, the yoga practitioner. He was the overweight drinker with high cholesterol and a swollen belly, the former chain smoker whose erratically beating heart fluttered with atrial fibrillation.

And now he was a widower. He had lost not just his "better half" (how he hated that expression!) but his hull, his keel, his anchor. What was he supposed to do now? Everything? Exactly. He would have to do everything for himself. Friends and relatives would be after him to remarry just to have someone to take care of him. Well off, well thought of, he was still handsome, healthy except for his mild heart trouble, and energetic, with a full head of silver hair, a ramrod-erect posture, a regal bearing. People said he lit up a room when he walked into it. But Paddy knew he wouldn't remarry; after Kathleen there could never be another woman for him.

He hadn't married until his mid-forties. From his father's side he came from a line of seafaring Irishmen congenitally unfit for marriage—a brawling clan of sailors with a taste for rum and whores. On land, just like them, Paddy was a fish out of water, dehydrated, a beached whale. Being married to the sea should've ruled out a wife and family; for six months of every year, a Navy Captain's home is his ship. No other military service demanded so much time at a stretch. But he had gotten married anyway. He did not relish the prospect of growing old and dying alone.

But now he was alone.

After twenty years, he'd retired from active duty. Had he extended for five more, a Rear Admiralty might've been possible, and Paddy wanted to be an Admiral, but some stronger need, one he could not identify, had towed him ashore. Instead he'd gone on to earn a Doctorate from the Naval Postgraduate School (NPS) in Monterey, California, and then returned to Annapolis, the only town he'd ever loved, to become a Permanent Military Professor of Leadership at $80,000 a year. That was when he'd met Kathleen Coughlin—Phi Beta Kappa Rice, M. A.

Georgetown, IQ in the stratosphere—at a National Catholic Laypersons convention in Baltimore. He fell in love for the first time and shocked everyone, especially himself, by marrying her within a month.

Their wedding, performed by a Naval Academy chaplain, a Captain like him, was held at 125-year-old St. Mary's Catholic Church on Duke of Gloucester Street in the heart of Annapolis. He and Kathleen bought a stately old house, a timber post-and-beam structure overlooking Chesapeake Bay, and lived there until they moved to Texas twenty years later. He'd liked to think of Annapolis as his kingdom by the sea. The Academy's campus stretched to the waterfront, where his favorite watering hole, Pussers Landing, was the official dock bar. He and Kathleen had loved the city's eighteenth-century buildings, their drives to London Town, their excursions to nearby Wisp Mountain (where he taught her to ski) at semester break in January. They'd loved Annapolis's ferries and graceful sailboats on the Bay, their day trips to Eastport and Cambridge and Edgewater, and the twilight strolls they took, hand in hand, through lyrical Quiet Waters Park as the colors changed every fall.

To be sure, though, he had loved Annapolis more than she had. If she'd sometimes been unhappy there, as a certain person suggested later, Kathleen had kept it a secret. Or maybe he'd been blind to it. They'd wanted children but had to settle for one, a child they christened Martha and called Marty and spoiled like a princess. Born the year his hero Ronald Reagan (who played a submarine captain in Paddy's favorite movie *Hellcats of the Navy*) was elected to a second term as President,

Marty had an even higher IQ than Kathleen's. For Paddy that proved a mixed blessing: Marty wielded her intelligence fiercely, like a lariat, smug in the suspicion, early on, that she was smarter than either of them.

Even though Kathleen seldom complained about the Eastern Seaboard, he'd known that her roots, the tendrils of her soul, were planted in the Southwest. The prairie, as he called it, was in her DNA. Born and reared in Texas, she had never stopped missing that damned state. She'd called it her Third Coast. She even subscribed to *Texas Monthly*. He'd promised to move them there when he retired again, though he'd have been content to live out their lives in Annapolis. He owed her something. He had always led, she had always followed, and he owed her. Paddy saw himself as not a boss or a dominator or a commanding officer but a leader. That's why he taught Leadership at the Naval Academy.

When he retired from teaching and he and Kathleen headed for Texas, he viewed the relocation as an heroic sacrifice on his part. He never let her forget it. They moved the year Marty entered Jesuit-run Loyola College Maryland (formerly Mount Saint Agnes College) with an academic scholarship. After that, it was downhill for him and Kathleen. He felt dwarfed in the sprawling ranch house he'd bought them in the Texas Hill Country. Having grown up in a port city — New Bedford, Massachusetts — he had never been a landlubber and couldn't adjust to being away from water. Nor was he keen on Kathleen's hometown, a sleepy bicultural city with two Air Force bases and an Army base but (being inland) nary a Naval base. The closest was in Corpus Christi, 150 miles away.

The sad thing was, even Kathleen seemed disappointed. The overgrown town she'd returned to was not the one she remembered from her girlhood. In its push to become a city, it had lost its charm and grown too big for its britches. Soon they both were missing Annapolis. But they couldn't go back. Huge decisions made that late in life are irreversible. Both realized that the move, her reward for a lifetime of loyal service, had been a mistake.

And then three years later, it hardly mattered, because Kathleen was gone. She was dead from an inoperable high-grade primary brain tumor unresponsive to radiation treatment administered by the finest oncologists in Houston. Often life is savagely cruel for no reason. Not just bad things happen to good people, monstrous things do. *"The Lord giveth, the Lord taketh away,"* Paddy stoically parroted as he delivered Kathleen's eulogy, but he was thinking, Why did He have to take away my wife? Why not take me? It was not even the cruelty but the unfairness, the rank injustice of life that created atheists and lapsed Catholics.

But Paddy refused to lose his faith. He was tougher than that. He saw himself as not just larger than life but stronger. He yearned for greatness. He saw himself as having the makings of a hero, standing tall in the face of whatever misfortune befell him.

⁂

After Marty graduated from Loyola Maryland, she joined him in Texas and didn't much like the city either. And he, God forgive him, didn't like her. The person she had become. When he confessed that to his priest—Francis Aloysius Monsignor Sheehan, a hoary-headed Dublin-born octogenarian—the old cleric chuckled. "Don't worry about it, lad. God does not command you to like the girl. He commands you to love her. And you do. Why? Because she's your daughter and you have no choice in the matter. Now go in peace and get your arse out of here. Don't come back without a real sin. Something worth the risk of hellfire. *Ego te absolvo a peccatis tuis in nomine Patris ...*"

And Paddy did love Marty. He loved her terribly. That's why it hurt so when she wouldn't do him proud and be more like her mother and less like that Steinem woman with the long hair and round glasses. Or Hanoi Jane Fonda. As a child, Marty had been impudent and imperious; as a teenager, bossy and pushy; as an adult, she didn't understand how important were a daughter's obedience and deference to a father who, during the 1962 Cuban Missile Crisis, had commanded a naval warship in the Caribbean that forced a Soviet B-59 submarine to the surface while helicopters buzzed overhead and the fate of Western Civilization hung in the balance. With her 170 IQ, why couldn't she understand that? Marty was thoughtless, ungrateful. *How sharper than a serpent's tooth it is to have a thankless child.* Was that Shakespeare or the Bible? Why couldn't Kathleen have given him a son instead? It was a question he was ashamed to ask, but he asked it all the time.

Marty had her good points, too. It never ceased to amaze him how much she favored Kathleen. It was eerie. She had her mother's wiry body, raven hair, creamy skin, and the bottle-green eyes of the Coughlins. Paddy carried both women's pictures in his billfold. Otherwise, Marty was nothing like her mother. Kathleen had been his helpmate; Marty was his drill sergeant. Kathleen had been open and transparent, Marty was private and opaque. After twelve years of parochial schooling by strict Irish nuns, Marty had entered Loyola Maryland as a feisty Reaganite, a Young Republican, and a Catholic Newman Club member; she had come out of it as a feisty SDS member and Young Democrat and militant atheist. Feminism, abortion, and gay rights had replaced God, flag, and family as her Trinity.

Paddy was devastated—had even the Jesuits been secularized? But Kathleen took Marty's transformation in stride: "She's not our little girl anymore, Paddy—she's her own person now." Paddy reminded his wife that Marty had always been her own person.

After Kathleen died, Marty almost redeemed herself by taking a Masters in child psychology from Baltimore's prestigious Morgan State University and establishing a practice in Texas to be near him. But then, for reasons he'd never understood, she'd left the practice to sell real estate: a calling he ranked somewhere between cocktail waitressing and nursing in a Planned Parenthood clinic. Even in a down market, she was a terrific realtor—her sales figures set records—but to him she was underachieving. Slumming. Wasting her gifts.

"Jesus, Mary and Joseph, Marty—why real estate?"

"To make some *real* money, Daddy."

"You could make even more as an embezzler or a bank robber. I thought you were a liberal. Money doesn't matter to liberals."

"Money matters to everyone forced to live under our corrupt Darwinian capitalist system. I enjoy real estate. I may start my own agency."

"But you loved your practice. You love kids."

"Not as much as I thought. Exceptional kids can be little monsters."

You should know, he wanted to say. He wondered if Marty would give him grandchildren. He yearned for some. Soon she'd be thirty—he'd begun to fear she was a lesbian. Nowadays everybody was "gay," it was the fashion. She had no beaus—he'd never seen her with a man—but she did have a female roommate, or housemate, someone he'd never met because Marty never invited him over. He knew the housemate was the reason she hadn't demanded he move in with her. Now *there* was a scary idea: having to live with Marty the martinet for the rest of his natural life.

"So it's all about the money," he said now. "The real money, as you put it."

"You're not one to knock money, Daddy. You've done okay with your two pensions and your goddam defense industry stock options."

"Watch your mouth, young lady. God gave you special gifts. Anyone can peddle real estate."

"Anyone can't. And screw God."

"Don't blaspheme."

"I'm sorry, but the God delusion is idolatrous and atavistic. And I can always resume my practice if I want. If it were up to you, I'd still be reading Father McGuire's *New Baltimore Cate-*

chism and saying the rosary."

"Maybe I worry about your soul."

"Don't. You're churchly enough for both of us."

He had risen and quit the room. How could a daughter of his say "Screw God?" It was depressing. Locking horns with Marty always depressed him. Not only did she not pray the rosary (he didn't either), she didn't even go to Mass and Communion at Easter or Christmas. She was one of those supercilious libs who listened to NPR, drank bottled spring water and nonfat lattes, and ridiculed the Church and the military, even the Navy. She was always whining about the "Military-Industrial Complex" and knocking America. She watched some cross-dressing lesbian anchorwoman on MSNBC every night.

After the funeral, Marty had insisted he move into the city, near her, and sell "that kitschy white elephant McMansion in the hills. It's way too much room for you, Daddy. It was too much for you and Mom. Four bedrooms, four bathrooms, a den, two offices, a library. . . All it needs is a bowling alley. It holds too many memories. Stop grieving. It's bad for your health. If you don't get out of there you'll never stop. You can't expiate your guilt with grief."

"What guilt, Marty? I don't feel any guilt." He was reluctant to pursue this, afraid where it might lead. "I happen to enjoy my home."

"Psychologists consider grief a stress reaction like fear. Grief increases the level of stress hormones like cortisol. It can damage the immune system. Chronic grief can trigger cognitive disorders and dementia. We're talking Alzheimer's, Captain."

"Stop. Let me grieve if I want. Maybe you didn't grieve enough."

She winced but pretended not to hear: "I want you to get out of that house. It's out in the middle of nowhere. You need to be around people. With your bum ticker, you shouldn't be isolated. And at your age, you shouldn't drive long distances."

"I have a perfect driving record, young lady. I've never gotten a citation or had an accident. I'm happy where I am." With a chuckle he added, "You just want to sell me a house."

"You don't need a house. I want to sell you a condo."

What she said made sense, but Paddy dismissed it because she said it. He already knew he should be more active (which meant vigorous exercise) and socialize with old people even though they bored the bejesus out of him. He tried to walk a mile every day. He'd joined a club for retired naval personnel, a bereavement club for widowers, a club for senior Catholic laymen, a chess club; he'd found them all on the Internet. He'd also found a singles club for seniors—there were flotillas of aging widows and divorcées out there. But he couldn't imagine stepping out and cutting a rug with some old bag. For company he thought of getting a pet—an "animal companion," they called it now—but a dog would be an expense and he hated cats and birds.

Marty was right about one thing: loneliness was a killer. As a boy he'd come home to his mother after school; as a man he'd come home to his wife after work; now that he had no one to come home to, and no place to come home from, a pit of loneliness yawned before him like an open grave. He would never love anyone as he had Kathleen; no one would ever love him the way she had; and he couldn't settle for less.

After the funeral, he'd done amazingly well for a month. Everyone but Marty was impressed. The first few days had been tough, the mornings especially. He'd always reached out to touch Kathleen on waking and couldn't break the habit: now he touched her pillow. On Sundays the two of them had dawdled in bed with the morning paper and read the funnies and sipped the rich Costa Rican coffee Kathleen made; now he drank instant coffee and scanned the papers by himself. He hadn't cooked his own breakfast since Nixon was president and now he had to. He thought of hiring a maid who could cook, or a cook who could clean, but that would cost money. Marty called him cheap, but he was simply frugal and thrifty.

He'd established a regimen and stuck to it. On Sundays he drove into the city for Mass, lunch at a cafeteria, and a boat ride on the River or a show at Sea World. At night he watched Fox News and "McHale's Navy" and "Sea Hunt" reruns or sports on TV, or the Catholic Channel, or read biographies of admirals like Chester Nimitz and Bull Halsey. He ate little and, except for some wine with dinner, never imbibed, though the wet bar in his living room was always stocked. Solitary drinking created alcoholics. Marty came by twice a week to check on him, and that was too often. He was always glad to see her but gladder when she left.

When that first month ended, he was still mourning. It was to be expected, given the magnitude of his loss, because Kathleen deserved to be mourned. He was proud to be coping as well as he was. He didn't know (though Marty did, Marty knew everything) that the worst was yet to come. Marty warned him that delayed reactions follow the trauma of a spouse's death. One handled the necessary practical matters and *then* one grieved.

As usual, Marty was right. When the delayed shock set in, he suffered a week of bad nights. They began with the midnight he woke to a cloying odor, sweet but stifling, in the bedroom. Instantly it was gone, but he'd recognized it as the smell of the funeral flowers at Kathleen's Rosary. He knew that the keenest sense memory is smell, but hadn't known that the unconscious could trigger it.

The next night, after taking his Metoprolol tablet for his irregular heartbeat and saying his prayers and crawling into bed, he heard a sound from downstairs. Clunky footsteps, heavy. From the drawer of the nightstand he took his shiny black Glock 17, with its 9-mm Luger cartridge, and tiptoed down the staircase. His poor heart was banging against his ribs. He found no one, but the door to the patio was open. Had he left it open? He must have. Gusts of cool air were sweeping into the kitchen.

He locked the door and returned to bed. Unable to sleep, he lay staring at the ceiling and wondered if old age reprised the night terrors of childhood. What would be next? Wetting the bed? Adult diapers? Night lights?

The third night, after taking an Ambien, he was almost asleep when he heard Kathleen's voice. Far off in the house, it sounded as if she were talking with stops and starts on the telephone. He lay thrilled with a crazed hope (had she come back to him?) until the talking ceased. He dared not move — he couldn't anyway. Then the sleeping pill kicked in, and on waking up next morning, he dismissed it as a dream.

By the fourth night, he dreaded going to bed. He read *All Hands* (the Navy magazine he subscribed to) and thumbed through Ronald Spector's history *At War at Sea: Sailors and Naval Combat in the Twentieth Century* until his eyelids were heavy. Then he switched off the lamp, drifted asleep, and woke to see Kathleen sitting on a chair in a corner of the bedroom. Her face was masked in shadow.

"Paddy? I'm sorry I woke you. Did you ever pick up your Dress Blues at the cleaners? They've been there for weeks, darling…"

He cried out to her. The sound of his voice woke him. It had been another dream. There wasn't a chair in the bedroom. But she was right—he did have some uniforms at the cleaners.

Each of the next three nights, he cried himself to sleep. *Jesus master please help me*, he prayed. For the first time in his life, fear was getting the better of him. Not even at sea, in no-fly zones or blockaded ports crawling with submarines, had he been so afraid. This fear had no object. He didn't fear Kathleen's ghost. Why should he? Wherever she'd gone, she was welcome to come back. What he feared was that he was hallucinating, losing his grip, losing his mind. Marty said that grief was deleterious to one's mental health. Grief and loneliness were driving him crazy, and his terror of going crazy shamed him. He came from a line of fearless seafaring Irishmen. He saw himself as the Greek Odysseus, the Roman Ulysses, a warrior, a leader. A sea wolf. He had been the brave "old man on a tin can," as the Navy called the Commander of a destroyer, and such men knew no fear and asked no quarter. In Gaelic the name O'Connell meant "strong as a wolf." St. Brendan was Ireland's patron saint of sailors.

Paddy longed for the open sea, with its flying fish, the salt spray on his face, the briny taste on his tongue, the heady smell in his nostrils. Crashing waves had a rhythm one could almost sing and dance to. The sea was addictive, like a drug. The sea proved to him that God existed. Not even during the Consecration at Holy Mass had he felt as close to God as he had gazing up at the twinkling black firmament, at 0300 hours, from the flight deck of the USNS *Oliver Hazard Perry*, the flagship of his destroyer flotilla. One night—and he'd never told this to anyone but the Monsignor—he'd heard God's voice in the rumble of the ocean. He'd never even told Kathleen about it. Yet he knew it had been God speaking to him. Like the lowest note of the pipe organ, it was a sound you felt rather than heard, and the words were in a language he didn't know. But he knew who was speaking.

But that was then and this was now, and what was he to do now? He could not go on like a child afraid of the dark, scared of his own shadow. It was demeaning. He was embarrassed for himself, ashamed.

On Monday morning, he drove to town to see Monsignor Sheehan at the archdiocesan office.

—⟐—

Paddy told the venerable sage, the wisest man he knew, what had been happening to him. The Monsignor was his confessor and knew things about him no one else did. When the old fellow nodded, with a benevolent smile, that he under-stood, since none of it was new to him, Paddy breathed relief.

He was in awe of the Monsignor. He wondered why the Monsignor wasn't a Bishop or an Archbishop, given his vast knowledge of history, theology, and philosophy. With his fierce mop of white hair, the Monsignor could have posed for God the Father as Michelangelo painted Him on that chapel ceiling. The creases in his Irish mug looked to have been made with a hammer and chisel. Paddy had heard that in his native Dublin, before becoming a priest, the Monsignor had boxed professionally and fought James J. Braddock near the end of the former heavyweight champion's career. Even now, in his eighties, the Monsignor was physically intimidating, a force of nature, with a prizefighter's huge gnarled hands and cauliflower ears.

"Tell me, lad," the old man was saying, "have you read the Danish philosopher Kierkegaard?"

"I have not, I'm ashamed to say."

"He was Protestant but a profound thinker. As a Navy man you'll relate to this. Kierkegaard compares a man's life to a ship sailing out to sea. His past is the shoreline. He must live in such a way that the shoreline recedes every day until it's gone if he looks back. Do you understand, Paddy? God commands us to go on living and leave the past behind. That includes the dead."

"How can I leave Kathleen behind, Monsignor?"

"Do as your daughter says. Get out of that house. Your dear wife is haunting you. And there's nothing wrong with that. She loves you and frets about you. She didn't want to leave. You said she promised never to. She wants you to know she hasn't completely left. God love her, she may feel guilty for having departed and be seeking your forgiveness. But she needs to let you go now. And you need to let her go, Paddy…"

<hr>

That afternoon, he called Marty at her office and told her he'd reconsidered. He asked her to sell his "McMansion" and find him a condo.

"Consider it done, Skipper. Why the change of heart?"

"You talked me into it, Marty."

"I never talk you into anything. Something's happened."

"I saw the light."

"You're having trouble in that house, aren't you. I won't say I told you so."

The girl was too damned smart, he thought after he'd rung off. Always being right did not make her any more lovable. No wonder she had no beau. But now he felt that a millstone had been lifted from round his neck. Maybe he was about to embark on an exciting voyage, gain a second wind, enjoy a sea change. He felt younger already.

Marty wasted no time. She was a real pro, with scores of local contacts. Watching her in action made him reassess his low opinion of realtors. Within a week, she'd sold his white elephant in the Hill Country and found him something in a trendy neighborhood on the edge of downtown. A condo in a skyscraper complex. It catered to younger people, but that was fine with him. Old people tried his patience. With its two floors, two large bedrooms, and two and a half baths, the unit encompassed 1700 square feet. After three phone calls, Marty negotiated a price of $260,000 (cash on the barrel, no penalties) and a $500 monthly maintenance fee. A real steal, she told him.

Compared to the McMansion, the place was small, but he could use one of the bedrooms as his library and study. There were armed twenty-four-hour security guards downstairs; workout facilities and a swimming pool upstairs; quality restaurants opening all over the neighborhood. The city's 200-year-old cathedral, San Fernando de Jesus, was within walking distance. Marty's own condo was a five-minute walk away—too close for comfort, really, but handy should he need her. An emerald forest of a public park, with walking trails and jogging paths, stretched just around the corner. What more could he need at this point in his life?

"Damn the torpedoes!" Paddy cried out like Admiral Farragut as Marty was showing him the condo. "Full speed ahead! Get me this one."

"Daddy, are you sure? There are others I can show you."

"I want this one."

There were just three things about it he didn't like: (1) the too-small elevator, (2) the metal front door from the hallway, thick and heavy as that of a bank vault and encumbered with a dead bolt and chain, and (3) the ring of the doorbell—instead of a *ding* or *ding-dong* it gave three chimes: *ding-DING-dong, ding-DING-dong*. But minor annoyances he could live with.

"When can I move in?" he asked her.

To celebrate they had lunch at a French bistro close by that Marty knew about. Paddy didn't like French restaurants—he found them overpriced—but Marty was treating and she insisted on the place. It was cozy and brick-walled, with fresh Morning Glory blooms in vases on the tables and Chopin piano music playing softly, almost subliminally. For starters Marty ordered them a $40 bottle of Pouilly-Fuissé, and minutes later, father and daughter were clinking their glasses of chilled white wine in a toast.

It was such a lovely moment that he knew the mood wouldn't last. Marty would find a way to ruin it. She'd been the sort of child who always says the wrong thing at the wrong time, a trait she had never outgrown. And sure enough, over their salades nicoise and out of the blue, she asked: "Daddy, why didn't you and Mom have more children? I mean, you know, being devout Catholics and all?"

He put down his salad fork and stared at her. "Why do you ask me this now?"

"I don't know. When should I ask you?"

"We tried," he said. "Believe me, we really wanted another child." She flinched, and he wanted it back, because she'd taken it as a slam.

"We couldn't have more children," he said. "The doctors weren't sure whose fault it was. There weren't the alternatives available you have now. Thank God we were able to have you."

"Thank you for having me" came her predictable response. "But I wish you'd paid me some attention. Mom did, you didn't."

He swallowed and dabbed at his mouth with his napkin. "Negative," he objected. "I even went to your soccer games and piano recitals."

"You went to one soccer game. Mom had to drag you to my recitals."

"I helped with your homework."

"So you could flaunt your knowledge. You wanted me to be valedictorian and get into good schools."

"It worked, didn't it?"

"Tell the truth, Daddy. Wouldn't you have preferred a son?"

Paddy stiffened. "That's not fair, Marty. Most men would prefer a son. Men know how to relate to little boys. They don't know how to relate to little girls."

"Well," she said, "I wish you'd spent time with me even if you couldn't relate. I sensed you were disappointed. I didn't complain, but I wanted to."

"And now that you finally have, could we change the subject? We all gripe about our parents. Your Grandaddy O'Connell made me take cold showers in January to toughen me up. If I was remiss as a dad because I was so busy with work, I'm sorry."

"It's okay," she said, trying to smile. She reached out and touched his hand. "Actually, you were a good dad. I'm being silly."

Now he felt patronized. She began to prattle about the condo, and her bubbly mood returned. But his appetite was gone. He could only pick at his coquilles Saint-Jacques au gratin (though he loved scallops) while she ate with gusto. It always went that way. She would ruin special occasions for him and not even be aware of it.

But then she'd redeem herself. Marty would prove indispensable to his move into the city, supervising it with breathtaking efficiency. She held an Open House at the McMansion and conducted showings; she handled the titles, contracts, financing, and closing costs; she oversaw cleanings and inspections. She decorated the condo. It couldn't accommodate a fraction of what filled the old house, so she put quality items in storage and held a weekend estate sale for others. Careful to safeguard, she took home fine art, jewelry, Waterford crystal, and Wedgewood china; other valuable items she put in his safety deposit vault at the bank. In the final tally, he came out $83,000 ahead and she did all right for herself.

Overnight, his morale improved. For whatever reason, the king-sized bed he'd shared with Kathleen felt more comfortable in the condo, and he slept soundly at first. He didn't see or hear things that weren't there. He stuck to his exercise regimen—in the ferny, fragrant green park, he walked a mile every morning, another in the afternoon. For his second walk, he'd take along a book in case he stopped to rest. Fatefully, on one of those walks, he encountered the little girl. Mary Martha.

—⁓—

It happened on a crisp, sunny fall afternoon with the smell of burning leaves in the air even though city ordinance outlawed the burning of leaves. That was strange. He wondered who'd dare to break the law in a public park. It was as lovely a day as he could remember, glorious enough to seem unreal. It felt great to be alive. Somewhere in the middle distance, a high school band was playing, but there were few people in the park.

When he stopped to read, Paddy always chose the same bench, near a precast-concrete drinking fountain with JOHN 3:16 painted in red on its grey stone base. Today he'd brought along Robert Southey's biography of Lord Nelson; he'd read it long ago as an ensign, but been too young fully to appreciate the Admiral's greatness.

He sat down to read. A skinny little girl came marching up the path, swinging her legs high, like a goose-stepper. A picnic basket hung from the crook of one arm. Her bizarre outfit resembled a Little League baseball uniform; her white jersey was striped with orange and red like a rainbow, and her white trousers ended at the knees, where her blue socks and red stirrups began. But her pink shoes were a ballerina's slippers, and she wore a snug white cap, fastened under the chin, like those of peasant maids in Renaissance Dutch paintings.

Paddy gawked at her and returned to his book. She plopped down beside him and set the basket between them on the bench.

"Don't play possum," she said. "I saw you looking at my shoes."

He looked up. "Excuse me?" he asked, a little irritably. He did not need any company. He wanted to read.

"I've seen you here before. Lots of times."

"That's funny. I've never seen you."

"You have beautiful silver hair. What are you reading?"

"Nothing you'd be interested in."

"I might be. Is it terribly atavistic?"

He had to smile. "Do you know what atavistic means?"

"Not exactly," she said, coloring. "I just like the way it sounds. Are you a voracious reader?"

Paddy sighed. "I read a lot." Strange kid, he thought.

"Read to me."

"It's not a book for a little girl."

"I'm not a little girl. I'm almost twelve. Do you like my baseball uniform?"

"Well, it's different."

"The jersey is Astros retro from the seventies. My parents bought it for me last month, when we went to Houston."

"You went to Minute Maid Park?"

She shook her head. "We went to M. D. Anderson Cancer Center. They say I'm sick."

"Oh." Now he saw that her complexion was sallow, her brown eyes darkly ringed. He felt a pang of regret. Poor little waif.

"I love baseball. I adore its mythology. Football I find uncouth. Too violent. If you're wondering about my shoes, I took ballet. I had to stop because of the physical demands it imposed."

"What's your name?"

"Mary Martha."

"That's a pretty name. My daughter's name is Martha."

"My name's not Martha. It's Mary Martha."

"Roger that, Mary Martha."

"May I ask your name?"

"Everyone calls me Paddy."

"I have a friend at school named Patty. Had a friend."

"Not Patty. Paddy. With two d's."

"What's in a name? That's Shakespeare."

"You're a very literate little girl, aren't you."

"Yes. Are you retired military?"

"I was a Captain in the Navy."

"I sensed that."

When Paddy chuckled, she asked, "How come you weren't an Admiral?"

The question took him aback. How come indeed. The kid was too smart for her own good.

He glanced around. "Are you here by yourself? Why aren't you in school?"

"I'm excused. I hate school anyway."

"You do? Why?"

"When you're sick nobody will play with you. They osterize you."

"Ostracize you. They shouldn't do that. We all get sick. Where are your parents?"

"In that building." She pointed toward a blue skyscraper half visible through the branches of a great live oak. "We live in the King William Towers. Don't worry, Captain. I'm not A-W-O-L."

He laughed. "In the Navy it's called 'U-A.' Unauthorized Absence."

"Why won't you read to me?"

"Don't you know how to read?"

"Of course I do. Last month I read *The Lion, the Witch, and the Wardrobe* by C. S. Lewis. But I enjoy being read to. My father read to me when I was little."

"He doesn't anymore?"

"He hasn't time. He's quite active in Democratic Party politics."

Paddy made a face but didn't say what he was thinking. "It doesn't mean he doesn't love you," he said. "I'm sure he loves you a lot. I didn't read much to my own daughter. Her mother read to her. May I ask what's in your basket?"

She pulled out a worn paperback: *Winnie the Pooh.* "My mother adores this book. She told me the idea was inspired by a teddy bear."

"It was."

The child was charming, even captivating, but Paddy thought it inappropriate to go on talking to her. "Listen, Mary Martha," he said, "let's make a deal. I'll read you one chapter of your book and then you run on home. Okay?"

"Okay."

Paddy read the first chapter of the A. A. Milne classic with all the feeling he could muster, which wasn't a lot, and when he finished he saw that she was gazing at him adoringly, brown eyes shining.

"Awesome," she said. "I'll say good-bye now. If you wish to see me again, I'll be here on Tuesday. Same time, same station." She giggled, as if she found the expression hilarious. "Will you come read to me?"

"Maybe."

"Please come. *Auf Wiedersehen,* Paddy. That's German for good-bye." She preened, stuck her book in her basket, rose from the bench, and goose-stepped up the path.

He met Mary Martha in that park four more times. Her bizarre costume never varied—she wore it like a uniform. Each time, he brought a new book to read to her. At the bookstore near his condo, on recommendations from a matronly clerk, he'd bought *Anne of Green Gables, Heidi, The Princess Diaries,* and a Nancy Drew offering, *The Hidden Staircase.* He read the child first chapters only. Her favorite was the Nancy Drew ("That was *totally* atavistic, don't you think?" she said), followed by *Anne of Green Gables.* After each reading, he urged her to keep the book, but she declined. Their visits lasted exactly thirty minutes. He asked once about her health and she changed the subject.

Before long, his grief was receding like Kierkegaard's shore-line, and he wondered if Mary Martha deserved credit. Not only was he sleeping soundly but his dreams just before waking were joyous and celestial. In one of them he was captaining his destroyer again as it patrolled the lucid blue waters of the Sea of Japan, northeast of South Korea. Once more, just as he'd remembered it, the incandescent vermillion sunrise of the Far East set the sea on fire, and the flight deck of his ship was aflame with a pool of crimson and gold. Boldly he strode through those leaping flames secure in the knowledge that neither they nor anything else could hurt him. He was invulnerable.

Waking up was a letdown—he'd wanted that dream to go on and on. He wondered why he'd ever left the sea. Had he not, of course, he wouldn't have had his family. But now his wife was gone and his daughter had grown up and he was away from the sea, away from water, marooned in a land vast and strange called Texas. It wasn't fair. All he had in his life now was Marty. And his kooky new friend little Mary Martha.

At the end of their fourth rendezvous in the park, as he and the child were saying good-bye, she stood on tiptoe and kissed him on the cheek. "Promise you'll come back, Paddy," she said with a worried frown.

"I promise."

"I love you." She turned and hurried off before he could think of a response.

But when he showed up—same time, same station—the following week, she wasn't there. Huddled on their bench instead, as though waiting for him, was a woman shivering in a camel hair overcoat. A norther had blown in, and Paddy was wearing his dark Navy pea jacket. He carried his latest purchase, a paperback of *Charlotte's Web*, in a white plastic bag. He took a deep breath, unsure what to expect, but with an ill sense of foreboding.

In a stern voice she asked, "Are you the man who calls himself Paddy?"

"People call me Paddy, yes."

"I'm Christine Van de Walle. Mary Martha's mother."

He nodded but withheld his own name. "May I sit down?"

"Please. We have to talk."

The woman had close-cropped pixie hair with bangs, a thin mouth, a beak nose, and Mary Martha's large brown eyes. She smiled, but the smile was hostile. "I understand you've been reading to my daughter. Mary Martha told us about you."

Paddy took out *Charlotte's Web* from his bag. "Then," he said, "she told you she asked me to read to her. She seemed lonely. I was glad to oblige."

"You've made quite a hit with her. Instead of candy, you ply her with books?"

"Stop right there, Mrs. Van de Walle. Mary Martha approached me, not the other way around. Nothing untoward happened."

The woman studied him. "Perhaps not," she said. "But my daughter has formed an attachment to you."

What luck is mine, Paddy thought. No good deed goes unpunished.

Then the woman startled him; she put her face in her hands and began to sob. "Mary Martha's dying."

Paddy felt a chill. "What?"

"She has A.M.L. Acute Myeloid Leukemia. She has just weeks to live."

"My God," Paddy gasped. "She mentioned that she was sick. I'm so sorry." He gave her his handkerchief.

"She wanted to come with me but felt too weak." When Mrs. Van de Walle raised her head, her eyes shone with tears. She dabbed at them. "My husband and I have been through hell. We've spent weeks with specialists in Houston. We practically live at the Medical Center here. She's taking massive doses of Pramipexole and Levodopa. She's incredibly brave."

"Is there anything I can do?"

"Yes. You can stay away from her. As I said, she's formed an attachment to you."

Paddy wanted to ask why a terminally ill child would be playing alone in a public park, but he held his tongue. The woman was in pain. "As you wish," he said, rising. "I'll find another place to walk. Again—I'm sorry." On impulse he offered her the book. "Would you give this to Mary Martha for me?"

He'd expected a No, but she snatched it and stuck in her handbag.

"Good-bye, Mrs. Van de Walle. I'll pray for your family. Mary Martha's a wonderful little girl and I hope she recovers."

Sniffling, the woman looked away. Paddy turned and lumbered up the path, a sad old man pulling his pea jacket collar tight against the wind, wondering why God would send him someone new to grieve about when he wasn't through grieving for his wife.

—⁓—

"Aren't you a little fuzzy on the details?" Marty asked him that evening. "A few things don't compute, Captain."

She eyed him doubtfully and took a bite of Moo Goo Gai Pan with her chopsticks. They were sitting at his dining room table. She had dropped by, uninvited, with dinner—Cantonese, in white takeout cartons with wire handles, plus a bottle of plum wine. He'd told her what happened in the park with Christine Van de Walle. Now he wished he hadn't.

"I'm not ever confused about details," he said as he squeezed soy sauce from a packet. "My memory is a steel trap. You know that."

Marty took a sip of wine. "Well," she said, "parts of the story don't ring true."

"Which parts?"

"First of all, what were you doing reading to some kid? You'd be the last person in the world to do that. You never used to read to *me*."

"Maybe that's why I was doing it."

"Two, if this kid was at death's door, she wouldn't be cavorting in some park in a baseball uniform. She'd be in a hospital, wearing one of those paper gowns. That mother sold you a sob story, Daddy. Everything she said was specious."

"The child herself said she was sick."

"The child also said she lived in the King William Towers. I happen to know you can't see the King William Towers from that park."

Paddy considered that. "But why would she lie?"

"And those drugs the mother said the kid was taking? Levodopa and Pramipexole? They're not for A.M.L. They're for Parkinson's."

"Oh, come on."

"Trust me. If that kid had A.M.L, they'd be giving her some chemo drug like Arabinoside. Or an induction agent to destroy the leukemia cells. Or bone marrow treatments. Or an allogenic transplant. Why would they give her stuff for Parkinson's?"

Paddy sighed. "I don't know."

"The woman was winging it and those were the first drugs that came to her mind. She doesn't *know* what you'd give a kid with A.M.L. You were being played, Daddy."

"For what? A paperback book?"

"Maybe she's a scammer. And so is the kid. Maybe they're a team. They're setting you up for a loan or something."

"Marty, that's crazy."

"Your whole story is crazy."

The exchange ruined his supper. Paddy couldn't eat another bite. He knew what Marty left unsaid: "And maybe *you're* crazy." Why had he told her about this afternoon when he hadn't told her about the haunting or the hallucinations?

"Also," Marty went on, "no real kid talks that way. '*I adore baseball — I love its mythology. Football I find uncouth.*' Did she really use the word atavism?"

"Atavistic. She didn't know what it meant."

"Few people do. Listen, Skipper, you're talking to a licensed board-certified child psychologist. What you've described was a child actress with a script and her acting coach. You were a mark."

"I'm not gullible, Marty. I'm suspicious of everyone. These people were real. I'm not making things up."

"Of course you aren't. *They* are. They were gaming you. Are you planning to eat your egg rolls?"

"They're all yours."

When supper was done, she cleared the table and disappeared into the kitchen. He heard her humming while she tidied up. He knew what that meant: she was marshaling for an attack.

He steeled himself. When she returned, she was wearing her drill sergeant's face. She sat down across the table from him, leaned forward, and looked him in the eye. "Now hear this, Captain. There are things I want you to do and things I want you not to. Don't go to that park again. It's not a healthy place for you. It's not safe. Use the gym and the pool here. Find another place to walk."

"I wasn't planning to go back. I promised that woman —"

"Screw that woman. She's not why you're not going. She's a goddam fraud. Second, I want you to read a book by Elisabeth Kubler-Ross. The Swiss psychiatrist?"

"I know who she is, Marty. I'm a university professor."

"You were one. She writes that many men react to a wife's death like a child does to a mother's desertion. I'll bring the book by tomorrow. Third, I want you to see Sandy Edelstein in Houston. I'll make an appointment for you."

"Who the heck is Sandy Edelstein?"

"I met her at a psychology convention. She's a Freudian psychotherapist who specializes in chronic grief caused by death or dying. You're still grieving over Mom, Daddy. This woman can help you."

"You want me to see a female shrink who calls herself Sandy."

"Sandy is short for Sandra. And why should it matter if a therapist has a penis? You *will* see her, dammit."

"Don't give orders. I'm the parent here, young lady. I don't need a mother."

She laughed testily. "Oh, yes you do. My mother was your mother. And she's gone now."

Here it comes, he thought. He closed his eyes and muttered, "I won't ask what that means."

"Mom mothered you. I don't care how many macho leadership courses you taught at the Academy, or how much younger she was than you. She told you what to eat and what to drink and how much. She cooked and cleaned for you. She washed and ironed your uniforms and laid them out for you every morning. She shined your shoes and your brass. She made sure you kept your appointments with your students and the deans. I know, because I was there."

Paddy felt his cheeks flush. "Your mother was an old-fashioned wife who regarded those things as her duties," he said. "Wives don't have time for such things today because they work. Your mother didn't have to work. I was the breadwinner. I think it worked out pretty well. Why is it always people who've never married that are experts on marriage?"

"Mom was not as happy as you thought. She hated those boozy parties with those boring naval officers and their wives you dragged her to in Annapolis and D. C. and Baltimore."

"She loved D. C. We'd go to the Kennedy Center."

"She thought you were a control freak and an egotist. She loved you anyway. Everything was always about you and your career even though she was more intelligent. Mom bypassed any number of careers because she put you first. And you wonder why I don't want to get married?"

Paddy felt a nerve twitch in his left eyelid. She had managed to hurt him with accusations he feared might be halfway true. Maybe he had put himself first. Leaders did that. Leaders went first.

"You were a selfish husband, Daddy."

"Stop right there, young lady. Or I'll have to ask you to leave."

She stood up. "I was leaving anyway. I love you, but sometimes it has to be tough love. I'll drop the Kubler-Ross book by tomorrow."

From the front door she said, "Think about seeing Sandy Edelstein?"

What a day, he thought when she was gone. A perfect storm of a day. *Dies irae, dies illa.* He hadn't gotten to see Mary Martha. He'd been accused of pedophilia by a stranger. His own daughter called him an egotist, control freak, mama's boy, and head case and informed him that his marriage to her mother had been a rotten marriage. He stayed awake for as long as he could to postpone the tossing and turning he knew lay ahead.

He watched a Dodgers-Astros game from the West Coast that lasted fourteen innings and four hours. It was two in the morning before he fell into bed. It took him another hour to fall asleep.

His dreams were in vivid Technicolor. He was back in Annapolis. The silver hair he was so proud of was falling out in thatches. Loose bridgework rattled in his mouth. In a panic he ran all the way from the campus to his dentist's office, but couldn't find the building. Then he was running faster, harder, in a park at dusk—the park he'd promised Marty to keep out of. Way up the path, in the same direction, Mary Martha was goose-stepping in her rainbow jersey and white cap. He ran after her till his lungs ached. When he caught up, she stopped and spun round and it wasn't Mary Martha but a middle-aged dwarfish woman he didn't recognize. She looked to be in pain—her face was twisted, her eyes wild. She yanked off her tight cap: her head was bald as an egg. From behind him came Marty's voice: "Didn't I tell you to stay out of this park, Daddy?"

He woke up panting, as if he really had been running. He was shivering, though the room was warm. He bounded out of bed and did something he'd never done before in the middle of the night. He crept downstairs, went to the bar, and fixed himself a drink: three fingers of rum, Mount Gay Rum from Barbados. Neat. In a tumbler.

He took the drink upstairs; he sat on the edge of the bed and sipped it—not to relax, though he was still shaking, but to get in a fighting mood. In his youth, drinking had made him want to fight. As a midshipman, he had boxed for the Navy and won more bouts than he'd lost. He'd been fast with his fists and nimble on his feet. A middleweight.

The rum knocked him out. Near dawn, he was wakened by a trill of laughter from downstairs, so girlish and childlike that he wasn't afraid. He heard it again. Had he left on the TV or the radio? He didn't care. He was sick of being spooked. Age should not rob a man of his courage after having robbed him of everything else. He started to get up and go downstairs. But he only turned over and went back to sleep.

The next night, he heard it again from downstairs: the carefree laughter of a child. He pushed his face into his pillow and covered his ears with Kathleen's pillow. When he woke next morning, he knew he had to do something right away. He was close to the edge, the point of no return.

He reviewed his choices. He could move back to Annapolis. But what would that accomplish? He could board a ship, any ship, and take a cruise. He had not been at sea in years. But he'd have to come back. He could consult Marty's *wunderkind* in Houston—Sandra Edelweiss or whoever—and spend a fortune on her. Or he could go see Monsignor Sheehan and channel God's help.

He chose the last option—somehow the old mick always made him feel better, closer to God, divinely protected. Marty's Freudian shrink would be a last resort. Marty the lapsed Catholic, Marty the militant atheist would scold him if she learned of his choice, but she wasn't going to.

He phoned the rectory and made an appointment for that afternoon. Then he showered and shaved, combed his hair, shined his black dress shoes, and donned his Service Dress

Blues. The uniform was a double-breasted navy jacket with six gold buttons; gold stripes on the sleeves for his Captain's insignia; a starched white shirt and a blue tie with a four-in-hand knot. He had not worn his Dress Blues since Kathleen's funeral. They were like a suit of armor to him.

The Monsignor offered him Bushmill's whiskey and a Cuban cigar. Paddy declined both. "Mother of God," the old cleric groaned, reclining in his black leather executive chair. He clasped his gnarled hands behind his neck. "Age is a penance, Paddy. Some days I hear myself creak. Be glad you're not old. You're not yet seventy."

"I feel old, Monsignor."

"What's troubling you, lad? What is it now?"

Paddy told him about Mary Martha and her mother; about his run-in with Marty; about his frightening dream. Every now and then, the old man would nod with empathy. But at one point, he frowned and shook his head and raked his fingers through his wild mane of white hair.

"Now listen, Paddy," he said gently. "I'm your confessor. This sounds to me like guilt and not just grief. Was there something in your marriage you need to confess?"

The question surprised Paddy. "Not that I know of. My daughter says I was a selfish husband and father. Maybe I was. But never consciously or intentionally."

"A crucial distinction," the Monsignor pointed out. "Holy Mother Church judges us by what we do, not what we are by nature. If we are naturally thoughtless or insensitive, there's no sin until we're aware of it. Not even a sin of omission."

"As a husband and a father I did my best. Maybe I should never have married."

"Malarkey."

"I could've stayed at sea and become an Admiral."

"Leave the past behind, lad. I've told you before. You say you live near the cathedral downtown?"

"Very near, Monsignor."

"What's to stop you from going to Mass and taking Holy Communion every morning?"

The question gave Paddy pause. "Nothing, I guess…"

"Try that for a start. You're in a wee bit of trouble, son. God waits for you in the Blessed Sacrament."

Paddy was disappointed. He'd hoped for more.

The Monsignor lit the cigar he'd offered and gazed up at the ceiling. "You know, Paddy," he mused after blowing a smoke ring, "in today's sophisticated world we no longer believe in evil or demons or the Devil. We chalk up the most heinous crimes to unhappy childhoods and poverty and being stressed out and not getting enough hugs. But you and I know evil exists. And not just symbolically or metaphorically. We know it exists as a concrete reality, a tangible *thing*, like cancer or famine or floods. We see the works of Satan every day."

"We do, Monsignor." Paddy remembered the Columbine massacre, the Oklahoma City bombing, the USS *Cole*.

"We mustn't live with evil, Paddy. Or with the Devil. We must cast them out. But sometimes we have to live with our demons for a while." The old man puffed on his cigar and frowned. "Now, I don't think you're in danger from the Devil. But I do think you're tormented by mischievous demons. The little buggers can't harm you if you ask God's help. Eventually they'll tire of you and pester someone else. In the meantime, keep the faith and live with them. Yes?"

"If you say so, Father."

"You're a brave man, Paddy. A tough guy, an old salt. A *sailor*. You boxed in the Navy, you said. I fought Braddock—Jim Braddock the Cinderella Man, the Pride of the Irish. That was in 'thirty-nine. He'd beaten Max Baer and knocked down Joe Louis. He beat me, too. But I lasted eight rounds with him."

"I knew you fought Braddock," Paddy said with a touch of awe.

"I know about your naval heroics, too. Though you've not mentioned them. Mother of God, lad, you look grand in that uniform! Fifty years ago, some little Canadian Jew wrote a song that said Jesus was a sailor when he walked upon the water. Jesus loved sailors. Peter was a sailor, a fisherman. Your demons can't sink you, Paddy, unless you let them. Learn to live with them. The best antidote is a sense of humor. Welcome them as your guests."

"I'll try, Monsignor." Paddy smiled with effort.

"Take heart, lad. Sure you don't want a drink? I have a bottle of Jamaican rum somewhere…"

—⁘—

When he got back to his condo, the security guard in the foyer handed him a brown paper bag. It contained the paperback Marty wanted him to read. A scrawled note inside read HI DADDY OFF TO GALVESTON FOR REALTOR CONFERENCE READ BOOK IT WILL HELP I'M AT HOTEL GALVEZ RM 1215 CALL ON MY CELL IF U NEED ME 210-829-8137 BACK THE 19TH LOVE U -- M

She'd be gone a week. He'd have preferred two or three. But he knew she meant well, and that in her own way she loved him. It was to be near him that she chose to live in a city she didn't like. He resolved to be kinder to her. He would read the Kubler-Ross book this afternoon, after his swim and nap.

He felt better now, thanks to the Monsignor and the Almighty. The old mick had confirmed that his demons were real and not (as Marty argued) imaginary. Marty had him senile, a victim of dementia. How infuriating. By God, he would not see her lady shrink in Houston unless he became suicidal. Maybe not even then.

Later that day, in the bedroom he'd converted to a study, he made himself comfortable by lying down and stretching out, beneath a tall lamp, on the leather sofa. Though he didn't want to, he began thumbing through the Kubler-Ross paperback, *On Grief and Grieving*. Marty had highlighted passages with a yellow marker and penciled red comments in the margins. He had no intention of reading the whole book, but he would scan those passages.

The first highlighted paragraph read that if the pain of one's loss is intolerable, the grieving party will do anything to negotiate a way out of it. A husband grieving for a dead wife may go through five stages, the third of which (after denial and anger) is "bargaining." Unconsciously, bargainers make deals to reclaim what death has stolen from them. A guilt-ridden bargainer may invent a way to say or do things he should've said or done when the loved one was alive. He may imagine someone to say or do them to, and even enter into an imaginary relationship to give himself a second chance and relief from his pain.

The skin at the back of Paddy's neck prickled. Marty had underlined the last highlighted sentence in red. Why? He had not sought or wanted a new relationship. Mary Martha was just a kid who'd approached him in a park. He had no desire to replace Kathleen with her, and couldn't if he wanted to. What did this "bargaining" business have to do with him? He would ask Marty when she got back from Galveston.

He struggled through five more highlighted passages before tossing the book aside. To him it was psychobabble, but he'd read more tomorrow. He had promised.

He left the condo and took a brisk long walk, steering clear of the park but passing attractive shops and restaurants in the neon twilight. Other pedestrians, mostly on the young side, smiled or nodded in respect when they passed him on the boulevard. When he got back, he turned on ESPN Classics and watched the 1964 Cotton Bowl game between Navy and Texas, in which Roger Staubach heroically quarterbacked the Midshipmen in a losing cause. Staubach was a devout Catholic and a Vietnam vet. Paddy loved Roger Staubach like the son he'd never had.

Then he was ready for bed. He slept soundly that night, and the next as well. He went to six o'clock Mass and took the Eucharist every morning until Marty got back from Galveston.

Being in that huge cathedral without Kathleen made him feel forlorn and abandoned, but he had to follow the Monsignor's instructions. By day he kept busy with his Navy club and chess club, and his exercise regimen in his building's fitness facility. He toyed with the idea of writing his memoirs; his Navy foot locker was filled with ship logs, journals, and papers from his teaching career. One's life acquired meaning if one left a record of it behind. But would he leave out the creepy post-Kathleen stuff? He'd cross that bridge when he came to it.

Marty showed up the first night she was back. She brought takeout food (Japanese) and a DVD for them to watch: *The Hunt for Red October*, a naval action movie in which Sean Connery played a Soviet submarine Captain. Paddy had seen it but didn't tell her. It wasn't Marty's vintage, and he wondered why she was being so nice. That made him uneasy.

After the movie, she talked about her trip to Galveston and of course asked if he'd read the Kubler-Ross. He hadn't finished it, he told her, then asked about the highlighted passages.

She cleared her throat, and her eyes took on the look of someone about to deliver bad news. "When I left Galveston," she began, "I stopped off in Houston and had lunch with Sandy Edelstein. I told her about your sessions in the park with the little girl. And meeting the mother."

"And?"

"She said it sounded like a grieving spouse bargaining for what he's lost."

Paddy started to protest but didn't. Hear her out, he thought.

"Sandy thinks you may have invented that little girl because you feel guilty for how you treated Mom. You needed someone sick and vulnerable to be kind and loving to. You imagined those visits with her. Sandy says mourners can delude themselves that their loved one is appearing to them as someone or something else. A person, a dog, even a bird."

"Rubbish, Marty." He shifted in his chair. "But go ahead."

"Sandy was just surmising things based on what I told her. She says the kid could represent me. That's why you gave her the name Martha. And why she's precocious, like I was at that age. And uses words I use, like atavistic."

"Now it's about you? I thought it was about your mother."

"You feel guilty about every female in your life, Daddy. In your subconscious they probably morph into each other, the way people merge in a dream. There's a textbook term for it. Overlap."

"Freudian psychobabble, Marty. And you reject Catholicism for this drivel?"

"The child hinted she was ignored by her father. Sandy says you feel guilty for ignoring me all that time."

It was too much—Paddy sat up straight and glowered. "I didn't ignore you, Marty! I just wasn't touchy-feely! Stop rewriting family history! And the kid's mother—who does she represent? *My* mother?"

"You'd gotten to the the stage where you realized bargaining was not going to work for you. You created the mother to end the relationship because you wanted out."

"Why would I kill a child off with leukemia?"

"To be sure you were rid of her. Maybe you needed another

cancer victim to grieve about."

"Oh, right! That's exactly what I needed! Jesus, Mary and Joseph, Marty. This Edelberg of yours—is she some kind of quack?"

"Edelstein. She studied under Kubler-Ross. But put her aside. Some of this occurred to *me* when I was here last time. Remember the things I said didn't add up? Remember my saying your little friend didn't ring true? And when you told me she used words few adults use, let alone a kid, I suspected what was happening."

"Which was what? That I'm going crazy?"

"Not at all. Delusions happen to perfectly healthy well-adjusted people when their grief becomes intolerable. They're simply defense mechanisms. Sandy wants to treat you. Please go see her in Houston. I'll go with you. She says apparitions are not uncommon among very old persons grieving for a dead spouse."

"I'm not very old, Marty. I'm sixty-seven. Reagan was almost seventy when he became President."

"Don't get me started on Reagan. He was demented half the time. The point is, a grieving mind can play tricks and invent people and scenarios."

Marty feigned a smile. "Daddy," she said softly. "It's your life. You don't have to see Sandy if you don't want to."

"Good. Because I don't."

"But think about it? Please?"

⁓

Paddy did think about it. But he didn't go see Dr. Edelstein. Instead he decided to follow the Monsignor's advice: *Learn to live with your demons.* He rejected Marty's theory that Mary Martha and Christine Van de Walle were imaginary. He decided not to write his memoirs—that would involve looking back from the stern of his ship rather than letting the shoreline recede. He read a best seller by a German-born spiritual writer about how crucial it is to live every waking moment in the present tense. He refused to read another word by Elisabeth Kubler-Ross.

Once he'd resolved to live with his demons, they went away. (The Monsignor, as usual, had been right.) He stopped having night terrors and hallucinating. For a solid month he went to Mass and Holy Communion every morning and Confession to Monsignor Sheehan every Saturday. He mingled with other seniors even though they tried his patience. He worked out in the exercise facility twice a day. He even signed up for a cooking course (Marty's idea) but dropped it after the second class. Marty offered to teach him to cook, and he actually considered it before declining.

He made his peace with Marty. She promised to give him his space and stop dropping by unannounced and telling him what to do. Now when she visited, it was her life they talked about, not his, and when she told him she was "coming out" and planning to marry her housemate, whose name was Suzanne, he surprised her by taking it in stride and not making a big deal of it. Inside, of course, his heart was breaking. Now he would never have grandchildren. His O'Connell line would die out. But he had a daughter who loved him, and for that he was grateful.

Winter came—an unusually cold winter for South Texas, bringing hard freezes and ice storms. Late one frigid night, channel-surfing after watching his Washington Wizards lose to the San Antonio Spurs, Paddy watched a PBS documentary about A. A. Milne, who wrote *Winnie the Pooh.* He found Milne fascinating—a Brit whose writing was more popular in America than in England, a pacifist who joined the British Army in World War I and distinguished himself as an officer. *Winnie the Pooh* was the book Mary Martha had in her basket the afternoon he'd met her.

Mary Martha! He'd almost forgotten that name. Not having thought about her in months, he wondered when and where she had died. The child had to be dead. There were many ways to confirm it—death records, coroner's reports, obituaries for a Mary Martha Van de Walle who'd expired during the past six months at age eleven or twelve. And the omniscient Internet, which (thanks to Marty) he'd learned to navigate. But he didn't want to confirm it. Nothing would give him more satisfaction than proving to Marty that the child had been real; yet he didn't want to be certain she was gone. It would make him grieve, and he was done with grieving. He had to let Mary Martha go as he had Kathleen. His little angel was just another figure on the shore now, waving good-bye as he sailed away to ports unknown.

That night, when he said his prayers, he said a special one for Mary Martha: *May her soul, and all the souls of the faithful departed through the mercy of God, rest in peace, Amen.* He had loved her and treated her with love. He harbored no guilt about her. He had a hunch that he would dream about her that night. He wanted to.

And he did. He dreamed he was in San Fernando de Jesus Cathedral, standing over her open white satin coffin. He heard mourners weeping and the heavy sea-like music of a pipe organ. Monsignor Sheehan was singing "In Paradisum," the Gregorian chant for the dead. In her pink gown of silk brocade, Mary Martha was a sleeping beauty. Her eyes were closed, but she wore a Mona Lisa smile. She wasn't bald—the curly brown hair that framed her head and shoulders was real. He reached out and touched it.

She opened her eyes and recognized him. Her smile disappeared.

The scream of the phone on the nightstand woke him. His eyes were wet—he'd been crying—and his vision was blurred. The digital clock beside the phone read 3:04. He switched on the lamp, wondering who'd be calling at this hour. Not Marty, certainly. Maybe some fool who'd dialed the wrong number.

He grabbed the phone and growled "Hello?" There was static—a bad connection. He heard a woman's laughter. Her hoarse whiskey voice slurred, "Is this the great Captain Patrick Brendan O'Connell?" Her words did not connect coherently.

"Who is this?"

"Mary Martha."

She sounded like a smoker, a drinker, a barfly. In the background a radio played country-western music. He couldn't speak. He tried to push himself up and out of bed but failed.

He fumbled with the receiver and almost dropped it.

"How are you, Paddy," the whiskey voice said.

"Who are you? How'd you get my number? How do you know my name?"

"I know where you live, too. I'm down in the lobby."

He closed his eyes and pinched himself on the forearm so hard his fingernails dug into the flesh. This was no dream. "You're not a little girl," he said. "You're a grown woman and drunk."

"I'm coming up. It's cold down here."

"Go away. The guards won't let you up unless they buzz me."

"They can't stop me. Why didn't you come back to the park?"

"I said go away."

"You promised you'd read to me."

His voice came in a croak. "Your mother said—" He couldn't finish.

"I'm coming up in the elevator. I want you to read to me."

"Your mother said you were dying."

"You thought I was dead? Are you disappointed?"

"Go away. Please. Whoever you are, leave me alone."

"You promised. Moth*erfucker*." She hung up.

Paddy yanked open the drawer of the nightstand. He took out the Glock 17, checked the Luger cartridge, and released the safety. He cradled the pistol in his trembling hands. Then he cursed softly and put it back in the drawer. Whoever or whatever it was—child, woman, demon—he couldn't shoot it. He thought of calling Marty, but No. He would not give her cause to call him crazy. Nor could he, a Navy Captain, cry for help from a woman in the face of an attack.

A sudden calm enveloped him. There is peace in certainty, he'd read somewhere, and now he could be certain that his torment would never end until he confronted the enemy in a fight to the death. The Monsignor said, "Don't fear your demons, welcome them as your guests," but the Monsignor was wrong. Damned if he'd welcome guests who terrorized his home in the dark of night. His sense of humor had run its course. Enough was enough. Paddy was ready to kill or be killed. He wanted a showdown.

It was zero hour: time to engage. He rose from the bed and squared his shoulders. Gingerly, he padded down the carpeted staircase in his pajamas, wishing he were wearing his Dress Blues. The living room was dappled in shadow. He remembered the old saw: *The Captain always goes down with the ship.* At the Naval Academy he'd learned the cliché wasn't true, but gone on believing it just the same. To guarantee their heroic deaths, Japanese naval Captains in the Second World War tied themselves to the beams when their ships were about to sink.

His doorbell began to ring, making that sound he hated: *ding-DING-dong, ding-DING-dong.* She had gotten past the security guards. The ringing grew louder, more frequent, and now he heard a pounding on the door like a tsunami crashing against the thick metal, loud enough to wake the building. Everything he feared was out in the hallway. Well, by God, whoever or whatever it was would soon be dealing with an Odysseus, a warrior, a sea wolf. In Gaelic the name O'Connell meant "strong as a wolf." St. Brendan was Ireland's patron saint of sailors. Paddy had not felt this strong in years. He marched across his living room to his front door. He removed the chain, unlocked the dead bolt, and pulled the door wide open. Darkness engulfed him like surging waves of black water. He felt himself drowning. He stood tall in the face of it.

Fomite
Burlington, Vermont

Fomite is a literary press whose authors and artists explore the human condition -- political, cultural, personal and historical -- in poetry and prose.

A fomite is a medium capable of transmitting infectious organisms from one individual to another.

"The activity of art is based on the capacity of people to be infected by the feelings of others." Tolstoy, *What is Art?*

Alfabestiario
AlphaBetaBestiario - Antonello Borra
Animals have always understood that mankind is not fully at home in the world. Bestiaries, hoping to teach, send out warnings. This one, of course, aims at doing the same.

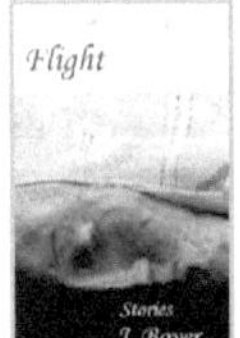

Flight and Other Stories-Jay Boyer
In *Flight and Other Stories,* we're with the fattest woman on earth as she draws her last breaths and her soul ascends toward its final reward. We meet a divorcee who can fly for no more effort than flapping her arms. We follow a middle-aged butler whose love affair with a young woman leads him first to the mysteries of bondage, and then to the pleasures of malice. Story by story, we set foot into worlds so strange as to seem all but surreal, yet everything feels familiar, each moment rings true. And that's when we recognize we're in the hands of one of America's truly original talents.

Improvisational Arguments-Anna Faktorovich
Improvisational Arguments is written in free verse to capture the essence of modern problems and triumphs. The poems clearly relate short, frequently humorous and occasionally tragic, stories about travels to exotic and unusual places, fantastic realms, abnormal jobs, artistic innovations, political objections, and misadventures with love.

Loisaida-Dan Chodorokoff
Catherine, a young anarchist estranged from her parents and squatting in an abandoned building on New York's Lower East Side is fighting with her boyfriend and conflicted about her work on an underground newspaper. After learning of a developer's plans to demolish a community garden, Catherine builds an alliance with a group of Puerto Rican community activists. Together they confront the confluence of politics, money, and real estate that rule Manhattan. All the while she learns important lessons from her great-grandmother's life in the Yiddish anarchist movement that flourished on the Lower East Side at the turn of the century. In this coming of age story, family saga, and tale of urban politics, Dan Chodorkoff explores the "principle of hope", and examines how memory and imagination inform social change.

Still Time-Michael Cocchiarale

Fomite
Burlington, Vermont

Still Time is a collection of twenty-five short and shorter stories exploring tensions that arise in a variety of contemporary relationships: a young boy must deal with the wrath of his out-of-work father; a woman runs into a man twenty years after an awkward sexual encounter; a wife, unable to conceive, imagines her own murder, as well as the reaction of her emotionally distant husband; a soon-to-be tenured English professor tries to come to terms with her husband's shocking return to the religion of his youth; an assembly line worker, married for thirty years, discovers the surprising secret life of his recently hospitalized wife. Whether a few hundred or a few thousand words, these and other stories in the collection depict characters at moments of deep crisis. Some feel powerless, overwhelmed—unable to do much to change the course of their lives. Others rise to the occasion and, for better or for worse, say or do the thing that might transform them for good. Even in stories with the most troubling of endings, there remains the possibility of redemption. For each of the characters, there is still time.

Loosestrife - Greg Delanty
This book is a chronicle of complicity in our modern lives, a witnessing of war and the destruction of our planet. It is also an attempt to adjust the more destructive blueprint myths of our society. Often our cultural memory tells us to keep quiet about the aspects that are most challenging to our ethics, to forget the violations we feel and tremors that keep us distant and numb.

Carts and Other Stories - Zdravka Evtimova
Roots and wings are the key words that best describe the short story collection, *Carts and Other Stories,* by Zdravka Evtimova. The book is emotionally multilayered and memorable because of its internal power, vitality and ability to touch both the heart and your mind. Within its pages, the reader discovers new perspectives true wealth, and learns to see the world with different eyes. The collection lives on the borders of different cultures. *Carts and Other Stories* will take the reader to wild and powerful Bulgarian mountains, to silver rains in Brussels, to German quiet winter streets and to wind bitten crags in Afghanistan. This book lives for those seeking to discover the beauty of the world around them, and will have them appreciating what they have— and perhaps what they have lost as well.

The Listener Aspires to the Condition of Music-Barry Goldensohn
"I know of no other selected poems that selects on one theme, but this one does, charting Goldensohn's career-long attraction to music's performance, consolations and its august, thrilling, scary and clownish charms. Does all art aspire to the condition of music as Pater claimed, exhaling in a swoon toward that one class act? Goldensohn is more aware than the late 19th century of the overtones of such breathing: his poems thoroughly round out those overtones in a poet's lifetime of listening."
John Peck, poet, editor, Fellow of the American Academy of Rome

The Co-Conspirator's Tale-Ron Jacobs
There's a place where love and mistrust are never at peace; where duplicity and deceit are the

Fomite
Burlington, Vermont

universal currency. *The Co-Conspirator's Tale* takes place within this nebulous firmament. There are crimes committed by the police in the name of the law. Excess in the name of revolution. The combination leaves death in its wake and the survivors struggling to find justice in a San Francisco Bay Area noir by the author of the underground classic *The Way the Wind Blew:A History of the Weather Underground* and the novel *Short Order Frame Up*.

Short Order Frame Up - Ron Jacobs

1975. America has lost its war in Vietnam and Cambodia. Racially-tinged riots are tearing the city of Boston apart. The politics and counterculture of the 1960s is disintegrating into nothing more than sex, drugs and rock and roll. The Boston Red Sox are on one of their improbable runs toward a postseason appearance. In a suburban town in Maryland, a young couple is murdered and another young man is accused. The couple are white and the accused is black. It is up to his friends and family to prove he is innocent. This is a story of suburban ennui, race, murder and injustice. Religion and politics, liberal lawyers and racist cops. In *Short Order Frame Up*, Ron Jacobs has written a piece of crime fiction that exposes the wound that is US racism. Two cultures existing side by side and across generations--a river very few dare to cross. His characters work and live with and next to each other, often unaware of the other's real life. When the murder occurs, however, those people that care about the man charged must cross that river and meet somewhere in between in order to free him from (what is to them) an obvious miscarriage of justice.

All the Sinners Saints - Ron Jacobs

A young draftee named Victor Willard goes AWOL in Germany after an altercation with a commanding officer. Porgy is an African-American GI involved with the international Black Panthers and German radicals. Victor and a female radical named Ana fall in love. They move into Ana's room in a squatted building near the US base in Frankfurt. The international campaign to free Black revolutionary Angela Davis is coming to Frankfurt. Porgy and Ana are key organizers and Victor spends his days and nights selling and smoking hashish, while becoming addicted to heroin. Police and narcotics agents are keeping tabs on them all. Politics, love, and drugs. Truths, lies, and rock and roll. *All the Sinners, Saints* is a story of people seeking redemption in a world awash in sin.

When You Remember Deir Yassin-R.L Green

When You Remember Deir Yassin is a collection of poems by R. L. Green, an American Jewish writer, on the subject of the occupation and destruction of Palestine. Green comments: "Outspoken Jewish critics of Israeli crimes against humanity have, strangely, been called 'anti-Semitic' as well as the hilariously illogical epithet 'self-hating Jews.' As a Jewish critic of the Israeli government, I have come to accept these accusations as a stamp of approval and a badge of honor, signifying my own fealty to a central element of Jewish identity and ethics: one must be a lover of truth and a friend to the oppressed, and stand with the victims of tyranny, not with the tyrants, despite tribal loyalty or self-advancement. These poems were written as expressions of outrage, and of grief, and to encourage my sisters and brothers of every cultural or national grouping to speak out against injustice, to try to save Palestine, and in so doing, to reclaim for myself my own place as part of the Jewish people." Poems in the original English are accompanied by Arabic and Hebrew translations.

Roadworthy Creature, Roadworthy Craft
- Kate Magill

Words fail but the voice struggles on. The culmination of a decade's worth of performance

Fomite
Burlington, Vermont

poetry, *Roadworthy Creature, Roadworthy Craft* is Kate Magill's first full-length publication. In lines that are sinewy yet delicate, Magill's poems explore the terrain where idea and action meet, where bodies and words commingle to form a strange new flesh, a breathing text, an "I" that spirals outward from itself.

Zinsky the Obscure-Ilan Mochari

"If your childhood is brutal, your adulthood becomes a daily attempt to recover: a quest for ecstasy and stability in recompense for their early absence." So states the 30-year-old Ariel Zinsky, whose bachelor-like lifestyle belies the torturous youth he is still coming to grips with. As a boy, he struggles with the beatings themselves; as a grownup, he struggles with the world's indifference to them. *Zinsky the Obscure* is his life story, a humorous chronicle of his search for a redemptive ecstasy through sex, an entrepreneurial sports obsession, and finally, the cathartic exercise of writing it all down. Fervently recounting both the comic delights and the frightening horrors of a life in which he feels—always—that he is not like all the rest, Zinsky survives the worst and relishes the best with idiosyncratic style, as his heartbreak turns into self-awareness and his suicidal ideation into self-regard. A vivid evocation of the all-consuming nature of lust and ambition—and the forces that drive them.

Love's Labours - Jack Pulaski

In the four stories and two novellas that comprise *Love's Labors* the protagonists Ben and Laura, discover in their fervid romance and long marriage their interlocking fates, and the histories that preceded their births. They also learned something of the paradox between love and all the things it brings to its beneficiaries: bliss, disaster, duty, tragedy, comedy, the grotesque, and tenderness.

Ben and Laura's story is also the particularly American tale of immigration to a new world. Laura's story begins in Puerto Rico, and Ben's lineage is Russian-Jewish. They meet in City College of New York, a place at least analogous to a melting pot. Laura struggles to rescue her brother from gang life and heroin. She is mother to her younger sister; their mother Consuelo is the financial mainstay of the family and consumed by work. Despite filial obligations, Laura aspires to be a serious painter. Ben writes, cares for and is caught up in the misadventures and surreal stories of his younger schizophrenic brother. Laura is also a story teller as powerful and enchanting as Scheherazade. Ben struggles to survive such riches, and he and Laura endure.

The Derivation of Cowboys & Indians-Joseph D. Reich

The Derivation of Cowboys & Indians represents a profound journey, a breakdown of The American Dream from a social, cultural, historical, and spiritual point of view. Reich examines in concise!detail the loss of the collective unconscious, commenting on our!contemporary postmodern culture with its self-interested excesses, on where and how things all go wrong, and how social/political practice rarely meets its original proclamations and promises. Reich's surreal and self-effacing satire brings this troubling message home.

The Derivations of Cowboys & Indians is a desperate search and struggle for America's literal, symbolic, and spiritual home.

Kasper Planet: Comix and Tragix-Peter Schumann

The British call him Punch, the Italians, Pulchinello, the Russians, Petruchka, the Native Americans, Coyote. These are the figures we may know. But every culture that worships authority will breed a Punch-like, anti-authoritarian resister. Yin and yang -- it has to happen. The Ger-

Fomite
Burlington, Vermont

mans call him Kasper. Truth-telling and serious pranking are dangerous professions when going up against power. Bradley Manning sits naked in solitary; Julian Assange is pursued by Interpol, Obama's Department of Justice, and Amazon.com. But -- in contrast to merely human faces -- masks and theater can often slip through the bars. Consider our American Kaspers: Charlie Chaplin, Woody Guthrie, Abby Hoffman, the Yes Men -- theater people all, utilizing various forms to seed critique. Their profiles and tactics have evolved along with those of their enemies. Who are the bad guys that call forth the Kaspers? Over the last half century, with his Bread & Puppet Theater, Peter Schumann has been tireless in naming them, excoriating them with Kasperdom....

from Marc Estrin's Foreword to Planet Kasper

Views Cost Extra-L.E. Smith

Views that inspire, that calm, or that terrify—all come at some cost to the viewer. In *Views Cost Extra* you will find a New Jersey high school preppy who wants to inhabit the "perfect" cowboy movie, a rural mailman disgusted with the residents of his town who wants to live with the penguins, an ailing screen writer who strikes a deal with Johnny Cash to reverse an old man's failures, an old man who ponders a young man's suicide attempt, a one-armed blind blues singer who wants to reunite with the car that took her arm on the assembly line -- and more. These stories suggest that we must pay something to live even ordinary lives.

The Empty Notebook Interrogates Itself-Susan Thomas

The Empty Notebook began its life as a very literal metaphor for a few weeks of what the poet thought was writer's block, but was really the struggle of an eccentric persona to take over her working life. It won. And for the next three years everything she wrote came to her in the voice of the Empty Notebook, who, as the notebook began to fill itself, became rather opinionated, changed gender, alternately acted as bully and victim, had many bizarre adventures in exotic locales and developed a somewhat politically-incorrect attitude. It then began to steal the voices and forms of other poets and tried to immortalize itself in various poetry reviews. It is now thrilled to collect itself in one slim volume.

Visiting Hours -*Jennifer Anne Moses*

Visiting Hours, a novel-in-stories, explores the lives of people not normally met on the page---AIDS patients and those who care for them. Set in Baton Rouge, Louisiana, and written with large and frequent dollops of humor, the book is a profound meditation on faith and love in the face of illness and poverty.

My God, What Have We Done?-Susan Weiss

In a world afflicted with war, toxicity, and hunger, does what we do in our private lives really matter? Fifty years after the creation of the atomic bomb at Los Alamos, newlyweds Pauline and Clifford visit that once-secret city on their honeymoon, compelled by Pauline's fascination with Oppenheimer, the soulful scientist. The two stories emerging from this visit reverberate back and forth between the loneliness of a new mother at home in

Fomite
Burlington, Vermont

Boston and the isolation of an entire community dedicated to the development of the bomb. While Pauline struggles with unforeseen challenges of family life, Oppenheimer and his crew reckon with forces beyond all imagining.

Finally the years of frantic research on the bomb culminate in a stunning test explosion that echoes a rupture in the couple's marriage. Against the backdrop of a civilization that's out of control, Pauline begins to understand the complex, potentially explosive physics of personal relationships.

At once funny and dead serious, *My God, What Have We Done?* sifts through the ruins left by the bomb in search of a more worthy human achievement.

As It Is On Earth - Peter M. Wheelwright
Four centuries after the Reformation Pilgrims sailed up the down-flowing watersheds of New England, Taylor Thatcher, irreverent scion of a fallen family of Maine Puritans, is still caught in the turbulence.

In his errant attempts to escape from history, the young college professor is further unsettled by his growing attraction to Israeli student Miryam Bluehm as he is swept by Time through the "family thing"—from the tangled genetic and religious history of his New England parents to the redemptive birthday secret of Esther Fleur Noire Bishop, the Cajun-Passamaquoddy woman who raised him and his younger half-cousin/half-brother, Bingham.

The landscapes, rivers, and tidal estuaries of Old New England and the Mayan Yucatan are also casualties of history in Thatcher's story of Deep Time and re-discovery of family on Columbus Day at a high-stakes gambling casino, rising in resurrection over the starlit bones of a once-vanquished Pequot Indian Tribe.

Travers' Inferno-L.E. Smith
In the 1970's churches began to burn in Burlington, Vermont. If it were arson, no one or no reason could be found to blame. This book suggests arson, but makes no claim to historical realism. It claims, instead, to capture the dizzying 70's zeitgeist of aggressive utopian movements, distrust in authority, escapist alternative life styles, and a bewildered society of onlookers. In the tradition of John Gardner's Sunlight Dialogues, the characters of *Travers' Inferno* are colorful and damaged, sometimes comical, sometimes tragic, looking for meaning through desperate acts. Travers Jones, protagonist, is grounded in the transcendent—philosophy, epilepsy, arson as purification— and mystified by the opposite sex, haunted by an absent father and directed by an uncle with a grudge. He is seduced by a professor's wife and chased by an endearing if ineffective sergeant of police. There are secessionist Quebecois involved in these church burns who are murdering as well as pilfering and burning. There are changing alliances, violent deaths, lovemaking, and a belligerent cat.

Suite for Three Voices-Derek Furr
Suite for Three Voices is a dance of prose genres, teeming with intense human life in all its humor and sorrow. A son uncovers the horrors of his father's wartime experience, a hitchhiker in a muumuu guards a mysterious parcel, a young man foresees his brother's brush with death on September 11. A Victorian poetess encounters space aliens and digital archives, a runner hears the voice of a dead friend in the song of an indigo bunting, a teacher seeks wisdom from his students' errors and Neil Young. By frozen waterfalls and neglected graveyards, along

Fomite
Burlington, Vermont

highways at noon and rivers at dusk, in the sound of bluegrass, Beethoven, and Emily Dickinson, the essays and fiction in this collection offer moments of vision.

The Good Muslim of Jackson Heights - *Jaysinh Birjépatil*

Jackson Heights in this book is a fictional locale with common features assembled from immigrant-friendly neighborhoods around the world where hardworking honest-to-goodness traders from the Indian subcontinent, rub shoulders with ruthless entrepreneurs, reclusive antique-dealers, homeless nobodies, merchant-princes, lawyers, doctors and IT specialists. But as Siraj and Shabnam, urbane newcomers fleeing religious persecution in their homeland discover there is no escape from the past. Weaving together the personal and the political *The Good Muslim of Jackson Heights* is an ambiguous elegy to a utopian ideal set free from all prejudice.

Signed Confessions - *Tom Walker*

Guilt and a desperate need to repent drive the antiheroes in Tom Walker's dark (and often darkly funny) stories:
- A gullible journalist falls for the 40-year-old stripper he profiles in a magazine.
- A faithless husband abandons his family and joins a support group for lost souls.
- A merciless prosecuting attorney grapples with the suicide of his gay son.
- An aging misanthrope must make amends to five former victims.
- An egoistic naval hero is haunted by apparitions of his dead wife and a mysterious little girl.

The seven tales in *Signed Confessions* measure how far guilty men will go to obtain a forgiveness no one can grant but themselves.

Meanwell - *Janice Miller Potter*

Meanwell is a twenty-four poem sequence in which a female servant searches for identity and meaning in the shadow of her mistress, poet Anne Bradstreet. Although Meanwell herself is a fiction, someone like her could easily have existed among Bradstreet's known but unnamed domestic servants. Through Meanwell's eyes, Bradstreet emerges as a human figure during The Great Migration of the 1600s, a period in which the Massachusetts Bay Colony was fraught with physical and political dangers. Through Meanwell, the feelings of women, silenced during the midwife Anne Hutchinson's fiery trial before the Puritan ministers, are finally acknowledged. In effect, the poems are about the making of an American rebel. Through her conflicted conscience, we witness Meanwell's transformation from a powerless English waif to a mythic American who ultimately chooses wilderness over the civilization she has experienced.

The Housing Market - *Joseph D. Reich*

In Joseph Reich's most recent social and cultural, contemporary satire of suburbia entitled, "The Housing market: a comfortable place to jump off the end of the world," the author addresses the absurd, postmodern elements of what it means, or for that matter not, to try and cope and function, and survive and thrive, or live and die in the repetitive and existential, futile and self-destructive, homogenized, monochromatic landscape of a brutal and bland, collective unconscious, which can

Fomite
Burlington, Vermont

spiritually result in a gradual wasting away and erosion of the senses or conflict and crisis of a desperate, disproportionate 'situational depression,' triggering and leading the narrator to feel constantly abandoned and stranded, more concretely or proverbially spoken, "the eternal stranger," where when caught between the fight or flight psychological phenomena, naturally repels him and causes him to flee and return without him even knowing it into the wild, while by sudden circumstance and coincidence discovers it surrounds the illusory-like circumference of these selfsame Monopoly board cul-de-sacs and dead ends. Most specifically, what can happen to a solitary, thoughtful, and independent thinker when being stagnated in the triangulation of a cookie-cutter, oppressive culture of a homeowner's association; A memoir all written in critical and didactic, poetic stanzas and passages, and out of desperation, when freedom and control get taken, what he is forced to do in the illusion of 'free will and volition,' something like the derivative art of a smart and ironic and social and cultural satire.

Love's Labours - Jack Pulaski

In the four stories and two novellas that comprise Love's Labors the protagonists Ben and Laura, discover in their fervid romance and long marriage their interlocking fates, and the histories that preceded their births. They also learned something of the paradox between love and all the things it brings to its beneficiaries: bliss, disaster, duty, tragedy, comedy, the grotesque, and tenderness.

Ben and Laura's story is also the particularly American tale of immigration to a new world. Laura's story begins in Puerto Rico, and Ben's lineage is Russian-Jewish. They meet in City College of New York, a place at least analogous to a melting pot. Laura struggles to rescue her brother from gang life and heroin. She is mother to her younger sister; their mother Consuelo is the financial mainstay of the family and consumed by work. Despite filial obligations, Laura aspires to be a serious painter. Ben writes, cares for and is caught up in the misadventures and surreal stories of his younger schizophrenic brother. Laura is also a story teller as powerful and enchanting as Scheherazade. Ben struggles to survive such riches, and he and Laura endure.

Raven or Crow - Joshua Amses

Marlowe has recently moved back home to Vermont after flunking his first term at a private college in the Midwest, when his sort of girlfriend, Eleanor, goes missing. The circumstances surrounding Eleanor's disappearance stand to reveal more about Marlowe than he is willing to allow. Rather than report her missing, he resolves to find Eleanor himself. *Raven or Crow* is the story of mistakes rooted in the ambivalence of being young and without direction.

Four-Way Stop - Sherry Olson

If *Thank You* were the only prayer,
as Meister Eckhart has suggested, it would be enough,
and Sherry Olson's poetry, in her second book, *Four-Way Stop*,
would be one. Radical attention, deep love,
and dedication to kindness illuminate these poems

Fomite
Burlington, Vermont

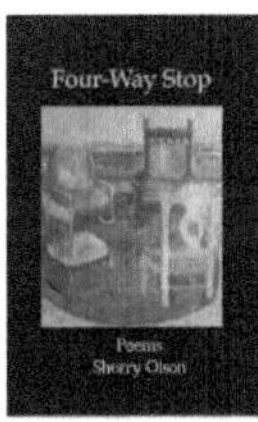

and the stories she tells us, which are drawn from her own life:
with family, with friends, and wherever she travels, with strangers –
who to Olson, never are strangers, but kin.
Even at the difficult intersections,
as in the title poem, *Four-Way Stop,*
Olson experiences – and offers – hope,
showing us how, *completely unsupervised,*
people take turns, with *kindness waving each other on.*
Olson writes, knowing that (to quote Czeslaw Milosz))
What surrounds us, here and now, is not guaranteed.
To this world, with her poems, Olson brings – and teaches –
attention, generosity, compassion, and appreciative joy.
 - Carol Henrikson

Did you know that you can write a review on Amazon, Good Reads or Shelfari? Just go to the
book page on the website and follow the links for posting a review. Books from independent
presses depend on reader to reader communications